Venault de Charmily, Adam Williamson

Answer, by Way of Letter, to Bryan Edwards, Esq., M.P., F.R.S.

planter of Jamaica, &c. containing a refutation of his historical survey on the French

colony of St. Domingo, etc. etc.

Venault de Charmily, Adam Williamson

Answer, by Way of Letter, to Bryan Edwards, Esq., M.P., F.R.S.
planter of Jamaica, &c. containing a refutation of his historical survey on the French colony of St. Domingo, etc. etc.

ISBN/EAN: 9783337331610

Printed in Europe, USA, Canada, Australia, Japan

Cover: Foto ©Andreas Hilbeck / pixelio.de

More available books at **www.hansebooks.com**

ANSWER,

BY WAY OF LETTER, TO

BRYAN EDWARDS, Esq., M.P., F.R.S.,

PLANTER OF JAMAICA, &c.

CONTAINING

A REFUTATION

OF HIS

HISTORICAL SURVEY

ON THE

FRENCH COLONY OF ST. DOMINGO,

ETC. ETC.

BY COLONEL VENAULT DE CHARMILLY,

KNIGHT OF THE ROYAL AND MILITARY ORDER OF ST. LOUIS,
PLANTER OF ST. DOMINGO,
MEMBER OF THE FIRST GENERAL ASSEMBLY OF THAT COLONY;
AND CHARGED BY HIS MAJESTY'S MINISTERS AND THE PLANTERS,
TO REGULATE AND SIGN THE CAPITULATION FOR THE FRENCH PART OF THAT ISLAND
WITH LIEUT.-GENERAL WILLIAMSON, LIEUTENANT-GOVERNOR OF JAMAICA.

London:

Printed for the AUTHOR, by BAYLIS, No. 15, Greville-street, Holborn;
And Sold by DEBRETT, Piccadilly; and BOOSEY, Broad-street, Royal-Exchange.

1797.

ADVERTISEMENT.

THE present edition was undertaken at the request of several of my friends, who imagined that my object would be better attained than by the original one in the French Language, particularly as Mr. Edwards' work is in English.— Some slight alterations have been made, and a cursory history of the Yellow Fever has been added, as remitted to me by a planter of Tobago, who has made the most particular researches on that pestilential disease, which was never known at St. Domingo before its unfortunate introduction by the Experiment frigate; it was as accidental there, as its appearance in Philadelphia some time since.—People's minds have been as much prejudiced against St. Domingo as if it was peculiar to that island: this has made me particularly attentive to that unhappy subject; and it gives me infinite pleasure to announce that it has entirely ceased its ravages.

I beg leave to add, that since the first edition of my work, I have been credibly informed, that in the Windward Islands there are as many Englishmen employed in the capacity of overseers as Scotch or Irish, except at Montserrat, where they are principally Irish.

PREFACE.

SEVERAL great events have taken place since the first edition of my letter, all of which corroborate the justness of my expressed belief, that a Peace with the French Republic would be impossible ; and I think no doubt can possibly now remain of *the good faith* which the agents of the Directory bear in their negotiations.

The last Revolution of the 4th of September, is likewise sufficient to convince the most eager partisans of peace, what degree of confidence can be placed in any treaty whatever contracted with such men; who neither respect *power or laws :* not even those which themselves have created. How much then does a regular government *endanger itself* in treating with such a factious collection, as that at the head of the Directory : who proclaim the *independance and sovereignty of the people*, and who at the same time *sell them* to other sovereigns : either to conclude treaties, or to satisfy their ambition, just as convenience suits their purpose. Three members of the Directory have had the boldness to arrest their colleagues, and without a trial (nay even the semblance of a trial, notwithstanding their *inflated bombast about juries)* have banished them. Perhaps themselves will be served in the same manner, or one amongst them more hardy than the rest, may assassinate the four others, to reign over a people *rendered abject by terror.*

The return of Lord Malmesbury, a second time sent away in the most insulting manner to England, ought to testify how dangerous it would be to treat conditionally with the French Republic.

The signal victory of Admiral Duncan, is one of the most favorable events that could have been wished, and its happy consequences invaluable. It has rendered England mistress and absolute arbiter of the seas, and reduced Holland from her rank among the maritime powers.

The French government has too openly manifested its intentions, for Sovereigns, (who are not in the most desperate necessity of submitting to a disgraceful peace) to consent to such treaties, as would be nothing more than a public adhesion to principles, *which contain the seeds of their own destruction.*

The peace which the Emperor has accepted, and the conditions that form its basis, evince more than ever the intentions of the French Republic, *to annihilate successively all the powers of Europe,* making use of each other till they eventually domineer over the whole. The Cis-Rhénane Republic affords a fresh and convincing proof, and leaves little to hope for the re-establishment of the German Empire.—The impolitic conduct of the Emperor forms new means of power to the French government, in obliging him to become the arbiter of the new Republics which it has created. The errors of the Continental governments likewise add more pressing motives for England to reject a peace which would have, relative to expence, all the inconveniences of war ; as the instability and bad faith of the Directory would necessarily force her to remain armed ; —besides, the danger of pestilential communication, which scarce any precaution known has been able to prevent ; with peace, it would most certainly destroy her domestic tranquillity.

Great-Britain may terminate an offensive war:

First, *in taking possession of Guadaloupe*, the only important asylum for privateers that torment her trade in the Windward Islands.

Secondly, in compleating *the Conquest of St. Domingo*, which I think is very easy, fromt he knowledge *I have of that colony, as will be seen in the sequel*. Thus, mistress of her enemies colonies, she may confine herself to a defensive, economical war.

I have read with astonishment in the public papers, (in their reports on the first day of the meeting of Parliament), a speech, there said to have been delivered by Mr. Bryan Edwards; if so, it fully proves, that he judged it easier to aggravate his errors, than frankly to avow that he had been misled in his information. If I am wrong, I am open to detection ;—but why fulminate *not only on the unfortunate colonists of St. Domingo, but upon the whole of the French colonists, in so cruel and unjust a manner*, all the ill humour, which, perhaps, I have occasioned, in exposing his numberless errors? which every man who had only lived a few months at St. Domingo, could as easily have noticed to the public as myself, and with the same advantage. Why carry his injustice *(to say no more)* so far as to rank *these brave and loyal colonists*, who have fought under the standard of Britain *for four years*, and who are numbered amongst English subjects, by the oath of allegiance which they took : Why, I say, does he rank them with a VICTOR HUGUES, whom he cited, who never was a proprietor, nor a colonist, nor ever known, but by his crimes, before his arrival at Guadaloupe? How, in the name of every thing honorable, could he conceive such an attack ? *An attack as indecent as unmerited by all the French colonists*, and which indicates the spirit that dictated the errors of the book I now answer. My countrymen and myself consider it as the effects of hatred and jealousy against a people *of generous, brave, and grateful colonists*, who, in devoting themselves to the interests of Great-Britain, have seconded the plan of *His Majesty's Ministers :* who have rendered the English nation the greatest service *in saving Jamaica, by carrying the theatre of war to St. Domingo*.—But the inconsiderateness which prompts Mr. B. E. to consent to the destruction of the English colonies (if I may so express it) where his fortune lies, in the fear of St. Domingo being re-established, leaves no room to doubt, that vanity with some men predominates over their interest. For, let it not be imagined, *that the colonies can be preserved with fleets or even garrisons ;* with such means it is true, towns and forts are defended; but the species of enemies we have now to combat, do not direct their attacks that way. It is the plantation establishments against whom their views are directed. The sugar islands are, as long as the French Republic exists, *so many powder magazines, which may be successfully attacked with only a lighted match.*

I firmly believe then, that Mr. Bryan Edwards is now very well convinced *in his own mind* of this forcible truth, which I think I have clearly demonstrated in the course of my answer, viz. THAT ON THE FATE OF ST. DOMINGO DEPENDS THAT OF JAMAICA, AND ON THE FATE OF THOSE TWO GREAT ISLANDS, (THE MOST PEOPLED WITH NEGROS) DEPEND ALL THE EUROPEAN COLONIES IN THE ANTILLES.

LONDON, November 15, 1797.

To *BRYAN EDWARDS, Esq.*

London, May 1, 1797.

SIR,

Having had an opportunity of conversing with you frequently, relative to the Colony of St. Domingo, I found that you knew but very little of its affairs, and that you had been badly informed with respect to the events that have happened in that Island. Indeed I believe I hinted this to you when you told me you had an idea of writing its history.

My curiosity was not, therefore, much excited to read your *Historical Survey of the French Colony in the Island of St. Domingo.* However, on the 28th of March last, being informed by a Member of Parliament with whom I dined, that my name had been introduced in your work, and, expressing a desire of knowing what was personal to me, he produced your book.

Judge, Sir, my surprise at the manner in which you mention my name, after having been (without any solicitation on my part) recommended to you by one of your intimate friends; having in consequence visited you out of civility, and having met you since at a common friend's. I desire you to be convinced that, by answering you, I pay no regard to this inconsistency. I wish I had only to upbraid you with errors personal to myself; but I am forced to notice the ill-grounded or malignant remarks you lavish upon those, who advised the British Cabinet to perform *one of the greatest and most useful operations of the present war.*

After having attentively read your publication, I find it necessary, in justice to the Colony, my own honour, and that of the brave and loyal inhabitants who have devoted themselves to the cause of Great-Britain, that I should make a public answer to it.

B

Among other persons who, like myself, have evinced to His Majesty's Ministers the great advantages of an attack upon St. Domingo, there are certainly some who could more ably have refuted your remarks on that Colony; but, fearful of exposing their wives and children to the furious vengeance of a people whose leaders have rendered cruel—and being the person whom you most directly attack —as you name me personally—as you own and stile me *the agent of* the inhabitants of the Grande-Anse—I take up the gage you have thrown for me, to demonstrate that your work, in the most material points, teems with errors and injustice.

As I freely declare to you, Sir, and to the public, that I endeavoured, more than any other person, to shew to the British Government the great utility that would accrue to the English from the possession of St. Domingo, it may be proper for me to say a few words to convince my readers how far I could speak of that Colony, so as to deserve the confidence of Government at that time, and, now, of the public at large.

After having finished my studies at the University of Paris, and having travelled through great part of Europe, I arrived at St. Domingo in the beginning of the American war. A few months residence in that Colony was sufficient to make me acquainted with its importance. Born with an activity hardly to be surpassed, and favored by Providence with a healthy and strong constitution, I was enabled to make myself perfectly acquainted with the affairs of the Island. During an uninterrupted stay twice, of seven years each, I may safely say that I have, in the full sense of the word, travelled over the whole Country, having been engaged in some important suits, having administred several great estates, and having had business of great consequence in all parts of the Island, which have made me acquainted with the principal planters in its various quarters. If you join to that the ambition also of becoming one of the richest inhabitants, you may judge if I was not in the situation of perfect information of the resources of its provinces, and the advantages of its different manufactures; besides my knowing personally almost all the officers, both military and civil; add to that, the generous hospitality of the *Creoles*, and my independance as a single man. From all these reasons you may easily conclude, that scarcely any inhabitant of the Colony had a greater opportunity of knowing its affairs than myself.

Returning to France at the end of the last war, I was grieved to see the baneful effects of those poisonous principles, which the French had sought for in America. I also saw, with deep concern, the establishment of that philanthropic sect, created at first in Philadelphia, and finally transplanted in Europe. I then visited England, where I remained a few months; from thence I went to Jamaica, where I also resided some time.

Since my return, in St. Domingo, having re-established several plantations on my own account, I was under the necessity of making myself perfectly well informed of every thing that related to the commercial resources of the Colony to its utmost extent: I also had, with Mr. de Marbois, the arrangement of the accounts of one of the most wealthy Contractors of St. Domingo. A long residence at Port-au-Prince and the Cape, enabled me still more to judge of every thing that passed.

On returning to my plantation, at the moment of the Revolution, it will not appear surprising, that I was nominated Member of the Assembly of my Parish, afterwards of the Province where I resided, and, finally, Deputy of the General Assembly of St. Marc.

From the very first publication of the *Rights of Man*, I foresaw, with the reasonable and well informed inhabitants, the miseries and misfortunes that awaited the Colony.

Residing in the South part of the Island, which was, in a great measure, indebted to the English and the inhabitants of Jamaica, for its establishment; and being also, by several voyages, acquainted with England, I early turned my views towards Great-Britain, to ensure the safety of St. Domingo. This sentiment never once abandoned me; from the first moment of the troubles, I constantly manifested it in my Parish, in my Province, and in the General Assembly of St. Marc, where all my thoughts and actions were continually directed towards procuring the success of my plan.

The torrent of revolutionary ideas had too much agitated every head, not to force the wisest people to conform to circumstances; and I freely own, that I was one of those who affected to believe the possibility of an absurd independance; preferring it, for the interests of the Island, *to a still more absurd idea*, of a Sugar Colony existing with the pretended *Rights of Man*. Unfortunately, the people of the greatest influence in St. Domingo were led to believe, from the remembrance of the commercial advantages they derived, during the American war, from their increasing trade with neutral nations; they were in hopes, and pretended, that it might well exist independent, under the general protection of the European Powers. My opinion has always been, that such a thing could never take place, and that the Colony ought to be under the protection of a *great metropolis*; and that it would be wisely judged to put it under the powerful patronage of England. The diversity of opinions frustrated all my plans, and obliged me, (mine being well known) to embark with the principal and well meaning proprietors on board the Leopard, with the view of flying from two parties; one of which saw in us the enemies of their ambition, and the other looked on us as enemies to that anarchy which they thought of establishing in our superb climates. Shortly after my arrival in Europe, I soon perceived that France was lost, and still more so St. Domingo, if a power interested to save her own Colonies did not timely succour her.

The melancholy intelligence of the disasters of St. Domingo were first brought to Europe by the *Daphne*, an English frigate. I was the only inhabitant, who came to England, to substantiate that

news;

news; a proof of which I found by 200 letters, delivered to me by Captain Gardner, who commanded that frigate.

I think it is the epoch of 1791, which you cite: I had, at that time, the honour of seeing the Ministers of His Britannic Majesty, and I proposed to them the means of saving *their Colonies*, by saving St. Domingo. The truth of my observations then, and which I have since repeated, are inserted in the Memorial which I submitted to Government. The revolutionary spirit, which had overturned the heads of the French people, furnished the justest and wisest reasons for the British Ministry to refuse an offer, which had been too late tendered, and had, on account of the conflagration of the Colony and the diminution of its revenues and productions, become of too little importance to risk a war with the French.

I repaired to Paris again; when soon, in 1792, the calamitous events, which affected France and the King, compelled me to look for an asylum in England. From that moment, I predicted the certainty of a war, and, continually occupied for the welfare of my countrymen and of the first Colony of the world, I reiterated my sollicitations to the British Government. In conceit with other inhabitants I have never ceased proving to the Ministers of Great-Britain, that, if St. Domingo, the most considerable of the *Antilles*, was not saved, it would be impossible to save any of their Islands.

War having been declared by the French in February 1793, then it was, that those, who had exerted themselves to preserve both the English and the French Colonies, were listened to. Many of them were no less zealous in the cause than myself; but, having the superior advantage of a thorough knowledge of the Colony, I was enabled to declare: " *such and such things must be done*; *I will* " *undertake them, or perish in the attempt.*" The British Ministers can judge whether I was so fortunate as to make good my promises: they were pleased to assure me of it, and His Majesty graciously

c

condescended to testify to me, personally, his approbation of the zeal and alacrity with which I exerted myself in that service.

I shall speak of what I relate as a person who has either advised, *executed personally*, or seen executed, whatever has taken place at St. Domingo, ever since the English, at the head *of whose operations I was*, took possession of it. You will then judge, Sir, whether I ought not to be better informed than you and many others; for as an eye-witness shall I speak about every thing the Ministry ordered me to do, ever since June 1793, until towards the end of 1794, when I left the Colony to return to England. That is the very period mentioned in your work; it was also about the same time, I was charged with the powers of the Colonists to come here, and lay their vows at His Majesty's feet, and to implore fresh assistance to enable them to finish what *I had so happily begun.*

As a Planter, well informed in every thing that relates to St. Domingo, I shall answer your work, and demonstrate its errors; and, finally, as a very active witness to every fact you advance, I take upon me to contradict whatever you pretend to have happened since the arrival of the English.

I expect but little justice, Sir, from a man, who has forgot the sacred duty of an historian, to calumniate brave, generous, and grateful Colonists, and unfortunate foreigners, who have faithfully fulfilled those promises and duties, which their honour as much as their interest dictated.

From a wise and liberal public who, I hope, will read this work, I expect the justice which is due to my fellow countrymen and myself. Though sensible of your injustice, truth and impartiality alone shall guide my pen, and the public will be our judge.

N. B. The passages quoted from Mr. Edwards' work are printed in *Italics*, with the pages from which they are extracted.

PREFACE.

IN the preface, you say :—*The present publication therefore is confined wholly to St. Domingo ; concerning which, having personally visited that unhappy country soon after the revolt of the Negroes in 1791, and formed connexions there which have supplied me with regular communication ever since, I possess a mass of evidence and important documents.*—Page ii.

In consequence of your assertion, the reader might be led to think that you are perfectly well acquainted with the colony ; that a long residence at St. Domingo has enabled you to study its political concerns, its commerce, its administration, its produce, and all its other resources ; to visit its several manufactures : and finally, that by living there several years, you had it in your power to collect the *important instructions you speak of*, in the various quarters of that extensive island ; the equivocal manner in which you mention your residence in that too unhappy country, will induce one to believe it. You should have said : " during a few weeks residence *only* that I remained shut up in the town of Cape François immediately after the rebellion of the Negroes, in 1791, I have, in a moment of great confusion collected all my materials;" you should have said that you could see nothing by yourself; that the inhabitants of the colony and town were, during your stay at the Cape, divided in several parties ; that you could speak but little French, &c. &c. &c.; the reader would then either have guarded against your assertions, or wholly put your work by.

And he saw (the Earl of Effingham) in its full extent the danger to which every island in the West Indies would be exposed *from such an example, if the triumph of savage anarchy over all order and government should be complete.*—Page iii.

If you had yourself known what Lord Effingham perceived, why did you not lay down your pen ? Why have you not endeavoured to know whether the Ministers had not seen as well as his Lordship ? Why have you not hesitated to accuse them of levity and want of foresight ? How, being a planter yourself, have you not pitied the unfortunate colonists, who, having providentially escaped from the daggers *of their murderers*, blessed the benevolent nation that saved them from destruction ?

And very earnest wishes were avowed in all companies (at Cape François) without scruple or restraint, that the British government would send an armament to conquer the island, or rather to receive its voluntary surrender from the inhabitants.—Page x.

The sensible and rational part of the inhabitants had long foreseen all the misfortunes which the publication of the pretended *Rights of Man*, would infallibly bring on St. Domingo, and they unanimously wished for England to seize on and take possession of the colony; wicked and ill-designed people only opposed that wise measure, and the barbarous associates to the *Amis des Noirs* prevented the surrender of the island. Since yourself heard the unanimous vows of the unfortunate inhabitants, reduced to despair, why did you not come forward as their advocate?

This circumstance (the attention shewn to Mr. Edwards) is not recorded from the vain ambition of shewing my own importance. The reader of the following pages will discover its application; and perhaps it may induce him to make some allowance for that confident expectation of sure and speedy success, which afterwards led to attempts by the British arms, against this ill-fated country, with means that must otherwise have been thought at the time, as in the sequel they have unhappily proved, altogether inadequate to the object in view.—Page xi.

Those marks of deference and respect then shewn, could by no means be addressed to you, as having no personal claim to them; but you were looked on as a person sent by the Governor of Jamaica; my too unfortunate fellow countrymen wished to convey their vows to those alone, who could effectually assist them.

Those vows expressed in the very height of their misfortunes, were not calculated to attract at once and fix the attention of the Ministers. When I renewed my solicitations, circumstances had then undergone a total change: my answers will in due time and place, amply serve to do away that consequence you draw from your own idea. Therefore, I refrain from doing it now.

They were even accused (the Spaniards) not only of supplying the rebels with arms and provisions, but also of delivering up to them, to be murdered, many unhappy French planters who had fled for refuge to the Spanish territories, &c. receiving money from the rebels as the price of their blood. *Of these latter charges, however, no proof was I believe ever produced.*—Page xiii.

The conduct of the Spaniards on this occasion, was investigated and fully proved to the Legislative Assembly of France by several documents and authentic pieces

3

brought from St. Domingo ; since that time, the proclamation issued by the President or Governor of the Spanish territories, the horrid *murders of the Gonaïves*, and still *more those of Fort Dauphin*, (no doubt, ordered by them), but most certainly executed under their very eyes, peremptorily shew that not too much was advanced on that subject, and that they were really guilty of all the atrocities committed at St. Domingo.

This Gentleman (Mr. Cadush) drew up, at my request, a short account of the origin and progress of the rebellion ; and, after my return to England, favoured me with his correspondence. Many important facts, which are given in this work, are given on his authority.—Page xv. ·

Mr. de Cadush, from his talents and knowledge of St. Domingo, was certainly capable to furnish you with excellent materials, respecting that colony : but you are not ignorant *that he successively embraced different parties*, and you should, of course, have attentively enquired into the truth of his assertions. You also ought to have known the charge brought against him, which he has perfectly well answered ; but that circumstance alone, was a sufficient reason for a prudent historian to be on his guard, and you might well be induced to think that in the notes and remarks he would transmit to you, caprice, chagrin, or vengeance, might guide his pen ; many reasons made me believe that your assertions, on the operations and proceedings of the General Assembly of the colony, were imparted to you by Mr. de Cadush ; I freely own that it is the most exact part of your book, and shews the merit and talents of the person you are indebted to for it ; but the details and particulars, are, by far, too much circumscribed, and imperfect to serve for a history ; it offers nothing to the reader of what is absolutely necessary to elucidate many facts, which may throw a light on the true and principal causes of the horrid atrocities and ravages perpetrated at St. Domingo.

Such are the authorities from whence I have derived my information, concerning those calamitous events which have brought it to ruin. Yet I will frankly confess, that if I have any credit with the public as an author, I am not sure this work will add to my reputation.—Page xviii.

Your bare assertion will enable the reader to judge how imprudent you were, in writing on such documents and authorities, given you by three individuals only, and on some other information collected, during a short residence of a few weeks, in a town of the colony, filled with troubles, and the most calamitous events.

After the perusal of this letter, the public I hope will be thoroughly convinced that by publishing your work on the colony of St. Domingo, *you have not studied your own reputation*; if you have any success as an author, the manner in which I shall demonstrate that you have very badly informed your readers, respecting St. Domingo, will *make them fear that, by the means of a* few agreeable phrases, you may have too previously misled them.

All therefore, that I can hope, and expect is that my narrative, if it cannot delight may at least instruct.

I will expose the lamentable ignorance of some, and the monstrous wickedness of others; among the reformers of the present day, who, urging onwards schemes of perfection, and projects of amendment in the condition of human life, faster than nature allows; are lighting up a consuming fire between the different classes of mankind, which nothing but human blood can extinguish.—Page xix.

I do not think that your narrative can give any information on the history of the colony. Would to God, that, prudently using the talent *of writing agreeably* allotted you by nature, you had empoyed it to instruct your countrymen, on the danger of the new ideas, which the reformers so zealously strive to propagate! You would have well deserved of your country, and of all Europe, if you had endeavoured to unfold the ruinous projects and schemes of those reformers; and you would be entitled to the gratitude of mankind, if you had employed your leisure hours, in protecting your fellow citizens of Jamaica, and the other colonies, from the rage of usurpers, who *quietly enjoying in Europe* all the advantages and pleasures of civilized societies, cooly and premeditately carry fire and sword among 3 or 400,000 white families, scattered in the Antilles, to make a trial in behalf of those unfortunate people, *who were really happy* before violent measures were adopted to procure their happiness.

Could you not, sir, instead of describing a country, which you are not acquainted with, point out the atrocious crimes which you know to have been there perpetrated, and when pointed out, tell the reformers, " *put an end now to your woeful experi-* " *ments: quench your thirst with that blood,* which you have shed, but require no " more; and allow mankind to seek under the ashes, with which you have covered " this fertile land, some means of relieving those wretched inhabitants, who have " escaped the carnage countenanced by you." Then mankind would have admired your talents; your name would have been sanctified among the wretched Creoles, and you would have acquired substantial glory, to which you can have no pretensions by writing on erroneous facts related to you, and which you set off, with the title of Historical Notes.

Let me not be understood however, as affirming that nothing is to be attributed on this occasion to the Slave Trade. I scorn to have recourse to concealment or falsehood. Unquestionably the vast annual importation of enslaved Africans into St. Domingo, *for many years previous to* 1791, *had created a black population in the French part of that island,* which 'was beyond all measure disproportionate to the white.—Page xxii.

If you had been well acquainted with the events of St. Domingo, you would have known that the greatest part of the Negros, who were imported there for some years, prior to the revolution in France, were brought into the Southern parts, *which were the very last to rebel:* no, the Africans were not the first to take up arms: they could not understand these barbarous philanthropists, who imbrued themselves in our blood, nor be understood by them : they could not understood those Mulattoes, whose passions were industriously raised, and who were already too susceptible of barbarity, on account of that mixture of blood, which flows in their veins.

No, let us say it, the Africans were not the first, who murdered their masters. The Creole Negro, seduced by villainous emissaries, longed (though kindly treated) to spill their blood : Paul Belin, Jean François, Marechal, Toussaint, and many others were Creoles. Let the *Amis des Noirs* learn to know mankind. Let them know that *the wretched Africans were, and still are, held in contempt* by the Creole Negros, who never make free with them: let them know, *that distinctions and prejudices existed and still exist more among the Negros,* than among the whites: let them know, *that a Creole Negress never granted her favors to an African Negro,* whom she denominated by the name of *Bosal:* that a Creole Negro *did not eat,* nor *does he now eat* in the company of an African ! Let the *Amis des Noirs,* let those philanthropists *read and learn if possible, the heart of man;* but, until they can account for *its inconsistencies,* let them spare our blood, and that of those wretched Negros, who knew no real misery, until they rebelled against their kind masters.

Such, sir, are the subjects on which it would have been beneficial both for us and all Europe, to have employed your pen ; to have performed this, there needed not memoirs and critical observations : a feeling heart alone would have sufficed, and not to have forgot that yourself was a planter in the colonies..

Having thus pointed out the motives which induced me to write the following narrative; the sources from whence my materials are derived, and the purposes which I hope will be answered by the publication; it only remains for me now to submit it to the judgment of my readers.—Page xxiii.

3

I do not see of what advantage your narration can be, even were it exact : th principles and causes of the events are not sufficiently detailed : the sources from which you have derived your knowledge, were not pure : your designs in writing remain, and would forever remain unknown to the world, if those, whom you endeavour to condemn, did not answer : and if they did not try to find out the reasons which induced you to write. I pledge myself in my answer, to prove, that you might have avoided publishing such a work as that which you have submitted to public curiosity ; by which we can learn nothing : wherein nothing is fairly canvassed, and in which no moral reflexion compensates for the mistakes you have made.

HISTORY of St. DOMINGO.—Chap. I.

And it must be attributed I presume to the greater discountenance which the married state receives from the national manners, that in all the French islands these people abound in far greater proportion to the whites, than in those of Great Britain.—Page 2.

If you had travelled the colony over, you would have discovered the reason of there being more people of colour in the French, than in the British colonies : you would have seen it, in the fertility of the colony, and in the manner the white workmen were there paid : you would have seen it, in the difference of those, who managed the plantations in St. Domingo, and those of the British colonies : and, above all, you would have discovered it in the manner of their trade.

You would have seen that at St. Domingo the superintendants and managers of property being very well and highly paid *(many of them receive a tenth part of the next produce of the plantations, others receive a tenth of the produce, on paying a tenth of the losess and expences)* young men of good families, carefully brought up, but of small fortunes, were sent to that colony, in order to get such employments. The overseers of plantations, with means of making a fortune, had particular care of the children they got by women of colour ; and very often they had them brought up in France, and granted them their freedom. The women in St. Domingo are in general mothers of numerous children.

The women of colour, are far from being disagreeable, in proportion as they have less mixture with the blacks. Tradesmen, captains of ships, and all others, who do not remain for any considerable time in the colonies, attach themselves to them, and previous to their departure, generally give them a share of their profits.

In some of the English Leeward Islands, the Irish are esteemed the best overseers. In Jamaica, the Scotch are the persons who most generally administer over the plantations ; both the one and the other being brought up in rigid œconomy and great mediocrity, repair to the colonies, in hopes of acquiring a limited fortune. They have settled salaries ; they have not the various resources of speculating, which a French overseer or manager of a plantation has ; the planters in St. Domingo being men of extensive landed property, generally allow their administrators and overseers, to have as many flocks of sheep, as many horses, mares, mules, and other cattle, as they can well bring up : it is not thus with the English overseers : they are limited to a certain number of cattle for their own use : all the provisions come from Europe for their own consumption, and that of the plantation : thus, they have very few opportunities of knowing what it is to speculate, which acquired means would have given them. They are not rich enough *for keeping free women,* and still less of granting freedom to their children, when they live with a slave ; the proprietor of the plantation generally has those children educated as workmen, &c... but they remain attached to the habitation and live happy, on account of the succeeding overseer generally bestowing on the children of his predecessor, the cares and services, which, in return, he expects to be conferred on his own.

These are partly the principal causes of there being many people of colour in the French colonies; to which we may add another, the many large cities, which are in St. Domingo ; one will easily suppose it, on reflecting, that there were four cities, which had constantly all the year round, a regular theatre, with each a pretty good company of comedians ; and that two or three other towns had play-houses, where performers from the other theatres acted occasionally.

These cities where inhabited by many wealthy merchants, by civil and military officers, by garrisons, of which the regiments called colonial, were settled at St. Domingo ; besides, by the officers of the merchant ships ; who, selling their own cargo, became inhabitants, having houses, warehouses, carriages, horses, during some years. Most of all these persons kept free female Mulattoes, which contributed much to increase the number of the people of colour.

Another reason for the population of the Mulattoes is, that these being qualified in the French colonies, *to possess habitations as well as the whites,* more of them are married here, than in the English islands ; because the white planter, who wished to benefit his children, during his life-time, caused them to marry, and gave them such property as he had a mind ; which he could not do by his will, as the French laws did not allow him to grant more than a yearly provision for illegitimate offspring.

E

Let us also observe, that the women of colour *are in general more elegant* in the French, than in the English colonies; which, doubtless, renders them more engaging; that the opulence of the colony contributed to this, because people sacrificed more for them, than they could do in the English settlements.

This is what you would have discovered yourself, if you had resided any time in St. Domingo, so as to examine thoroughly the different habitations, to be enabled to speak with propriety of the manners of the inhabitants. There were, however, more white people of both sexes, married in the French, than in the English colonies, because the planters reside there, in a far greater number, than they do in the English islands. I shall confine myself to that very just observation, made by yourself, that out of the 85 members of the Assembly of St. Mark, *who embarked on board the Leopard*, 64 were married, and had between them 183 white children.

In St. Domingo the whites were estimated at 30,000, the Mulattoes at 24,000, of whom 4,700 were men capable of bearing arms, and accordingly, as a distinct people actuated by an esprit de corps, they were very formidable.—Page 2.

The white people of St. Domingo, owners of habitations as well as householders were estimated at 30,800; but, in this estimation, you should have observed, that the two colonial regiments of the Cape and Port-au-Prince, and the corps of artillery were not included, neither were those who belonged to the royal navy, the crews of merchant ships, and a vast number of tradesmen, such as masons, carpenters, and others, who daily leaving their places of abode, were never rated. Without exaggeration, one may venture to affirm, that the number of whites, usually residing in St. Domingo, amounted to more than 50,000 souls, of which more than 16,000 formed the white militia of the colony (and that was not the totality of them, who were capable of bearing arms; as all persons in the law, physicians and surgeons were exempted, as were likewise all those in either a military or sea faring employment, and, especially all persons in the European navy and trade).

Such a population ought not certainly to have deemed formidable 4,700 people of colour, capable of bearing arms, scattered all over the colonial parishes, without chiefs, without ammunition and energy; *they were never so, until* the unhappy moment, when the whites ceased to be united; then they gained that strength, which they owed to the different parties, who employed them; they never could do any thing alone; had it not been for their coalition with the Negros, they would have been soon annihilated, for they are not half *so brave as they*: if the Negros had been allowed to proceed, there would not have been left a single man of colour in all St. Domingo, *and I can prove* that, if the Negros were desired to extirpate them all from the colony, they would do it in a very short time, and cheerfully execute the mandate given for the purpose.. The Mulattoes proved only dangerous, on account of the differences of the Whites, and because their villainy is by far more cruel and barbarous then that of the Negros, either Creoles or Africans.

They enacted the laws, nominated to all vacant offices and distributed the Crown Lands, as they thought proper.—Page 2.

It is surprizing that a colonist, distance only 30 leagues from St. Domingo, could not have known to a certainty, that a general never enacted one single law. All edicts came from France : complaints were often made by the planters that the council of the colony sometimes registered a letter from the marine minister as a law ; but the mere and simple orders of generals and intendants, never had the energy of a law, except in cases of general police, and that provisionally. You little knew the vanity and pretensions of the two councils of the colony, of the Senechals and inferior judges, which would never permit them to subscribe to the arbitrary laws of a governor.

Generals named but provisionally to vacant posts : one may rightly suppose that the marine ministers in France, in which department were the French colonies, were careful of losing no opportunity of placing their own dependants ; sometimes the general's choice was confirmed by the minister, but generally it was not.

To obtain a grant of lands, it was expedient to submit to necessary expences and formalities, and the person, who first fulfilled these conditions always obtained the preference ; to speak otherwise, betrays an ignorance of the most common laws of the colony.

If you meant to speak of the new grants of lands *reunited* to the crown, you are strictly true ; but, it must be owned, that the *reunions* were deemed in the colony, a robbery committed on the first grantee ; and though it may have happened sometimes that he who had sued for the *reunion*, did not obtain it, yet, it was generally granted to him.

Against the abuse of power, thus extravagant and unbounded, *the people had no certain protection.*—Page 3.

Nothing but prejudice or ignorance could have advanced to you so false a proposition. The inhabitants would never have submitted to live under such a tyrannical yoke : with one dash of your pen, you bring a whole colony into a state of the most abject servility. I challenge you to mention one single fact in support of your assertion, excepting that of the embarkation of the council ; and that expedient *then* saved the colony from anarchy and confusion. The governor, and the

2

the superintendant, were subject to the same laws in common with the rest of the inhabitants, in all discussions relating to private affairs, property, or habitations.

He was, in truth, (the Governor) an absolute Prince, whose will, generally speaking, constituted law : he was authorized to imprison any person in the Colony, for causes of which he alone was the judge.—Page 3.

This is as unfounded as the foregoing article : it is true, that the governor-general issued orders to oblige the indebted planter to appear before him ; but for what reason ? because the inhabitants of St. Domingo were, in general, wealthy, brave, and accustomed to command their Negros in a very imperious manner. Whence it resulted, that, far from being, as you suppose, *the slaves of a despot*, they were often inclined to submit to no law : that the judges were not obeyed, and few inferior officers durst repair to the house of a rich planter. The consequence was, the act of justice could hardly be carried into execution.

As the greatest part of the French in St. Domingo were in the military service, and deemed it an honour, it was usual that, without the assistance of civil officers, whenever an inhabitant refused to obey a judgment or sentence of the judges, or pay his creditors, the general sent an order to the commandant of his quarter, who immediately forwarded it to the inhabitant ; the latter held it an honour to repair alone, without hesitation or delay, to the governor's, to give in his reasons : if then they were not approved, the inhabitant was ordered to apply to the court of justice, or to settle with his creditors, and to remain under arrest in town, on his parole : if there were heavy complaints against the inhabitant, he was confined in a military prison, where he was treated with all due regard.

On some occasions, people who fought duels, or who, by their bad and restless conduct, were inimical to the tranquillity of the colony, were ordered to embark for France ; but those orders were rare, and were only granted upon the request of the inhabitants themselves.

On the other hand, no arrest by any other authority was valid without the Governor's approbation ; thus, he had power to stop the course of justice, and to hold the courts of civil and criminal jurisdiction in a slavish dependance on himself.—Page 3.

Your work is a chain of errors. Why did you not know that judges of the higher courts, the general and King's attornies, daily ordered the convicts to be imprisoned as well as debtors, except the great owners of plantations ? The governor's

sanction

sanction was never requisite, neither had he any right to impede the execution of any act issued from a court of justice. I repeat to you, Sir, that you are but very little acquainted with the pretensions and tenacity of the French civil courts, if you seriously believe they would have put up with such a gross abuse; on the contrary, *they too often clogged* the wheel of government, on purpose to shew their power and importance. Never did governors interfere with criminal causes, they even were seldom present at the deliberations of the councils (a right they had as the King's representatives) except in cases where the administration or interest of the colony was concerned.

All these officers were wholly independent of the civil power, and owned no superior but the Governor-General, who could dismiss them at pleasure. It may be proper to observe too, that the counsellors held their seats by a very uncertain tenure.—Page 4, note B.

You pass from one error to another still worse! Why do not you define to your readers *what King's lieutenants were?* you should have told them, they were military officers, who could have nothing to do with the civil power: they commanded in garrisons and the militia; but, except in cases which related to military service, the King's attornies and seneschals would have made them sensible, that they had no power whatever, either over them, or the inhabitants.

You are also wrong, Sir, when you pretend that the *King's lieutenants* could be dismissed by the generals: you ought to have known, that they both received their commissions from the King; and you should also know that, *under the ancient government*, a French military officer could not be deprived of his commission without a court martial. The first French officer you might have addressed on that head, would have saved you the trouble of setting forth an error, which will appear palpable and absurd to the least discerning reader: if, in London, where there is every opportunity of getting such good information, you have neglected to do so, how much more *ought your readers to think* you have done it upon matters at a distance of 2000 leagues from you?

Your observation on the counsellors is also an egregious mistake. They received their credentials from the King, as the military officers did their brevets. The governor had no power whatever over them individually. They were, as to their functions, submitted to the controul of their own company; and, as to the rest, they enjoyed the same rights as the other inhabitants of the colony.

Seven members constituted a quorum for the hearing of appeal causes; but a hint from the Governor-General *was always sufficient to render much investigation unneces-sary: and it is asserted (with what truth I pretend not to determine) that, besides their slavish dependance on the executive power, the members of those courts* were notoriously and shamefully open to corruption and bribery.—Page 5.

I submit to the indignation of every unbiassed reader an author, who, without the least proof, boldly presumes to attack *respectable courts of justice,* and who, with-out any inquiry or reflection whatever, giving way to the wilful misrepresentations of individuals, who, perhaps, *had been stigmatized by them,* does not blush to publish such a paragraph; what answer could he make to one of those judges, who should challenge him to give even probable reasons for his assertions, and should sue him for damages? Unfortunately for the author, he would find himself under the same predicament as to many other parts of his pamphlet, wherein he himself candidly owns, as he does now, that he is not at all acquainted with the truth of what he ventures to set forth.

The officers, both of the regular troops and the militia, were commissioned provisionally by the Governor-General, subject to the King's pleasure and approbation; but the militia received no pay of any kind.—Page 5.

You just now said, that superior officers, such as King's lieutenants, town-majors, &c. were liable to be changed at the governor's discretion, who could dispose of every employment, so far, that he was, in your own opinion, *an absolute prince; here,* you own, that the appointment of all troops, who received any pay, as well as militia, were submitted to the King's sanction, whose commission was absolutely requisite. How do you reconcile *two facts so very contradictory?* and, above all, how can you have the assurance of placing them so near each other?

Who always was (the Governor-General) selected from the army.—Page 6.

The governor was often chosen out of the navy, such as Count d'Estaing, the Prince of Rohan, who were superior officers in that corps, the Marquis of Vaudreuil was likewise appointed Governor-General of St. Domingo, and others; finally, when the Revolution of France began, Commodore Count Peynier was Governor-General of the Colony. This plainly indicates *your slender knowledge of the affairs of St. Domingo;* you advance every thing without examining, regardless whether you mislead your reader or not.

While the lower orders among the Whites derived the same advantage from that un-conquerable distinction which Nature herself has legibly drawn between the White and Black inhabitants ; and from their visible importance, in a country where, from the disproportion of the Whites to the Blacks, the common safety of the former class depends altogether on their united exertions.—Page 6.

Instead of writing a history, with which you are unacquainted, why did you not unravel the principle of that distinction, which you own that nature has traced, of the necessary influence of all that is white in the colonies over every thing that belongs to, or originates from slavery ? By explaining this true principle as it ought to be done, you would have deserved the unfeigned and lasting thanks of your country, and of all the Whites in the Antilles ; but it was expedient to reflect and work on your own foundation : you preferred describing the most absurd stories, according to your own fancy, as will be seen throughout the following pages of this letter.

I mean, however, only to account for in some degree, not to defend the conduct of the Whites of St. Domingo towards the coloured people, whose condition was in truth much worse than that of the same class in the British colonies, *and not to be justified on any principle of example or reason.*—Page 7.

I call upon you to prove to the public what you advance ; which, if you do not, I shall invoke the judgment of all honest men on you. Produce more substantial proofs, than your mere *ipse dixit,* of the bad treatment experienced by the Mulattoes from the Whites ; or I shall give what you here advance, as a peremptory proof of the egregious ignorance with which the whole of your pamphlet is written. *That the condition of the People of Colour was more wretched in St. Domingo than in the English islands,* I deny, and now appeal to the impartial reader.

The free Man of Colour at St. Domingo enjoyed all the rights, which truly constitute the liberty of a man in society : he could inherit, sell, or purchase *to what amount he pleased* ; make his will, leave his residence, quit the colony, come back to it, *bear testimony* for or against the Whites and people of his own colour: he might marry, and transmit freedom to his children : in short, he enjoyed every privilege that the Whites had ; he served in the militia as they did, for which he had no pay (they likewise had none). What then was the difference between free Men of Colour and free White Men ? I will explain it : custom, afterwards sanctioned by law, ordained that the Whites should form themselves into companies of militia ; that the *Metis,* the *Quarterons,* the *Mulattoes,* should be promiscuously incorporated ; and that the *free Negros,* the *Grifs,* and the *Marabous,* should form distinct companies: that the companies should be commanded by White officers. There was no law that prohibited Men of Colour from being judges or lawyers; but they never indulged the idea of being so. The law did not hinder the Whites from marrying Women of Colour; neither did it forbid Men of Colour from taking White women amongst the French in marriage: custom alone and prejudice were the only laws. *In the distinct service of militia* consisted all the difference, which customarily distinguished, in the civil and military employments, the Men of Colour from the Whites: add to this, the prejudices which the meanness of birth generally imprinted in the minds of the Whites.

As the French islands had no colonial assemblies, the rights of the People of Colour were never discussed, and never was the necessity of the question started about limiting to any generation the duration of such prejudices. Let the reader keep in mind, that the colony was, in common with all the French, under a monarchical and military government, *where nobility is necessary, and where it was numerous.* This last reason is the best of any that can be adduced for the prolongation of the prejudice, which lasted against the mixture of blood in the different families, however opulent they might have become. It should be remarked, that custom, becoming a law, only said, that a Man of Colour should be in a distinct corps of militia. The reader, after what I have just observed, may judge the advantages of the Whites, and the disadvantages of the Men of Colour, in the French colonies.

Let us now consider the condition of the Men of Colour in Jamaica. They have, as in the French colonies, the liberty to marry, to manumize their children, to sell, purchase, and make their will; but not to inherit more than 2000 l. currency: they cannot bear testimony but according to the degree of their colour. *If a man be degraded, surely it is in this circumstance!* They serve distinctly in the militia; they are neither judges nor commanders; their fourth generation only can be members of the colonial assembly; there is no antecedent advantage in their behalf. All the difference is to the disadvantage of the Men of Colour in that British colony, where he can neither inherit, nor be a witness, without being subject to conditions unknown in the French colonies. What, then, are the laws of the colony of St. Domingo that cannot be justified, by example or reason, in their treatment of the Men of Colour? Does an author, who falsely alledges a fact, without any proof, to criminate unfortunate men, deserve any share of confidence? I leave the question to the determination of the reader.

In many respects, their situation was even more degrading and wretched than that of the enslaved Negros in any part of the West Indies.—Page 7.

My

My task becomes every moment more arduous. The above mentioned truths prove the falsity of this assertion. Discarding notorious and criminal malevolence, I am willing to impute it to downright ignorance. Incensed as I am by this phrase, I content myself with requesting my readers to remember, *that you are a party concerned against St. Domingo*, as a Jamaica planter, and that you bring forwards no proofs whatever of your absurd and ridiculous assertions.

Although released from the dominion of individuals, yet the free Men of Colour in all the French islands were still considered as the property of the public, and as public property they were obnoxious to the caprice and tyranny of all those whom the accident of birth had placed over them. By the colonial government they were treated as slaves in the strictest sense; compelled, *on attaining the age of manhood, to serve three years in a military establishment called* Maréchaussée.—Page 7.

Nothing of the like nature ever took place. I appeal to all those, who have been in the French colonies; Men of Colour were there full as free as the Whites.

I have already said, that all free Men of Colour were obliged, as well as the Whites, to serve in the militia; such was the public duty to which they were subject: but there was, in every parish, a brigade of horse, composed of Men of Colour, denominated *Maréchaussée*: in the cities and large boroughs, these brigades were numerous; but in small parishes, they consisted of four men only. This cavalry had a settled pay, and was commanded by brigadiers, Men of Colour, but their superior officers were Whites.

The first part of what you here alledge is very true, and I should be very wrong not to embrace the rare opportunity, allowed in your history, of paying homage to your veracity.

It consisted of certain companies of infantry, which were chiefly employed as rangers in clearing the woods of Maron *or runaway slaves.* This establishment was afterwards very prudently dissolved, *and the companies disbanded: it appearing, that the Mulattoes acquired, by communication with each other, a sense of common interest and of common strength, which was beginning to render them formidable to their employers.*—Page 7.

It may be easily seen, by what I have observed, that one reason of the great population of Men of Colour in St. Domingo was, that tradesmen, merchants, who remained there for some time, officers of trading vessels, the many overseers, who

G

were often discharged; in short, that all the Whites, who resided for any time on the plantations, had what, in the colonies, is called a *menagere*, that is, a woman, to take care of their apartments and effects. These women often became mothers. Many of those Whites had it not in their power to purchase their children from the planter, and pay the government the lawful fees of the ratification of their liberty, then they confined themselves to the purchase of their children from their master. The inhabitants, who sold them, continued to maintain them, to bring them up, and keep them on their plantations, with all that goodness so natural to the planters: they were *taught a trade*, which would more than support them, when they attained the age of twenty. At this age, the old master requested leave from the commandant, to enroll them in the *Maréchaussée*, or the horse-patroles of the parishes: they were paid out of the taxes called *Municipal*. After three years duty in this corps, the King granted, according to law, and *gratis* to him who had finished his time, a ratification of his liberty, which cost considerably to all other Men of Colour, or their parents.

The reader now perceives that what you deem a burden, was an advantage; for there was a compensation allowed the brigadiers and troopers, on the taking of the Maron Negros, &c. &c. exclusive of the gratuitous ratification of their liberty and the parish pay.

There was likewise a duty on foot, fulfilled by Men of Colour, which was in particular designed for the police of the cities, and also for the use of the councils and jurisdictions. They reaped the same benefit as the Maréchaussée. An appointment of this nature was eagerly sought after. How can you therefore, Sir, venture to affirm, that free men were treated in the French colonies as slaves, *in the strictest sense of the word?* Where are your proofs? you cannot contradict clear facts, proved by unquestionable regulations.

I do not know where you have heard the idle tale of the fears, which occasioned the disbanding of the Maréchaussée, where there were as many free Negros as Mulattoes. I can assure you that they in general behaved very well, that they were embodied, until the government of the colony was dissolved, and that the greatest part of the inhabitants of St. Domingo have demanded them back since the English have taken possession of the colony.

On the expiration of that term, they were subject great part of the year to the burthens of the Corvées; a species of labour allotted for the repair of the highways, of which the hardships were insupportable. They were compelled moreover to serve in the

2

militia of the province or quarter to which they belonged, without pay or allowance *of any kind, and in the horse or foot, at the pleasure of the commanding officer, and obliged also to supply themselves at their own expences, with arms, ammunition, and accoutrements.* Their days of muster were frequent, *and the rigour with which the King's lieutenants, majors and aide-majors enforced their authority on those occasions over these people, had degenerated into the basest tyranny.*—Page 7.

Here is an inconceivable mistake, and really unpardonable, as you might easily have learnt better. By your description of the *Corvées,* you represent the burthen as insupportable, *designedly to render more odious,* those who prescribed them : but, what will the reader think of you, when he finds that you are totally unacquainted with the nature of the task *of the Corvées* at St. Domingo ? I will here give its explanation.

All the inhabitants in the colony were compelled to send annually to the public works, called *Corvées,* a certain number of their Negros, in proportion to the number of slaves registered, as being on the plantations : they were employed in repairing the highways of the parish. The surveyor pointed out to the commander of the militia, the necessary repairs to be made : the latter sent to every inhabitant the assessment, which fell to his share to work ; or, if the labour was considerable, all the Negros sent to the *Corvée,* worked together, under the inspection of a certain number of White overseers, who the inhabitants likewise sent to direct them. They often repaired there themselves ; *an inhabitant,* who was an officer of the parish militia, was appointed weekly by the commandant of the district, to go and verify the muster of the Negros, and maintain good order among them ; *all the inhabitants, without exception of colour, were obliged to send to the Corvée ;* and the Negro slaves of the free Mulattoes were employed without distinction, with those of the Whites : a Man of Colour was appointed by the commandant, to accompany the officer of the militia, in the inspection of the works. And when he had mustered the Negros, he sent to the commandant, by the Man of Colour on duty, the list of the absentees. He often sent to the inhabitants themselves to let them know that their number of men was incomplete. *These men* were not under the direction of the militia officers, when disengaged from this *Corvée;* their duty and that of the officer of the militia lasted a week, when they were succeeded by others. *Such and such only* was the burthen, imposed on Men of Colour *at the Corvée,* and on my honor, I declare, that, during 20 years, I never knew them do any other duty. They had an equal right with the officers to be reimplaced, for there never was but one officer of the militia commanded for the *Corvée,* neither was there but one inhabitant of *colour on guard* in the week, and it was a matter of indifference who he was.

Once more, I declare that all free men of every colour, who resided in St. Domingo, were obliged to serve in the militia, as is customary in the English colonies, lawyers, physicians, surgeons, &c. excepted. Militia corps of whatever colour, had no pay, every man was by law obligated to provide himself with arms, uniform, &c. according to the company he served in, which was absolutely optional with the inhabitants; the wealthy served in the horse, and the lower class were in the foot. Men of colour likewise had their choice of serving in what corps they preferred, and their inclination generally led them to give the preference to the horse.

You are, sir, very little informed, even with the most trifling circumstances; in time of peace or war, *there was but one review of the militia, every three months,* that is to say four reviews in the year, and it was the same, and took place on the same day, for all the free people of every colour.

They were forbidden to hold any public office, trust, or employment, however insignificant. They were not even allowed to exercise any of those professions, to which some sort of liberal education is supposed to be necessary. All the naval and military departments, all degrees in law, physick, and divinity, were appropriated exclusively by the whites. A Mulatto could not be a priest, nor a lawyer, nor a physician, nor a surgeon, nor an apothecary, nor a schoolmaster. Neither did the distinction of colour, terminate as in the British West Indies with the third generation. There was no law nor custom that allowed the privileges of a white person to any descendant from an African, however remote the origin. The taint in the blood was incurable to the latest posterity. Hence, no white man, who had the smallest pretension to character would ever think of marriage with a Negro or Mulatto women: such a step would immediately have terminated in his disgrace and ruin.—Page 7.

I am eager to acknowledge that what you here say, is partly true: to prove, sir, how mortified I am to be under the necessity of contradicting you; but there was actually no law which rendered the Mulattoes incapable of these employments and professions. Previous to the Revolution, they never dreamt of the pretended misfortune of filling them, as they never had received a suitable education for it. They were through gratitude respectfully submissive to the laws, or rather the customs, under which *they received their liberty.* It is only within a few years, since the sect of reformers broke those bonds, which were the very basis of society, that they wished for new advantages: no laws in any part of the universe, were better framed than those, which the European colonies in the Antilles, and
particu-

particularly in St. Domingo, enjoyed to a degree of prosperity, unprecedented in the annals of history.

When the European planters left their native country, to go and inhabit the islands of the torrid zone, and when they placed their capitals in the acquisition of persons, of whom they stood in need, in their new establishments, they did it agreeably *to the laws of the mother country.* If death has mown down a great many among them, whilst they were accomplishing their design; if, by the perseverance and industry of those who escaped part of the dangers, the inhabitants of metropolitan cities, have arrived to such a degree of eminence, through the advantages accruing from commerce in the colonial commodities; they cannot *attack the charter,* which the Whites have purchased with their blood: and all the laws respecting their property, are as respectable and ought to be as religiously observed, as those in virtue of which the European proprietors possess their lands and their houses. *To attempt to invalidate or overturn this decree,* would be seeking to annul the first principle which constitutes the social law *of all united people.*

Admitting even, that European nations have a right to make, in their own constitution, what changes they please, not one of them has a right to tell its colonies: " We shall regulate, at 1,500 leagues distance from us, what best suits the nature of " your property, and, at our pleasure, alter the foundation of your social con- " tract."

You might and you ought, being a colonist, to have employed your talents, in defending our rights, telling the European nations, " *if your principles alter, you may* " *propose to us to adopt them; but if, better judges of what maintains our possessions,* " *and preserves our existence, and that of our families, we refuse to change the basis* " *of our constitution, rendered invariable by nature and necessity; then we cease being* " *the same people; we cease being your fellow citizens; we cease forming a part of your* " *nation; we become a distinct people; we break every bond that united us to you.*"

This privilege is incontestable, and if the laws of slavery be absolutely necessary in the Antilles, the mother country cannot have the right to change them without our approbation. It is in that *absolute necessity of slavery in the colonies,* that we must look for the origin of the laws, customs, and prejudices, against the People of Colour. They are indebted for their existence to the humanity of those Whites, who, after having *given them life, liberated them likewise from slavery,* to which they were *by laws* subjected. Those well informed travellers, who minutely examined the colonies, have observed that the prejudices of the Whites, against the People of Colour, are lawfully, absolutely grounded on the laws of personal safety: they have seen that the Mulatto

H

has received his liberty under the *tacit restriction* imposed on him, which is *by the Europeans called a prejudice*; he knew that he would *neither command nor judge his father*, who was *his master. If the agreement between the master and the slave*, which is so advantageous *for the latter, ought not to have been perpetually executed*, it would *never have been begun.* Men of Colour would have remained *in slavery*, and the planters would not have loaded them with favors, by granting them a share in their rights, and by excepting those few only, which are calculated to maintain subordination among those who remain slaves.

You might, sir, have employed your abilities in proving how necessary it was in the sugar islands to keep up subordination, among the various classes of inhabitants, and in shewing that, what is in Europe *termed prejudices*, is very useful and even necessary; for no white planter ever attempted to do them away, however attached he might be to his children of colour. You might, sir, have proved that the generosity of the Creoles would have done away the prejudices, if it depended on them; but they are absolutely necessary on account of the Negros, who, through jealousy, hate and despise the People of Colour. Whereas the Whites, thus distinguishing them from the others, loved them, and showered down favors upon them.

Finally, sir, you might have proved that the greatest number of these new people, called Men of Colour, are entirely indebted for their existence to the generosity of the planters: you might have demonstrated, that, if those prejudices did not exist, the planter would have been obliged to renounce *the pleasure of doing good:* you might, and ought to have, by explaining what often occurs, put the European readers, who are little acquainted with the colonies and their customs, in a state of judging for themselves.

For example, could you not have told those who affect to be philanthropists, who have sought and that with success, *to plunge the dagger into our hearts,* that, a stranger received in a plantation with an open and hospitable goodness, so universally displayed at St. Domingo, often gave way to the influence of the climate, and the allurements of a young Negro girl of fifteen; that, becoming the father of a Mulatto, he received as a gift, his child, on condition that he would procure the ratification of his liberty from the King. If no prejudice had existed in the colony, and if this child had been brought to Europe, and carefully educated, if (what is very uncommon) *he had profited by it,* at the age of 18 or 20, having returned to the colonies, and become the equal of his master or his successors, where his mother remained a slave, and proved in the interval, the mother of two or three black children, it would follow, that this Negro woman, aged 36, when her son completed his 20th year, would be still in the prime of life, and well able to work with her three black children.

But, what would be the consequence, in the colonies, if the Mulatto becoming free, could also become the superior of his former master? Let us suppose, that, this mother encouraged by the condition of her Mulatto child, had, through her own bad conduct, or that of her children, brought on herself, or on them, a punishment, necessary to be inflicted for the support of order. Let the philanthropist answer, what would the Mulatto, son of that black women have done, if he happened to be either the judge or commanding officer over his mother's master? Where would this son's resentment stop? Let the philanthropist judge what would be the tranquillity of the colonies in a similar arrangement of things. And let them tell us what would be the conduct of brothers, sisters, nephews, and cousins, in short, of all the kindred of a free Mulatto, who might be the champion of his relations.

Of the many other circumstances, which I might adduce in proof of the necessity of an intermediate class of people in the colonies, I confine myself to this one. Let the prudent and worthy man reflect on this example, and let the impartial man, who studies mankind, judge, if prejudices, which distinguish Men of Colour, from White ones, are not useful; as, without them, the White man could not have granted *one single liberty, without creating an enemy for himself.*

Then, this new race of men could never have existed, because cohabiting with the Blacks, from the first generation, it has lost the greatest part of that colour, which distinguishes it from Negros. Can the generous man, who bestows *a great kindness on a moderate stipulation, for his own and his family's safety, be blamed?* And, he who receives so signal a favor, *as liberty,* is he not bound to fulfil this condition which only *vexes his vanity,* which ought *not to be indulged as his colour hourly reminds him* of the valuable present conferred on him by the Whites? Let the philanthropist, who merits to be so called; let the man, truly a friend to his fellow-creatures, now judge what the Europeans call a prejudice in the White Creoles.

This is, sir, what you might have explained, rather than copying false or exaggerated anecdotes. The immense fortune of several People of Colour, in every quarter of the colony, prove far better than all arguments, how truly happy and protected they were.

A Man of Colour being prosecutor (a circumstance on truth which seldom occurred) must have made out a strong case indeed, if at any time he obtained the conviction of a White person.—Page 9.

The courts of justice were never free from law suits concerning rights of possessions, between the White inhabitants and the free Mulattoes, and justice was administered in their favor, as well as in the behalf of the Whites; for *you ought to know,* that the father and the White relations of the *Men of Colour, always protected, and often supported them* in their ill-grounded claims, which gave rise to many law suits.

To mark more strongly the distinction between the two classes, the law declared that if a free Man of Colour presumed to strike a White person of whatever condition, his right hand should be cut off; while a White man for a similar assault on a free Mulatto was dismissed on the payment of an insignificant fine.—Page 9.

The most ancient law of the colony did, indeed, ordain the penalty which you have mentioned, but I must say, that, during all the time I resided at St. Domingo, I never knew that offence to have taken place more than once; which was, after the campaign *of Savannah.* The Mulattoes were, for the first time (very inconsiderately) formed into regiments of colour; this was one *of Count D'Estaing's impolitic plans.* To that must be ascribed the first cause of the misfortunes of St. Domingo. A Mulatto, who had been a subaltern in his own corps, playing at billiards with *un petit Blanc,* first struck him many times, with the *queue* which he played with. The White man brought him before a magistrate. The commander of *Petit Goave,* being informed of it by the judge, ordered the Men of Colour to be imprisoned eight days, taking the matter up in a military way, and preventing thereby, the civil power having cognizance of it; and the affair was attended by no worse consequence than that punishment. During a long abode at St. Domingo, prior to the Revolution, this is the only instance I ever knew of a Man of Colour having presumed to strike a White.

I must allow, that I have often seen White people sent to prison, for having struck Men of Colour, and have myself, without any difficulty, obtained that justice for a Mulatto, who had been ill-used by a White.

I now repeat here, that the free people of Colour, were so very little vexed, that they were always protected by the White families of their father, who assisted them in all their affairs.

In extenuation of this horrible detail, it may be said with truth that the manners of the White inhabitants, softened, in some measure, the severity of their laws; thus in the case last mentioned, the universal abhorrence which would have attended an enforcement

forcement of the penalty made the law a dead letter. Manners, not law, prevented the exertion of a power so unnatural and so odious.—Page 9.

You ought to have observed, that these laws had been established at a time, when the colony was still weak, and could hardly support itself by it's own means ; that the force of opinion was then much more necessary. As you allow, that this law is become obsolete, why do you mention it, as a proof of the servility of the Mulattoes, since, on the contrary, the extinction of the law proves, that opinions, respecting them, were altered on account of the natural, *but too real partiality*, which the Whites generally bore for the Men of Colour ?

But the circumstance which contributed most to afford the coloured people of St Domingo protection, was the privilege they possessed of acquiring and holding property to any amount. Several of them were the owners of considerable estates, and so prevalent was the influence of money throughout the colony, that many of the great officers in the administration of government, scrupled not secretly to become their pensioners. Such of the coloured people therefore as had happily the means of gratifying the venality of their superiors, were secure enough in their persons, although the same circumstance made them more pointedly the objects of hatred and envy of the lower order of the Whites.—Page 10.

When a person proposes to write a history, can he reasonably bring forward an accusation of this nature, without adducing some proofs ? Especially, when persons of distinction, who ought to have been, and generally were chosen from among the best people, and those whom public opinion had never stigmatized, become the object of crimination. I can safely say, that, since my arrival in the colony, none of the public officers were ever accused of a crime, which you so very inconsiderately charge them with.

But there is this misfortune attending this, and must attend all other systems of the same nature, that most of its regulations (the Code Noir) are inapplicable to the condition and situation of the colonies in America. In countries where slavery is established, the leading principle on which government is supported, is fear, or a sense of that absolute coercive necessity, which leaving no choice of action, supersedes all question of right. It is in vain to deny that such actually is and necessarily must be the case in all countries where slavery is allowed. Every endeavour therefore to extend positive rights to men in this state, as between one class of people and the other, is an attempt to reconcile inherent contradictions, and to blend principles together which admit not of combination.—Page 11.

This is what you ought to have thoroughly explained ; as a planter, as a proprie-tor of slaves yourself, you should have employed your talents in establishing the necessity of a system existing in the colonies : you should, by pointing out it's ne-cessity, have protected your countrymen against the aspersions of those, who, for these ten years past, have been endeavouring to ruin them ; by proving the truth of what you assert : that, to be desirous of seeing the colonies under any other laws, but those already made, is aiming at the uniting *of incoherent principles* ; then, you would have obtained the esteem of wise and worthy men, and had a just and lasting claim to the gratitude of the planters.

It was so very easy for you, sir, to answer fully the declamations of the sect of the *Amis des Noirs*, and to convince all sensible and virtuous men whom they have mis-led, by presenting them with a true picture of the condition of the slaves, in our co-lonies, in opposition to that of the same men in Africa, and I will go still farther, with the condition of the day-labourers and peasants in Europe. Why did you not relate what happened in Africa, before the European repaired there for Negros to bring to our colonies, which is renewed every time a tedious sea war in Europe suspends that trade ? Why did you not offer to your readers the contrast of the wretched subjects of the petty tyrants, who swarm in Africa, and who are ever engaged in wars ? Why did you not speak of prisoners cruelly butchered by the conqueror, before the European visited those countries, and of those same prisoners, brought now to the Antilles, on a plantation, the master of which, interested in their welfare, con-tinually watches for them ; supplies that foresight, which nature has denied the Ne-gros ; surrounds them with enjoyments, which attach them to the new country they inhabit, and assuages those sorrows, which always naturally remind them of their na-tive country ; a master, in short, who is a second Providence for his slaves. These facts are strictly true, with regard to the French colonies ; and you pretend (but I know not on what ground) that the Negros are better treated in the English colo-nies. However, facts ought to have been fairly stated ; they would have been more welcome to the greatest part of your readers, than the metaphysical reason-ings of the friends of the Blacks, which they answer successfully enough.

Doubtless, Sir, it was an action worthy of you, to convince the friends of the Blacks, and all the European philanthropists, of the injustice and exaggeration of fears which the word slavery causes among them, by enabling them to compare the condition of the free planters of Europe, with that of the slave planters in the colo-nies. You would have removed their anxiety, by pointing out the Negro as certain of his subsistence and that of his family ; nursed during illness : free from care, and seeing old age approaching, unaccompanied with wretchedness and misery: subject to labour, it is true, but comforted in repose, by enjoyments which the fears of futurity do not disturb.

At St. Domingo, the Negro had a garden of his own, which produced the support of life : but, if dry weather, or any other accident, deprived him of its produce, the planter supported him and his family. On every plantation, there was a warehouse of provisions, in case of scarcity : there likewise was an hospital, furnished with the best medicines, and a physician, who attended two or three times a week, and oftener, if required. The Negro, by working only a quarter of an hour each day in his garden, might bring up pigs, poultry, &c. &c. He was also allowed to have mares, which, in common with those of the plantations, brought him in a yearly income, which was entirely his own.

If to these real facts you had added some observations, on the physical nature of the Negro's skin, which gives him an invaluable advantage in work over the White men ; transpiration piercing with difficulty the cellular and greasy tissue which his epidermis covers, he preserves that moisture, necessary for his blood, and is not liable to the inflammatory and putrid diseases, which attack and prove fatal to the Whites ; in particular, to the Europeans, in whom the radical humidity is less retained, which renders their blood more inflammatory. If you had directed the notice of your readers to the moral character of the Negro, you would have convinced every unbiassed man : in the first place, that, in lieu of natives, the Negros were the only persons fit for such works, as the European establishments under the Tropics and in the Antilles require. 2d. That men scarcely civilized, obliged to continual labour, *in a climate averse to it*, and in a number, which bears no proportion to the superintendants of that work, that these Negros were to be slaves through necessity ; you would thus have set the nations and governments of Europe in their true point of view, where the very nature of things placed them, in regard to their colonies, in the Antilles ; that is to say, in the alternative of *absolutely renouncing* the advantages accruing to them, or of their supporting slavery.

In short, you might have said, that the Negros were *grown up children*, with the wants of men ; if you had made a proper use of those talents, which nature gave you, by observing them, you would have easily discovered that every childish passion was implanted in their souls. Fickle, inconstant, vain, timid, fearful, jealous, generous ; without foresight ; superstitious, and always guided by the impulse of the moment : to these they unite all the vices of the slaves ; lazy, gluttonous, thievish, liars, vindictive, as all weak beings are, injustice driving them to despair. On the whole, you would have proved, that this race of men is naturally good : and if nature has denied them attention, observation, reflection, perseverance, and all the other advantages which give the Whites a superiority over them, she has proved exceedingly kind to them in respect to climate, *physical advantages, and even that of the heart* ; for, she has allowed them *that exquisite sensibility for women,* which makes man forget so many toils, and she has inspired them with *the most tender affection* for their children, which induces man to support every thing. You might have proved, Sir, that, if the Negros enjoy those advantages in their country, and on the burning sands of Africa, though under the despotic and barbarous governments of the petty tyrants of that country, their happiness must be still greater in the sugar plantations, where the air, though in a like climate, is constantly refreshed by regular breezes ; and where, having made hasty strides towards civilization, they partly enjoy the advantages of European customs, without losing those of their native climates. You might have well represented their lot in Africa, and, comparing it with that which they enjoy, under very different masters, you might have enabled your readers, who are just, humane, and skilled in the knowledge of social life, to decide, that, every thing duly considered, there were few people in general, more happy than the Negros in the colonies.

I have travelled over the principal states of Europe, and paid great attention to the habits and customs of the common people. No people on earth have visited more foreign countries than the English ; the colonies have not remained unnoticed by them ; to the English traveller, therefore, in particular, do I appeal for the proof, that the Negro in the Antilles *is not so wretched as the greatest part of the peasants in Europe.* The Negro is no longer the slave he was in Africa, and subject to the arbitrary whims of a cruel tyrant, whose will, founded on caprice, was the only law ; who is not even (as the planting colonist) defended against himself *by personal interest,* the acting principle of men in society.

In the colonies, the Negro is a slave, according to the acceptation of the word ; but he is, more properly speaking, what is called *a servant in Europe :* under the laws of a master, whose interest is attached, not only to his existence, but even to his happiness ; under the laws of a master, who is himself subject to those of his country, and also subordinate to the ordinances of religion, morality, and public opinion. The Negro is, moreover, under the protection of general laws, which are always awake to shelter him from that violence and cruelty, which might make an attempt on his life.

If the reader hears, that, in the colonies, the slave becomes one of his master's family, is domesticated therein, and looks upon himself to be a member of it, then

3   I com-

I compare him, not with the barbarous inhabitant of Africa, but with every description of day-labourers and workmen in Europe, who are far *greater slaves* than the Negros: not the slaves of an individual, whose interest it is to protect them, and whose neglect *of them* is attended by loss on his side, doubly so, as he must make an advance to replace the loss of them; but with those who are really slaves, to *necessity and to work*, which they often find great difficulty in getting.

One of the chief reasons for the establishment of men in society, is, the inequality of their means of strength, activity of mind, and health, which requires their closer union and the mutual aid of each other; that the weak might reap advantages from the superiority of the strong: it is, in short, the inequality of their means, which has prescribed to mankind an obedience to the laws of society, that they might be protected from oppression, want, jealousy, and idleness; in short, from all the misfortunes of a solitary being, and that he might the better enjoy all the blessings of Providence. Let the judicious observer reflect, whether it be the Negro or the peasant, the day-labourer or the European handicraft, who more enjoys the blessings of nature, through the channel of the laws of society.

The Negro inhabits a country, the heat of which renders it useless for him to provide himself with that quantity of clothes so necessary in Europe; he is, therefore, better able to regulate his motions. He is, by the climate, invited to enjoy pleasures little known among European peasants; water and coolness are the Negro's chief enjoyments. To the intense cold of Europe he is a stranger, he does not sit during a great part of the year, near a solitary fire. He enjoys more of himself, nor is he obliged, during his leisure hours, in summer time, to provide against the melancholy prospect, which presents itself, in the approaching winter, to the European peasant.

The Negro's master is obliged to take care of, and support him and his family: in times of bad harvest or famine, he must be fed; and, if he is forced to labour, he need not be uneasy respecting the goodness of the harvest, as it is his master's business to look to that.

The Negro, without the least inquietude for his own and family's support, *enjoys the blessings of life* under the most pleasant climate, and he has great plenty of good, wholesome, and varied food.

If the Negro be ill, a physician belonging to the plantation, administers him every relief that benevolence can suggest. The best drugs, the best medecines, the most suitable regimen, a most commodious hospital, convince the Negro, that interest and humanity induce the master to wish for his recovery, and that the greatest care shall be taken of him. By no means uneasy about his family, futurity gives him no anxiety, nor does it, in the least, add to his pains.

The climate is favourable to the Negro's labour, which is never exceedingly great. The privation of the Negro's work for the next day, would prove a sure punishment to the planter in the colonies (as it cannot be done by another journeyman). His children's births are, for him, days of uninterrupted pleasure. If the Negro cannot work, he *is fed, supported, and maintained, as if he laboured*, and with so much care, that his not working becomes for his master a real loss, which increases daily with his illness.

The Negro has no notion of those ideas, which plague philanthropists. The word *liberty*, in the sense and acceptation of it in Europe, is of no value to him : he knows that he was born to work, he sees his master busy in the management of his plantation : he sees his master's anxieties to be far greater than his own; he is submissive *through custom, habit, and weakness*, to the most common laws of society, and wishes only to be protected by them, in consideration of his labour ; he devotes it with pleasure, for the enjoyment of real happiness. A stranger to the principal wants of life, with rapture he enjoys pleasure, *which he prefers to his life*. He was born an inconstant being ; an hour allowed him to work for himself, will procure him *as many women as his passions require*, and he loves his children to distraction. After having enjoyed life in his youth, he sees old age approaching, *unaccompanied with cares, and never attended by those diseases*, which the European peasants are overwhelmed with.

His master loves and takes care of him ; his companions respect him *(for the Negros bear to old age the highest deference)* ; winter and hunger give him no uneasiness ; he sees, without any emotion of pain, an increase in his family : to his last moments, *his master's interest requires*, that every attention should be paid him, to convince his children that they will, in their turn, experience the same care, and that their old age will receive from his gratitude, the recompence and kindness due to their services. The labourers in the colonies are happy all their life time ; old age, especially, is to them a sure and comfortable port.

I now leave to the discerning and judicious readers, the comparison of the condition of the peasant with that of the Negro.

The most simple observations on the nature of man, plainly evince, that he is born a *slave to want, to labour*, and of course to society. Climate and individual constitution have brought in some changes in the different societies, but every one of them has sooner or later adopted those laws, manners, and customs, which best suit them. The colonies of the Antilles, had attained that degree of prosperity, which evidently proved that the regimen they pursued, was the best calculated for their happiness, and that abstractions and moral calculations, when compared with experience, are very often absurd.

I have therefore only to observe in this, that in all the French islands the general treatment of the slaves, is neither much better nor much worse, as far as I could observe, than in those of Great Britain. If any difference there is, I think that they are better clothed among the French, and allowed more animal food among the English. The prevalent notion that the French planters treat their Negros with greater humanity and tenderness than the British, I know to be groundless.—Page 11.

Inform the public on what ground you assert, that the prevailing and general notions of the French *treating their Negros more kindly than the English,* are false. Produce your proofs: your mere thoughts are, by no means sufficient to convince your readers.

You pretend to know yourself that the common opinion is ill-grounded: your knowledge is then owing to your own personal observations; but, pray, when and where have you made them? Since you only made a stay of a few days at St. Domingo, without being able to repair to any habitation; no one being then allowed to go out of the town, wherein you landed. You surely do not intend to give your readers as exactly true, the observations you might have made during your residence in a town where nothing but disturbances and disorder prevailed. Detail then your knowledge with some proofs: but since you have published your pamphlet without any, I am under the necessity of requesting the notice of your readers on your continual and inconsiderate propensity to impeach and decide on your bare assertion, and moreover to submit yourself to the verdict they must have already pronounced against you.

If you wish to be acquainted with some of the reasons, which enabled the French to use their Negros far better and kinder than the English, give me leave to observe: 1st. That the planters by residing much more on their habitations, than the English, are thereby better acquainted with their Negros. 2d. The produce accruing from their land, being far greater, they are of course richer: and you ought to know that rich people are inclined to make all around them feel the benefit of their opulence. 3d. The English overseers receiving less pay than the French have less means of making those expences, which the latter do at St. Domingo. 4th. In that island, the planters being possessed of a vast quantity of land, allow their Negros more ground for their private gardens, and a great plenty of water. If to these you add that the French planters from national character, are more willing than the English to communicate with their Negros, you will easily be convinced of the reasons which lead every unbiassed mind to acknowledge that the Negros belonging to the French colonies are more kindly treated by their masters, who more usually reside on their plantations, than they are by English masters, who are unacquainted with their Negros, on account of their mostly residing out of their colonies.

Yet no candid person, who has had an opportunity of seeing the Negros in the French Island and of contrasting their condition with that of the peasantry in many parts of Europe, will think them by any means the most wretched of mankind.

On the whole, if human life, in its best state is a combination of happiness and misery, and we are to consider that condition of political society as relatively good in which not-withstanding many disadvantages the lower classes are easily supplied with the means of healthy subsistence, and a general air of chearful contentedness animates all ranks of people—where we behold opulent towns, plentiful markets, extensive commerce and increasing cultivation—*it must be pronounced that the government of the French part of St. Domingo (to whatever latent causes it might be owing)* was not altogether so practically bad, *as some of the circumstances that have been stated might give room to imagine. With all the abuses arising from the licentiousness of power, the corruption of manners and the system of slavery, the scale evidently pre-ponderated on the favorable side, and in spite of political evils and private grievances* the signs of public prosperity were every where visible.—Page 11.

I have already mentioned the reasons of your assertions. You would have done much better by writing on this subject, since you had talents for it, and the power of truth brings you to that confession, which I have endeavoured to unfold.

Why, Sir, a total stranger at St. Domingo, will you set yourself up as a judge of those laws with which you are unacquainted, and instead of trusting to the observations which a little experience has allowed you to make, why do you at-tempt to establish an ideal theory, to confess afterwards, that facts are against your theory itself? The prosperity of St. Domingo, which you have yourself noticed, and you own to be obvious every where, ought to have convinced you that your notes were erroneous: why then, Sir, have you translated them? Why did you not wait until time and your own enquiries had made you acquainted with the latent causes you mention? You would have easily discovered there was none; but that you alone were mistaken in whatever you wrote on St. Domingo: since the prospe-

rity

rity of that colony was entirely owing to public and natural causes either of the soil, laws, or industry of its inhabitants.

The. meetings were held in spite of the governor, and resolutions passed declaratory of the right of the colonists to send deputies to the States-General. Deputies were accordingly elected for that purpose to the number of eighteen.—CHAP. II. Page 14.

You should have been informed that there were but very few meetings to chuse the deputies who were to be sent from St. Domingo to the States-General of France; that many inhabitants first wished to consider whether it was useful to send any *at all on this subject*; that many planters protested against that nomination, (I was of the number); that lists came from Europe ready made and were privately signed ; that there were only 4,000 names written down, more than half of which had not been signed by the real persons. You should have been informed that the judicious inhabitants, and especially those of the South, were averse to the sending any deputy to the States-General, on account of such a measure being quite contrary to the interests of the colony, which being itself overwhelmed with *debts of her own*, had no business to interfere with those of France. They were sensible that eighteen deputies only were too few to gain an influence over an assembly, who knowing us to be rich, would not have failed to lay accordingly heavy taxes upon us. This was the motive, which induced several planters to protest against those lists forwarded through the colony, and which an inhabitant, express from Paris, handed about at St. Domingo. Whoever attempts to write on the revolution of a country ought to be perfectly acquainted with its very origin.

Some of these were young people sent thither for education, others were men of considerable property.
Unhappily there was too much to offer on the part of the Mulattoes.—Page 17.

Be consistent with yourself, Sir, and do not advance that the Mulattoes were sent to Europe for education, that they were possessed of considerable property in the colonies, to say, a few lines afterwards, that unhappily they had great grievances to complain of. You are continually speaking of their misfortunes, and (as I have demonstrated) you only ground your reasoning on laws, either extinct, or which did not exist; and, finally, on mere fictitious facts.

In this disposition of the people of France towards the inhabitants of their colonies in

*the West Indies, the national assembly on the 20th day of August, voted the cele-
brated declaration of rights.*—Page 17.

To this ought to be ascribed all the misfortunes of the colonies ; the would-be
philantropists must rejoice on hearing the very name of that day.... the 20th of August was the fatal day, when the destruction of St. Domingo and other colonies
was pronounced ; and when were doomed to death more than 300,000 men of every
colour, the greatest part of whom expired in the most excruciating torments. Such
is the triumph of the reformers, and those miscreants who vainly attempt, by foolish abstractions, to bring men back to a pretended natural equality, which does not,
nor ever did exist, and which it would be impossible for them to define. Are the
ashes of the colony imbrued in the blood of so many unfortunate victims, not
sufficient for their woeful experiments ? and are not so many millions of men destroyed,
by the poisonous doctrine they have propagated through the whole world, sufficient
to prove the falshood of their principles, and the dreadful consequences which attended them ? When and where will they at last stop their cruel rage against the
human race ?

*To promulgate such lessons in the colonies as the declared sense of the supreme govern-
ment was to subvert the whole system of their establishments.*—Page 18.

The pretended Rights of Man, which were *quite absurd in Europe,* were *barbarous*
in the colonies, and have put the dagger and firebrand into the hands of the Mulattoes, who, afterwards, placed them in those of the Negros. These latter are still ignorant of what was meant to be said to them ; but, what they feel, to a certainty, is,
that they have lost very kind masters, who had for them a paternal tenderness,
whereas they are now under the awe of tigers, who wantonly spill their blood,
whenever they please.

*And this measure crowned the whole : they maintained that it was calculated to convert
their peaceful and contented Negros into implacable enemies, and render the whole
country a theatre of commotion and bloodshed.*—Page 18.

The *Amis des Noirs* certainly knew that the colony would be overthrown : but
such was their wish ; for, those pretended *Amis des Noirs,* who were downright Jacobins, were convinced that the first families of France had considerable property
in the colonies, and they wished to destroy, at once, all the means they might have
to oppose their designs.

A recital of the conduct and proceedings of these provincial assemblies would lead me too much into detail. They differed greatly on many important questions.—Page 19.

It is, however, in the conduct and proceedings of the provincial assemblies, that an historian ought to look for the origin and causes of those disturbances, to the baneful effects of which was owing the devastation of the most flourishing colony. The discerning and judicious reader might also, perhaps, discover in those assemblies, the motives which led to a proposal for the British government to take possession of St. Domingo.

The Mulattoes determined to claim without delay the full benefit of all the privileges enjoyed by the Whites. Accordingly large bodies of them (the Mulattoes) appeared in arms in different parts of the country.—Page 20.

The first insurrections of the Mulattoes were immaterial, and very little to be feared ; none of them precisely knowing what they were to lay claim to. By claiming the rights of the Whites, what did they aim at ? they had not the very first necessary notions to enable them to change their condition. The Mulattoes when they acted alone *were beaten every where* ; that race is cowardly, cruel, and too full of prejudices to succeed in any attempt. A few individuals, *whatever may be said* in their behalf, owed to circumstances, more than substantial talents, the degree of reputation they enjoyed.

Monsieur Ferrand de Beaudière, a magistrate at Petit Goave, was not so fortunate. This gentleman was unhappily enamoured of a Woman of Colour, to whom as she possessed a valuable plantation, he had offered marriage. Apprehensive that, by this step, he might be displaced from the magistracy—Page 21.

The unfortunate Mr. Ferrand de Beaudière had not acted, as a magistrate, for almost six years before ; he lived on his habitation near *Petit Goave*. He became enamoured of a pretty Woman of Colour ; and being more than 60 years old, and unable to obtain her otherwise than by marrying her (though she was not rich, as you advance) he drew up the memorial which cost him his life, to lessen the prejudice that would, if he had married her, have relegated him in the class of the Men of Colour. It must be observed, that Mr. Ferrand had been long before forced to give up his place as a magistrate. In general, he was looked on as a man of very little judgment. His love and partiality for that *Quarteronne* prompted him to write the memorial, which he presented to the Men of Colour, who *were base enough* to confess that it was not their own, but that they had received it from him.—This is strictly the truth; let it be contrasted with your assertions.

In the mean while, intelligence was received in France of the temper of St. Domingo towards the mother country. The inhabitants were very generally represented as manifesting a disposition either to renounce their dependency, or to throw themselves under the protection of a foreign power.—Page 22.

Why did you not enquire into the origin of those reports? you would have discovered that, from the beginning of the disturbances, the wise inhabitants of the colony had foreseen the misfortune which awaited on St. Domingo, whose only resource was, to be put under the protection of Great-Britain, that was interested in its preservation: for they were thoroughly convinced of a *constant truth*, which cannot be too often repeated, viz. that if St. Domingo *should be destroyed*, the destruction of *Jamaica would soon follow*; and that, in order to save its own colony, England ought to take possession of St. Domingo.

It was said, that they were no longer subject to the French empire, but members of an independent state.—Page 23.

I freely own, that a few inhabitants seemed to aim at a state of independency; but the opulence of the colony and its prosperity had misled some sanguine persons, who, thereby, much prolonged the salutary effects of the cares of those, who, wiser and better informed, wished to put it under the protection of Great-Britain. This diversity of opinion *may be deemed* one of the causes to which the overthrow of St. Domingo is owing; for, had it been entirely delivered to the British government from the beginning of the disturbances in France and in the colony, its own importance would, no doubt, have merited and obtained those endeavours, which would have effectually saved and preserved it.

The assembly concurred in sentiment with the orator; and one of their first measures was to relieve the People of Colour from the hardships to which they were subject under the military jurisdiction: it was decreed that, in future, no greater duty should be required of them in the militia than from the Whites; and the harsh authority, in particular, which the King's lieutenants, majors, and aide-majors, commanding in the town, exercised over those people, was declared oppressive and illegal.—Page 23.

I think, Sir, you pretend to prove by that proceeding of the colonial assembly, that the People of Colour were really very unhappy: the planters knew the contrary;

3   but,

but, either parents or relations to the Mulattoes, they wanted to increase both their happiness and fortune, which the French laws, in some circumstances, opposed. That occasioned great inconveniences in the colonies; it is on that account that the object of the first deliberations of the assembly at St. Marc, was directed towards improving the condition of the Men of Colour, in several points, susceptible of it; such as fixing the epoch when, as in the English colonies, the Man of Colour might cease being deemed an African; to find out means of enabling the Mulattoes to inherit their mothers' property, without being legitimated. As the momentaneous residence of the Whites in the colony, had induced the inhabitants to suffer (as necessary under such a climate as the Antilles) the concubinage which was there practised; it seemed but just, that the offspring of such a connection should inherit their mothers' property, which was forbidden by the law (called *coutume* of Paris) that regulated the colony. The laws of France prohibited natural children from inheriting the effects of their parents.

Humanity and true philanthropy, *and a still more natural sentiment*, had led many inhabitants, protecting the Men of Colour, to consider it just to find out some means of reconciling the prejudices necessary in the colonies, with the necessity of representing the Mulattoes in the assembly, either by allowing them to chuse, among the Whites, a certain number of deputies, or, in a still more direct way. I can assure you, that such a measure was a chief object of attention, and that the assembly was greatly inclined in behalf of the Men of Colour.

It is true, that some King's lieutenants or town-majors, exercised over the People of Colour an oppressive authority, by compelling some of those serving in the cavalry to be on duty for the service, respecting the communications between the several commanders; *and custom, not law*, had prescribed that a Man of Colour should be on guard at every King's officer who had the command.

In the overthrow of all former notions and ideas, which took place in the beginning of the French Revolution, it seems *that all departmental assemblies*, surprised at their new and sudden power, sought to make a trial of it, against the ancient authorities, by plaguing and tormenting them: this is the usual and natural mode of proceeding in a revolution.

The assembly of St. Domingo *itself* was not free from such folly; and the aversion they had imbibed, in the colony, *to the marine minister*, who had till then governed it, added to the hatred all the inhabitants bore to the *intendant of the colony*, (Mr. de Marbois,) caused an exaggeration in the lawful subjects of grievances, and induced the assembly of St. Marc to issue the decree which you mention.

Some military officers certainly deserved it, but the aversion to a few of them, and especially the desire of shewing some regard to, and attention *for ameliorating the condition of the People of Colour*, led the assembly to make it general against every King's commander.

The ship Léopard was brought from Port-au-Prince to St. Marc for the same purpose (to protect the representatives).—Page 35.

You are, Sir, but very ill informed respecting the truth of this fact. The arrival of the Léopard at St. Marc was a very extraordinary event in the history of St. Domingo, the particulars of which are too long to be here related; but I can affirm, that this ship, far *.from* landing with a view of protecting the assembly, *threw it -into a real panic.* It was one of those many astonishing occurrences, which have taken place since the Revolution, and seem to have brought it forward, in every respect. The embarkation of the assembly on board that ship, *was neither less surprising* nor less unforeseen. As one of those members who were on board, I ought to know every particular concerning it. I assure you, that the arrival of the Léopard was quite unexpected. That ship was so far unable to protect the assembly, that it was impossible for her to come into the bay of St. Marc. No human power could possibly have saved her, if a South wind had risen. I shall only tell you, that, if you had wished to get true information, you would have been told, that the ship came to the entrance of St. Marc's bay, to give the assembly notice of her departure for France, and to wait under sail for her dispatches to the King and the National Assembly; and that what followed was in consequence of the fear which seized on *some of the members of the assembly*, and that such an event was neither foreseen, nor even probable.

Here it was that he first learnt (Ogé) the miseries of his condition, the cruel wrongs and contumelies to which he and all his Mulatto brethren were exposed in the West Indies, and the monstrous injustice and absurdity of that prejudice.—CHAP. IV. Page 41.

The *Amis des Noirs*, may ascribe to themselves alone Ogé's misfortunes, whose brain they had turned. But how could that young man *help being deceived*, when even *you, sir*, who are both a colonist and planter of Jamaica, (which is about thirty leagues distant from St. Domingo), have yourself been deceived so far, as to advance and repeat vague and groundless facts, at a time when the prejudices of the colonies contributed to the preservation of your property? Ogé may have been deceived, *but ought you, sir, to have been so yourself?*

The first white man that fell in their way they murdered on the spot : a second of the name of Sicard met the same fate ; and it is related that their cruelty towards such persons of their own complexion as refused to join in the revolt, was extreme ; a Mulatto man of some property being urged to follow them, pointed to his wife and six children, assigning the largeness of his family as a motive for wishing to remain quiet. This conduct was considered as contumacious, and it is asserted that not only the man himself, but the whole of his family were massacred without mercy.—Page 44.

Such is, Sir, the effect of the exaggerations of those who, being little acquainted with men, presume to destroy the sacred principles and basis on which societies repose. Such is the dagger put into the hands of those, whom the reformers so ardently wished to impose on. The murder of the unfortunate *Sicard* was owing to the *hatred of a prejudice* ; but, when the ill-fated Mulatto, pointing to *his wife and six children,* and, no doubt, alledging his age, met the same fate, *in whose blood* have the monsters imbrued their hands ? In their own, in that of a Mulatto, like themselves, who was without arms and defenceless.

What opinion ought to entertain of you *all the White children, who have lost their fathers and mothers ?* What ought to think the fathers who have lost *their children,* and all those who are reduced to all the horrors of want and misery, mournfully lamenting the death of their friends and relations ? What ought to think all those, who overwhelmed by the atrocities, which they fell victims to, read in your pamphlet, that the misfortunes of the Men of Colour *were such that Ogé and his associates could not help being revenged on those by whom they were exceedingly oppressed.* By your groundless assertions, *you are yourself guilty towards them and your country,* whose subjects they are now, as well as you : the public will judge.

They soon invested the camp of the revolters, who made less resistance than might have been expected from men in their desperate circumstances.—Page 44.

Had you been exact in considering the conduct of the Men of Colour under every circumstance, you would easily have discovered that the foundation of their character is a mixture of every vice, governed by cowardice ; the little resistance which astonishes you in men who, at the moment you describe them, were surrounded by the Whites, sullied already by the most atrocious crimes, and having every thing to fear, suffered themselves to be carried off with less resistance than in fact one might have expected ; every thing should have convinced you of a great truth, which is, that in what was executed *on the part of the Men of Colour,* nothing of importance was done by them.

The Mulattoes have in general more finesse and knavery than the Negros; they have moreover a barbarous and ferocious character, which displays itself on all occasions. It is from a thousand proofs, which I offer to produce, that I declare, that almost all the atrocious acts which have been committed at St. Domingo since the Revolution, have been advised, commanded, and still more frequently executed, by the Mulattoes; this proves more than any thing their cowardice, although cowards are always cruel. Few instances of kindness and humanity in them can be adduced in exception to this rule, whilst many may be cited of the Negros towards their masters or towards the Whites.

The Negro is by far more simple than the Man of Colour; but he is braver, more feeling, and more generous. It may be said with truth that few traits of barbarity can be imputed to the Negros. In general they are courageous, and very susceptible of attachment; they often suffer themselves to be killed, if they cannot escape with their chief, rather than surrender themselves or desert him.

But Rigaud, the leader of the Mulattoes in that quarter, openly declared that it was a transient and deceitful calm, and that no peace would be permanent, until one class of people had exterminated the other.—Page 46.

Rigaud has unmasked the grand secret of the *Amis des Noirs*. A vain prejudice could not be the cause of this hatred: the destruction of the colony was the plan which had been devised, as tending to deprive the Emigrants of the means of preventing the accomplishment of the Revolution in France. The Jacobins and their disciples knew much better than the Mulattoes, that it was impossible the colony could subsist without the Whites; and the Mulattoes were ignorant enough not to perceive that their small number could not keep the Negros of the colony in subjection; and that their weakness would soon engage the Negros, *who hate them much more than the Whites*, to destroy them. They did not discover this truth till it was too late.

It is proper to observe here, that the Men of Colour were more severe towards their Negros than ever the Whites had been towards them; and in general the greatest threat that was pronounced against a slave, was, that he should be sold to a Mulatto. In short it was the greatest punishment he could be made to endure.

The Mulattoes, too vain and too ignorant, in thinking as Rigaud (even admitting all their successes to be complete did not perceive that they were putting an end to their political existence; for, had they succeeded in destroying the Whites, they would have found themselves in less than twenty years incorporated with the

Negros,

Negros, and the few that might have escaped the vengeance of the Whites or the hatred of the Negros, would have seen their first offspring of a colour, entirely different from themselves. The design of Rigaud which you mention was absurd; because he knew the small number of his comrades. By what you even say you must consider him as pronouncing his own death; the White planters were more than three times sufficient in number and courage, as well as talents, to destroy the whole race of the Men of Colour, if the Negros had not been called to join them.

But if the Men of Colour were incapable of making all these reflexions, *the innovators*, the *Amis des Noirs*, reflected for them, and troops of Jacobins, particularly monsters called *civil commissioners*, were sent from Europe. It is them, it is the Whites, who would have completed the destruction of the colony, and not the Mulattoes.

A sentence, on which it was impossible to reflect, but with mingled emotion of shame, sympathy, indignation, and horror.—Page 47.

The sentence against Ogé may appear severe to a man ignorant of the horrors that have taken place at St. Domingo and the crimes this young man committed. But you, Sir, admit all that accompanied his revolt; and you know, that by all the laws in the universe, the murderer is condemned to death. *How many murders had not Ogé either committed or caused to be committed?* In what respect was his punishment a disgrace to his country? How can it inspire horror, since he only underwent the penalties by which the law punished murderers, incendiaries, and in fine those, who, like Ogé and his accomplices, had made *their wretched victims suffer more than a thousand deaths.*

Consult the father who has escaped the massacre of his family! Consult the numerous families ruined by the ridiculous vanity of the Mulattoes and the absurd principles of the innovators! Consult the children who have lost their parents, and who, *ruined and wandering in countries far distant from their heritage*, are incessantly cursing the crimes for which Ogé and his accomplices have been punished! Unite, Sir, with all good and sensible men in eternally execrating the monsters who have instilled into the atrocious minds of the Men of Colour all the crimes which desolate the zone under which your fortune lies; and, above all, do not augment the wretchedness of my unfortunate countrymen by suffering them to feel that they have found in you more tenderness towards their tormentors than for their disasters! *Oh colonist! Oh planter!* do not attenuate the crime in the Man of Colour, by giving him reason to think that he may find *minds in Europe* that comprehend not the extent of his cruelties!

N

Barnave alone (hitherto the most formidable opponent to the prejudices and pretensions of the colonists) *avowed his conviction that any further interference of the mother country in the question between the White and the coloured people would be productive of fatal consequences. Such an opinion was entitled to greater respect as coming from a man who as president of the colonial committee must be supposed to have acquired an intimate knowledge of the subject, but he was heard without conviction.*—CHAP. V. Page 58.

This is, Sir, what ought to be repeated every day, and in a different manner, to the pretended philantropists of Europe, particularly to the cruel *Amis des Noirs*, and still more to every government. The distinguished but misapplied talents of this young man were too generally known not to occasion profound reflexions concerning the confession which the force of truth extorted from him : which was, *that the mother country ought not to be desirous of regulating the laws of the colonies, nor to interfere with the laws established between the different colours of men that inhabit them.* We ought never to cease repeating, *that those in Europe* who are the best informed concerning the affairs of the colonies, *know but little what concerns them* and are as much filled with prejudices against them as Barnave was ; who, being president of the colonial committee, was at last obliged to admit it, after all his efforts to the contrary.

Let the colonies perish, said Roberspierre, rather than sacrifice one iota of our principles.—Page 61.

Thus then the grand plan of the *Amis des Noirs* is known. *Let the colonies perish sooner than their new principles !* What, Sir, being a colonist and planter yourself, have you not discovered all the barbarity contained in this impudent and cruel confession ? Why has not your indignation against those who sought *to send you, your family, your friends and your countrymen to the grave, given your soul all the energy necessary to undeceive the universe concerning this tribe of persecutors,* who, in one word, have indifferently devoted to destruction all the colonies and their unfortunate inhabitants?

Some of the ladies (as I was told) even ridiculed with a great deal of unseemly mirth *the sympathy manifested by the English at the sufferings of the wretched criminals.*—CHAP. VI. Page 78.

This then is the gratitude you offer to those inhabitants who, in the height of misfortune, received you with *such eagerness !*

What ! *you have been a husband and a father ! you have friends and fellow-citizens,* and yet can have been unfeeling enough in the midst of this deluge of disasters that overwhelmed the Cape, and of which you were witness, to employ your time in selecting a barbarous aspersion ! Instead of sharing the calamities of those that surrounded you, you have lived secure enough in the midst of so many misfortunes to draw from them a calumny which you have since *reflected upon so little* as to venture to print.

I will appeal to all disinterested and feeling men, and tell them *that amongst the unhappy people at the Cape, in the midst of whom was Mr. BRYAN EDWARDS, there was not one that had not lost a father, a mother, a brother, a sister, or some friend or relation. Almost all had lost their property, and yet they received him with kindness and eagerness. The father forgot the death of his children, the child the loss of its parents; the husband the loss of a wife, perhaps dead, dishonoured in the arms of the monsters; the disconsolate mother forgot for a while the loss of her daughters, delivered up to a thousand torments more cruel far than death. But they forgot every thing, both the loss of their families and fortunes, in order to receive and welcome a stranger from a generous nation ! In the midst of so much affliction, this stranger, cold to the miseries and wretchedness of their situation, which he knew could not reach him, employed himself in slandering the women !*

Let those to whom I have appealed, judge.

That the whole body of the latter in St. Domingo had solid ground of complaint and dissatisfaction, cannot be denied. There is a point at which oppression sometimes arrives, when forbearance under it ceases to be a virtue: and I should readily have admitted that the actual situation and condition of the Mulattoes in the French islands, would have made resistance a duty, if it did not appear from what I have already related, that the redress of their grievances occupied the very first deliberation of the first General Assembly of representatives that ever met in St. Domingo.
—CHAP. VII. Page 81.

I have already answered what you advance ; I here again request the proofs of what you venture to write, and I repeat, *as I have already proved it,* that the Mulattoes were more happy in the French than in the English islands. I wish for no other proof than your own words (in confessing that they had great property), and what you here add proves still more that the principles and attachment of the Whites were very favourable to the Men of Colour. Never did the annals of any

people furnish proofs of ingratitude equal to that of the Mulattoes towards their be-
nefactors, all of whom where either their parents or relatives.

*It was the Mulatto people themselves who were the hard hearted task-master to the .
Negros.—Page 62.*

Philanthropists ! answer, yourselves, one of the most ardent friends of the Mulattoes.—I am ignorant, Sir, of the proofs you have to support this assertion, and whether they give you greater reason to expect to be believed, than those you have hitherto made use of in your work. But I will answer for it, that what you say is
very true ; twenty years experience has convinced me of it. The following are the
reasons which the Men of Colour gave, and still give, for their conduct towards
their slaves ; namely, that they know the Negros better than we do, and that they
are better acquainted with all their wickedness and vices, having more inter-
course with them, and having been bred up with them. The fact is, the Mulattoes mistake the hatred and disgust the Negros have to serve them, *for charac-
teristical vices.* But the Men of Colour are too ignorant, and too little accustomed to reflexion, to discover in the human heart the justice of the impatience and
horror of the Negros towards them, who see them freed from slavery, in order to
become their masters, only through the libertine caprice *of the common master,* who
is the White.

*The Negros apprized that it was only through the agency of the Mulattoes, and the con-
nexions of those people in France, they could obtain a regular supply of arms and ammunition, forgot or suspended their ancient animosities.—Page 86.*

You here admit, Sir, of what I have said in the preceding remark, and I will answer for it, there has been no change in the hatred and animosities which exist between these two classes of men ; I have proofs too numerous to state here. I shall
perhaps have an opportunity at some future period, to lay them before the public in
the History of St. Domingo.

*And publicly declared (the Mulattoes) that one party or the other, themselves or the
Whites, must be utterly destroyed and exterminated. There was no longer they said
an alternative.—Page 91.*

This declaration is a repetition of Rigaud's, which I have previously answered.
I shall add here, that the Mulattoes have already acknowledged the error into
which

which they had been plunged, and that they felt their own destruction approaching. Those that remain employ their power in amassing great fortunes, that they in their turn may escape ; none of them expecting to remain in the colonies *after their own declaration*, which will be certainly executed, whatever may be the fate of the colonies, though not so cruelly as you relate ; but it will be absolutely necessary that they quit it, if they should not succeed in exterminating the Whites, and still more so if the Negros were left to themselves and continued free ; for they would very speedily massacre them all.

And all parties as well among the Republicans and the Royalists, concurred on this occasion, in reprobating the folly and iniquity of the measure.—CHAP. VIII. Page 110.

The civil commissioners Polverel, Santhonax and Ailhaud, had quitted France, charged by the Jacobins and the *Amis des Noirs*, to do every thing in their power to introduce this measure. The inhabitants of all parts were much surprised when it happened, although they were forewarned by many. I had wrote to the colony ever since 1792, that this was the plan entrusted to those men sent to the colony. Vigorous measures might have been employed to prevent it ; they were pointed out : the number of ships, troops, &c. were described ; but that *mad brained spirit* that accompanied every thing that was done to prevent the evils of the Revolution, attended this circumstance as well as many others. You might have known that the colony had again been informed four months previous to the arrival of the civil commissioners, and have said, that it was the difference of parties that contributed most to prevent the effects of the measures pointed out and prepared. You ought to have mentioned the surprise of the Men of Colour when they learnt that they had been tricked by the *Amis des Noirs*, and that they only served *as active instruments* for executing their destructive plan ; but it was too late, every thing ceded to the torrent.

In the mean while the new governor (d' Esparbès) began to manifest some signs of dissatisfaction and impatience.—Page 111.

The unfortunate Count d'Esparbès, was the most incapable man to govern a colony like St. Domingo, particularly during a Revolution. The civil commissioners knew it well ; this was the reason they demanded him. But if this general had had the smallest portion of talents, necessary for his situation, the civil emmissaries would have been caught in their own net. It was proposed to Count d'Esparbès to have them arrested, and this might have been done, at the time it was proposed; in twenty-four hours after it was too late, he was seized himself and immediately embarked.

To one of these gentlemen I am indebted, for more valuable and extensive information, than I have been able to collect through any other channel.—Note d. Page 112.

I have already, Sir, answered your pretended collection of materials relative to the History of St. Domingo, and its Revolution. I have only got through a third part of your work, and the reader is capable of judging of the value and extent of these materials. I shall again prove how much you wanted new ones, particularly in the inaccuracy of those you have made use of, and how much wiser it would have been in you, to postpone the execution of a work, which you will certainly regret having published, since it will cause you to be reproached with a frivolity which neither becomes your situation, nor the subject you treat of.

I cannot refrain from giving my readers a proof how few the materials were that you have succeeded in collecting at St. Domingo, by telling them, that during your stay there, you even neglected to procure a good map of the island, to adorn your work with; but, in order to supply the defect, you have taken *Faden's*, even without his permission. Your printer is now at law with him upon the subject. Imperfect as this map is, it is the most correct thing in your work: we may suppose that had he been at St. Domingo, he would doubtless have procured one more exact. Since you, Sir, wished to write concerning the island, why did not you provide yourself with one?

On the 10th of June 1793, the civil commissioners having reduced Port au Prince, and Jacmel arrived at the Cape.—Page 114.

Being desirous of writing concerning the History of the Colony of St. Domingo, and its Revolution, you ought to have here stated what these civil commissioners were, and to have fixed the opinion of your readers respecting their character and talents; for they had a great deal of both.

As they had conquered Port-au-Prince by their courage, it was your duty, *even for the honour of the British arms*, to speak of their energy, since *these very conquerors* of Port-au-Prince were obliged *to abandon it to the English*, without having fired a single gun, and that they not only *fled from that town*, but from the *whole colony*.

In stating what you ought to have said, I do not pretend to give now the history of the colony; you may judge, and you will judge still better, as well as our readers, whether I shall be capable of it when the time comes. In the mean time, I shall continue, as briefly as possible, to answer all your errors. My answers shall be dictated by the knowledge I have of facts, as having been *an active and advising witness.*

There existed, it seems a decree of the National Assembly, *enacting that no proprietor of an estate in the West Indies, should hold the government of a colony, wherein his estate was situated.*—Page 114.

You might easily have learned from the first proprietor and inhabitant of St. Domingo, that the law which you seem to think was made by the National Assembly, was, on the contrary, made by the French Monarch; you might have been easily informed, that this law prohibited a governor-general from holding any estate or plantation in the colony he governed; you might have observed, that this was a precaution taken by the old government to prevent injustice, which a general, being a planter, might have been tempted to commit against his neighbours.

The proclamations which they published from time to time in palliation of their conduct, manifest a consciousness of guilt, which could not be suppressed, and form a record of their villainies, for which the day of retribution awaits, but still lingers to overtake them.—Page 117.

You have published your work in March, 1797, and you here still write your predictions. You are even unacquainted with the most simple facts, relative to the history you have published. The great criminals Polverel and Santhonax, not only escaped punishment, but on the contrary were declared free from blame. You do not state the reason, which is by far more certain than your prophecy. It is the treasures they carried off with them, those they sent to North America, and to France. This is what has destroyed your prediction, which is so far from being fulfilled, that Santhonax was sent back in triumph to the colony he had astonished with his barbarity; and your note is as surprising, as your prophecy is false, *for you there make Polverel die in some part of St. Domingo,* when he died in France in the midst of his friends and comforted by medical art; *tranquil in appearance,* but a victim to excessive pains, the consequence of his excesses at St. Domingo; *and doubtless a prey to remorse,* if it were possible for such a man to have any.

There is not a single colonist, but what could have informed you of these particulars, which a man, desirous of writing the history of their country, ought at least to know as well as them.

Nevertheless it appears certain that the population of the Whites has been entirely destroyed, and that not a single White was left at the Cape; it is estimated that if 12 or 1500 persons were saved, it was more than could have been expected.—Note, relative to the event of the Cape.—Page 121.

I beg of you, Sir, to notice what you say here, and which you declare to have received *from a person* in whose veracity you place the greatest confidence. You admit that the population of the Whites is destroyed. The period is very essential; this was before my arrival at Jamaica, before I began the necessary operations for putting the English in possession of the colony, and you allow that there remained not a single White at the Cape. For a long time past there were scarcely any upon the plantations belonging to this dependency. You will perceive by the succeeding answers, that you are not accurate in saying that no Whites remained there. It had certainly nearly caused their total flight; but it did not happen all at once. You will remember the state of the town, and the wish of the commissioners to call in the brigands. In short you at least admit that the population of Whites has been destroyed there. You will, however, soon bring them to life again, in order to *to prove how wrong it was* to propose to undertake to put the English in possession of this fine colony.

The possessions of France in this noble island were considered as the garden of the West Indies; and for beautiful scenery, richness of soil, salubrity and variety of climate, might justly be deemed the paradise of the new world.—CHAP. IX. Page 123.

If, having well reflected *on the truths* contained in this paragraph of your book, you had deduced the necessary consequences, being a colonist and proprietor of a plantation, and consequently capable of judging of the advantage of such an important colony to the mother country, you had, as a legislator, considered its interests, you ought to have felt the advantages Great-Britain *would derive* from keeping possession of St. Domingo, which has been delivered up to her by such unforeseen and favourable events. Had you employed your talents in stating *the immense advantages which must result to her* from this possession, you would have consoled and re-animated *the hopes of the planters in the different Windward Islands,* the soil of which *being dried up, exhausted, and swept away,* by the rains,

no

no longer repays their labour the advantages *their industry merits,* and which *the extent of their capitals requires.* You might have shewn them the paradise of the new world, St. Domingo, as a promised land, which waited only their arrival in order to triple their fortunes, and double the activity of the manufactures and commerce of England. You needed only, Sir, to have allowed yourself to have been guided by truth, which wrests from you the true and precious confession you here make, and which I shall make use of hereafter.

Of the territories which remained exclusively in possession of the original conquerors, the Spaniards, my information is very imperfect.—Page 123.

Why, Sir, have you undertaken what was beyond your power to perform? Because you have written the History of Jamaica and the English Windward Islands, was it necessary that you should write the History of St. Domingo; and that, by referring to such imperfect materials as you acknowledge you possess, *you should risk the reputation you may have acquired* by publishing the fables or tales that have been given you by two or three individuals, who were perhaps interested in deceiving you? Can we imagine, that all you really say concerning the History of St. Domingo can be contained in a dozen pages? You ought never to have written concerning this colony, as you are in the same situation with respect to the French part of St. Domingo, as you acknowledge yourself to be respecting the Spanish; that is to say, you absolutely know nothing about it; for certainly what you say concerning it amounts to nothing, when it is known, that the size of the French part is only half the size of that called the Spanish; that the latter is more fertile than the French part, and only wants cultivators, without being, as you say, and seem to believe, covered with *wild beasts* without masters. The Spanish inhabitants own the lands upon which they have *Hates* or *Corails* for their beasts and herds of horned cattle and horses, which are all marked and perfectly known, and with which they carried on a very considerable trade with the French part.

These noble plains only want cultivators, in order to repay *a hundred fold* the advances that may be made on them. This is what, in an intelligent work, you might have set forth, supported, and demonstrated. You would then have been the true friend of man; your labours would have been useful, and far from being dangerous, they would moreover have been instructive to your readers, instead of giving them ideas replete with errors.

F.

(54)

The Buccaneers.—Page 124.

You speak of the Buccaneers, in order to support the common passages, which *you repeat after so many others*, and which you wish should avail as a proof of the punishment of the cruel Spaniards. But it is not the Buccaneers who have punished the Spaniards; it is the Freebooters, who have retaken a part of the gold from these barbarous conquerors; which, in the very heart of St. Domingo, they tore from the unhappy inhabitants that peopled these countries. The Buccaneers were the first Europeans who sought to establish, and did establish themselves in St. Domingo, after the Spaniards; but all were or had been Freebooters; and it is particularly by sea, that their exploits have been (with so much reason) celebrated: for their conquests upon the continent, were only the consequences of their maritime expeditions. It was long after, that they established themselves *at Port-de-Paix*, and became Buccaneers, a name which originated from their custom of drying up their meat slowly, over a fire made with green wood, thence called *Boucan*, a custom that is still in use amongst the Spaniards.

They did not follow those great pursuits in hunting, which supplied them with subsistence and commerce, until freebooting became less productive. They never attacked the Spaniards by land, but for the purpose of pillaging their ports with their fleets. At St. Domingo, they were fixed too far from their establishments; they only fought when the huntsmen of the two nations met each other.

They consisted originally of a body of French and English planters, whom in the year 1629 a Spanish armament had expelled from the island of St. Christopher.—Page 124.

I am far from approving of the barbarities of the Spaniards; but, according to the custom of those times, they took possession of the Antilles *they had discovered*, and where they had formed more or less establishments. I approve of, and admire the courage of the Freebooters, who attacked them; but I do not admit, like you, Sir, that their right was founded in justice. It is unbecoming *a philanthropic historian* to make right consist *in power*. The Spaniards became masters of the Antilles, through a cruel barbarity; but the Freebooters, who attacked them their with so much bravery, *were not the avengers* descended from the Caribbees, and the aborigines of these countries; and the defence of the Spaniards against those who attacked them was legitimate. An historian should not, by his reflections, establish such dangerous principles in an age, and at a time *when their falsity* have almost overturned and brought *Europe to the brink of ruin*.

If the government of Spain had been actuated at this time by motives of wisdom, it
would indeed have left those poor people to range over the wilderness unmolested.—
Page 125.

You certainly, Sir, are very little acquainted with the human heart, and have reflected very little upon the species of men of which the enterprising people called
Freebooters and *Buccaneers* were composed ; since, forgetting the state in which Europe then was, and the courage and passions which guided these surprising adventurers, you above all forget their history ; for you make them to be peaceable huntsmen,·that might have been allowed to rove about the Antilles, without recollecting
the nature and basis of the plans and projects which made these extraordinary men
undertake every thing. It was the desire of seizing upon the treasure which the
Spaniards had found in the new world. It was the Freebooters that attacked and
the Spaniards that defended. They were obliged to support this war *in spite of*
themselves ; and to have suffered the Buccaneers to rove about the Antilles, would
have been giving them the desire and means of seizing upon what might have suited
them. *If, notwithstanding this cruel war, which lasted fifty years*, the Freebooters,
become Buccaneers, had compelled Spain to cede a part of St. Domingo, what
might they not have done, had they been left masters to ravage every thing ?

From a party of these adventurers (chiefly natives of Normandy) the French colony
in St. Domingo derived its origin. By what means they were induced to separate
from their associates in danger, to relinquish the gratification of revenge and ava-
rice, and exchange the tumults of war for the temperate occupation of husbandry, it
is neither within my province nor ability to explain.—Page 127.

The history of the Freebooters, imperfect as it is, would have given you that information which you pretend it is not your *business to possess.* Who then has compelled you to write concerning that of St. Domingo ? The duty of an author is
to instruct for the sake of his reputation, if it is not for the trouble and expence
his readers have been at to buy and read his book ; they ought not to be deceived
by a pompous title, in order to be told in the course of the work, that he has not
the means of *keeping his promise.* You might easily have learnt, that the increase
of the Freebooters, their wounded, their children, the advantages of their victo-
ries, their truces, and the habit of hunting in the island, were the causes of their
establishment : every thing would have given you the necessary clue for discovering
the reasons which first induced the Freebooters to establish themselves as Buccaneers at St. Domingo, and afterwards as cultivators. *Port-de-Paix* which they had

frequented since their arrival at *La Tortue*, was the first place they inhabited. The terror they inspired caused the principal Spanish planters to retire and settle upon the continent, and the rest to abandon those parts lying at a distance from the capital of the island. You might have easily known that at the Peace of Ryswick, the Freebooters or Buccaneers were settled in the bay called *Liguana*, whence Léogane derives its name. They were numerous at *Petit-Goave*, &c. These first beginnings are known to all the Creoles and planters of St. Domingo. Besides, if you were desirous of writing the history of this colony, you ought to have done every thing to inform yourself of the earliest foundation of the country concerning which you wish to write, in order that you may not say to the readers who have purchased your book, *I have not the ability to inform you*. The reader deceived by your pretended views, was not the dupe of his own vanity ; he became a dupe to yours, because you were desirous of writing concerning what you avow yourself ignorant of.

Of the towns and harbours in the Northern provinces the chief were those of Cape François, Fort Dauphin, Port Paix, and Cape St. Nicolas. I shall treat only of the first and the last.—Page 130.

In the preceding paragraph you confess you have not the knowledge necessary for the information of your readers ; in this you tell them you will not speak of two of the principal divisions of the Northern parts of the French colony; why then have you written, or if you wished to write, why not consult people in a situation to give you the information you want ? You should have known that *Fort Dauphin* in particular is a quarter very important on account of its productions, its situation, &c. *Port-de-Paix* deserved your attention the more as being the first establishment of the Buccaneers in the island, and the place where the republican forces in the Northern part assembled under the command of Laveaux, in order to oppose the English forces.

The Jesuits' College converted (after the revolution) into a government house, and place of meeting for the colonial and provincial assemblies.—Page 131.

I should not stop, Sir, to expose the trifling errors with which your book abounds, did I not think it necessary to put *your readers* upon their guard against assertions of very different moment. I must tell you then, that since the extinction of the Jesuits in France, their house, which *was not a college but a convent*, is become the *government* ; and it was in this house that the governor, in 1783, had the honour of receiving his Royal Highness the Duke of Clarence, which was *long before* the revolution.

It

It was built at the foot of a mountain called le Haut du Cap.—Page 131.

The town called *Cap François* was, and what remains of it is still, built upon a small plain, inclosed by a high mountain called *le Morne du Cap*, which forms almost a semi-circle; the bay completing its chord or base. The Morne has only a narrow passage for the road that leads into the plain; a great deal was obliged to be cut away in order to make the road good, for at high tides or the overflowings of the river, the sea washes the foot of it. On the South, the *Morne du Cap* is joined by the Northern mountains, which run along to the point of the rock where the *Fort of Picolet* is built, which defends the entrance of the road.

Unfortunately for what you here advance, what is called the *Haut du Cap* is a village, at the distance of a small league from this town; it is situated upon a very small hill which you gradually descend till you come to the Hospital of *la Charité*, which is a full mile distant from the Cape. If you had not announced that you remained there, where you collected various materials which have assisted you in writing concerning the colony, one might have thought you had been deceived; but, intending to write about St. Domingo, you ought to have travelled as an observer. If you so imperfectly place the first town of the colony, *and of all the colonies of the Antilles*, where you have been, and where you assert yourself to have collected your materials in order to write your Historical Views on the History of St. Domingo, what ought such an error to be attributed to? I beg my readers will recollect this in other cases where you may not yourself have furnished me with such strong proofs in order to refute you.

I am obliged, Sir, to fulfil a very painful task in exposing the very numerous faults which your pretended Historical Views concerning my unfortunate country contain. If in the two preceding articles I have proved errors which you ought to have avoided, having been upon the spot yourself, that which follows is still more surprising. It is of another kind, and is equally inconsistent in an historian as well as a Fellow of the Royal Society of London to have committed.

It is situated (the town of Cape St. Nicholas) at the foot of a high bluff called the Mole.—Page 131.

All who have travelled and those who have only visited their own country know that a Mole is a projection or jutting out of earth or stone into the sea, whether natural or artificial, of whatsoever extent, in order to break the waves, support the weight of the ocean, and sustain the shocks of this raging element. A mole then is any projection which separates a port from the main sea. That part of the sea thus separated by the projection called the Mole forms the port. You never should have written that the town of Mole St. Nicolas was situated *at the foot of a mountain called the Mole.* The Mole of Cape St. Nicholas is formed by a very even tract of land running four miles into the sea, called the peninsula, joining by its largest part the continent of the island of St. Domingo, with the hills behind the Mole town; the Mole is the peninsula on the North West; which, with the chain of mountains on the island on the North East, forms the gullet or bay of the Mole, nearly six miles long, at the bottom of which is the finest port of all the Antilles, and best sheltered from every wind. I shall now leave our readers to judge what confidence they can place in what you have hitherto written, if you make such mistakes as these, and how much they can depend upon you in every thing that follows. The contents of your tenth chapter are still more extraordinary.

It was destroyed (Port-au-Prince) by a dreadful earthquake on the 3rd of June 1770, *and had never been completely rebuilt.*—Page 132.

The town of Port-au-Prince destroyed in 1770 was very inconsiderable; it has been entirely rebuilt and increased to double its former size, several streets having been formed for that purpose by causeways raised upon the sea shore. You might have easily refuted the memorandums given you upon this subject yourself, by reflecting upon the degree of prosperity to which the colony has arrived since 1770; and by recollecting that Port-au-Prince was the capital, the residence of the governor-general and the *intendant* or administrator-general of the colony and the town where the two councils had been united. You should have considered that it did not require twenty years to rebuild it, when you know that the houses are built with wood.

Which makes the number of Negro slaves throughout the colony 480,000.—Page 135.

Had you taken the trouble, Sir, to consult any planter of St. Domingo, he would have told you that you might state the number of Negros at 500,000, at least; for, besides those you have given an account of, which have been entered upon the statement of each plantation by the inhabitants, you must know that in general the planters never entered children and old men upon these statements, that they might have less duty to pay, and furnish a less portion of service to the *Corvée*; a great many planters used to put in their statement only those who would *Maroon* or desert, and whose capture would have subjected them to the

2

penalty or confiscation of the Negros, if they had not been entered upon the statement of the plantation.

The total value at the port of shipping, in livres of St. Domingo, was 171,544,606.—
Page 136.

When a person wishes to inform the public of the produce of a colony, it is necessary to inform him of the entire nature and diversity of its revenues : after which, when he presents them with any estimate whatever, he should inform them of the number of years upon which the produce is calculated. After having produced the accounts upon which your estimate is founded, you should inform your readers that, without exaggeration, one-fourth more might be added to the accounts of the average you produce, which are calculated upon the amount of the colonial produce that had paid the customs, &c. As a correct historian, who really wishes to be useful to his readers, you ought to mention *the enormous contraband trade* carried on at St. Domingo, whose immense coasts are every where open to the commerce of Jamaica, Curaçao, and the American ships. As a colonist of Jamaica, you surely knew, and ought to have said, that three parts of the cotton of St. Domingo was smuggled into Jamaica ; that upwards of two-thirds of the crop of indigo went the same way ; that Curacao received a great part of the coffee from the Southern and Northern coasts, with some cotton, indigo, and white sugar ; and that the Americans, from the North, likewise carried off a great quantity of contraband sugar and coffee. Continuing likewise your calculations, you will observe, that this must amount in value to upwards of 1,500,000 l. sterling, which is a greater return than many of the Windward Islands make to their mother countries ; and which, for a commercial and manufacturing nation, is worth the trouble of reckoning, particularly by a writer holding a seat in the Senate of his country.

I am induced to think, Sir, that you have made these calculations as well as me : certain reasons, which I shall discover to my readers at the end of this letter, will give room to suspect the cause of your not publishing them.

For this difference various causes have been assigned, and advantages allowed and qualities ascribed, to the French planters, which I venture to pronounce, on full inquiry, had no existence.—Page 136.

You have certainly, Sir, hitherto displayed by far too much inaccuracy in what you have written, to make yourself easily credited. You ought to have laid before the public the proofs you have procured, and the information you speak of, since you hazard an opinion contrary to what, *by your own confession*, generally existed. Depend upon it, your assertion will not be admitted upon your bare word.

Being a planter, like yourself, and having resided more months at Jamaica than you did weeks at St. Domingo, I must tell you, that the planters of this colony possess the qualities attributed to them ; that they draw a greater produce from their lands than is drawn from the English colonies, from many other causes than those you very improperly attribute to the art and care with which they are watered at St. Domingo. You give your readers reason to think, that all the plantations in the French part of St. Domingo are watered, which is an error ; for in all the Northern part, forming the dependancy of the Cape, and the greatest province in the colony, there are not six inhabitants who water their lands. Those in the Western part are the only ones that are almost entirely watered ; and in the Southern part more than a third are not ; by which, when added together, it does not appear that half the sugar plantations are watered. This is a proof that you have not received the necessary information to enable you to determine. The following are the advantages, Sir, which the inhabitants of St. Domingo possess over the planters of Jamaica :

1st, Almost all the proprietors reside, or have resided upon their plantations more generally than the English planters ; the presence of the master attaches the Negro more to his work.

2dly, The proprietors make more experiments upon their soil than can be made in colonies where the proprietors do not reside so frequently.

3dly, At St. Domingo the sugar plantations, lying all in plains, the canes are more frequently replanted than at Jamaica ; where, being planted upon the hills and in the mountains, the proprietor is obliged not to plant so often, and to uncover his land less ; in order that the rains, so violent under the Tropics, yet so necessary to make the suckers thrive and the young canes sprout up, may not wash away the earth that has been newly dug up.

4thly, For more than twenty years past, there has been an emulation amongst all the planters of St. Domingo, which has occasioned the greatest improvement in the cultivation of the cane and the fabrication of sugar.

5thly, The great salaries allowed to the managers of estates who had talents, preserved these advantages established by the rich proprietors, who had added that theory to practice which fortune furnishes the means of acquiring to those desirous of instruction.

I feel no hesitation in declaring, that the situation of the plantations at St. Domingo is the principal cause of the difference in the produce, because the canes being

being planted on a plain, those that are called *great canes* (that is, the first production of a new plantation) may, without inconvenience, be more frequently replanted and rolled; they yield nearly one-half more than the young sprigs (or the canes which sprout out from the stock that has been previously cut); whence it results, that, by planting more frequently, we have a greater produce. But, in order to prove incontestably that the prosperity of the colony was owing to the planters, I shall bring proofs which ought to come within your own knowledge; one is, the account given to the assembly of Jamaica, by one of its members, Mr. Henry Shirley, on the 23d of November 1792. He says: " That throughout the whole Colony of Jamaica there are only 1047 small establishments, and 767 sugar plantations." According to your account, there are 793 sugar plantations at St. Domingo; but there are 7743 small establishments. Whence arises this difference, if it does not consist in the qualities you deny *to the French planters?* for it must be observed, *that the extent of the French colony of St. Domingo* ought not by any means to be considered as the cause of the extent of its culture, since there are many lands at Jamaica which only wait for the industry and labour of the cultivators, in order to yield a considerable produce. The qualities of the French planter are, his activity, his courage in undertaking new establishments, his industry, his sobriety, and his judgment in well considering the proper culture for his soil.

Another proof of the superiority of the talents and industry of the planters of St. Domingo over those of Jamaica, is, that the former have almost *always been in want* of the necessary hands for cultivation, whilst the English islands have always abounded in Negros, both better and cheaper, and the English planters have never been in want of any. Nevertheless, the small plantations, *which prove the general industry and activity of a people,* have not increased there in the proportion of one-seventh with those of St. Domingo. This is what in candor you ought to have stated. I shall add, Sir, that, after many observations, I think the fabrication of sugar at Jamaica tends to diminish its produce; because, generally, in order to have a clear sugar, agreeable to the eye, they do not lime it sufficiently, nor bake it enough; which makes a considerable part of the sugar *go into the sirups or molasses.* The planters at Jamaica are not ignorant of this loss; but they think they recover it *in the rum* proceeding from the sirups: which, certainly by that means, produces more and of a superior quality, but which, nevertheless, does not indemnify them for the considerable losses sustained in the first fabrication of sugar.

In the French colonies a good sugar-maker, or refiner, was sought after and well paid; in the English colonies a distiller, or a man that manages a still-house best, is in great estimation.

R

I shall add here, Sir, that many lands in Jamaica might be watered, if the proprietors pleased ; and there is even a considerable and excellent track of land lying between Kingston and Spanish-Town, having water, of which no use is made for culture ; which excites the astonishment of the planters of St. Domingo, who cannot comprehend why the other lands are preferred to this plain ; *the state of which is,* I think, one of the best proofs of the superior industry of the planters of St. Domingo over those of Jamaica.

*Having made diligent enquiry into the average produce of the French sugar-lands while on the spot—*Note F. Page 137.

You should have observed that the cane of St. Domingo is not, as at Jamaica, the only flourishing production ; that the produce of other articles surpasses that of sugar ; for there are a great number of plantations of coffee, cotton, indigo, cocoa, &c. ; that, according to the account given by M. de Marbois, and that of 1791 presented by you, there are 8536 plantations or establishments in the French part of St. Domingo, and that at Jamaica, according to the account I have already mentioned as having been given to the assembly of this island in 1792, there are only 1824 plantations or establishments of any kind whatsoever, working to raise the crops of the colony. I shall add, Sir, what you have not thought proper to state, although you have written relative to the History of St. Domingo at the time a part of this colony belongs to the English, which is, that the French part of St. Domingo *alone* returned to the mother country, in one year, DOUBLE *the produce returned by the* WHOLE *of the English colonies in the Antilles.*

In order to prove it, Sir, I shall make use of your own calculation (or *average,* page 136 of your work) ; and, balancing it with the account stated by a planter, your countryman and friend, Mr. Shirley, member of the colonial assembly of Jamaica, I shall relate what he states in the account he presented to it, which is, that in the years

$$\left.\begin{array}{c} 1788 \\ 1789 \\ 1790 \\ 1791 \end{array}\right\} \text{Jamaica only returned} \quad - \quad \begin{array}{c} \text{Cwt. of Sugar.} \\ 5,130,856 \end{array}$$

Add to this, that 2,563,228 cwt. have been produced in the same space of time by all the other English colonies ; which makes the total amount of sugar produced by all the English colonies in the Antilles to be 7,694,084 cwt. during the above four years, in which every thing was collected together that could contribute to raise these colonies to the highest pitch of prosperity.

Without examining, Sir, upon what memorandums you have founded your *average*, I shall content myself with remarking, that if to your calculation of the produce of sugar in St. Domingo you add one eighth for contraband trade, and 9 lb in the 100 for the difference between English and French weight, you will find that the colony has produced in four years 8,140,804 cwt. of sugar, which is 2,035,201 cwt. each year; whilst Jamaica and the other English colonies have produced annually only 1,923,521 cwt.; the surplus of 111,687 cwt. of the annual produce of St. Domingo may serve to balance the errors of the calculation, if there are any.

If you add, Sir, according to your *average*, the coffee, cotton, indigos, &c. together, you will perceive that the produce of these commodities, amount to a sum of more than 95,000,000 livres of St. Domingo, being much greater than the amount of its sugars. If you then add the contraband trade (which is *easier carried on*) for these articles, you will find in the whole, wherewithal to furnish *double the general produce of all the British colonies of the Antilles*; even including the three millions of coffee that was made in Jamaica in 1792, and likewise the produce of the other small plantations, in all the English colonies. *This observation is too important*, for an historian to have passed over in silence—this object is of too much *political interest*, not to be laid before the eyes of the nation, for which a book is written, and under whose power, the inhabitants of St. Domingo, have voluntarily placed themselves. Such a truth clearly demonstrated must prove, better than any thing that can be said, the advantages of this fine colony, *which is too little known* in Europe.

Being nearly two thirds more than the general yielding of all the land in cane, throughout Jamaica.—Note F. Page 138.

I repeat it, Sir, your confession is not sufficient in saying, that the lands of St. Domingo, produce twice as much as those of the colony of Jamaica. The whole English nation should be informed what the French colony of St. Domingo really is, and the advantages it will be of to the commercial and manufacturing mother country, that may keep possession of it. It must be observed, that if this fine and great colony *is destroyed, all the other colonies,* particularly Jamaica, *will necessarily and speedily share the same fate*; as a planter of that island, you ought to know and fear it more than the Europeans; the reflection ought to have stopped you when you wrote the succeeding chapter..

And such in the days of its prosperity, was the French colony in the island of St. Domingo: I have now presented to my readers, both sides of the medal.—Page 138.

Certainly, Sir, the nine chapters I have just read over, give but a very faint idea of the French colony of St. Domingo. The exhibition of the remains of one of the sun's rays going to be obscured by clouds, is not giving an idea of its splendour ; in like manner you have given but a very imperfect idea of what St. Domingo was during the time of its prosperity ; it is absolutely unknown to you, and for which I appeal to the testimony of your own countrymen, who have been there since its disasters. What has escaped from its overthrow, has struck those who came there after a long residence in the English colonies, with astonishment. Even its ruins have surprised those who have long resided at Jamaica, the most considerable and most flourishing of your islands : and in the wretched state to which the colony is reduced, it has still returned considerably more productions, than any of the other English islands that have not been ravaged.

You ought to have informed yourself of the present state of St. Domingo, and not to have forgot that the misfortunes of that superb colony have doubled your revenues. As a planter of Jamaica you ought to acknowledge that the diminution of the productions of St. Domingo and the disasters of the Windward Islands have doubled the price of your produce, and raised your colony to the highest pitch of prosperity. The re-establishment of St. Domingo cannot be very agreeable to you : you even seem to fear it : and I believe this is what has induced you to write your Historical Views, and to throw blame upon the proprietors of this colony. *I beg the reader will once more recollect, that, being a proprietor of a sugar plantation at Jamaica you cannot be indifferent concerning the fate of St. Domingo, and it is your personal interest that has prevented you from being impartial.*

To Great-Britain above all other nations of the earth, the facts which I have related may furnish an important lesson : and it is such a one as requires no comment.—Page 138.

Why, not expose, Sir, to all Europe, and to England in particular, the great lesson which the misfortunes of the finest colony present to the universe ? Why not call forth the ideas and attention of your country to its interest and to what it has to fear from that cruel sect of the *Amis des Noirs* ? Why not present to her the example of what she must expect, if, listening to innovators and their perfidious systems, she suffers them to carry their flaming torches into her colonies ? Why not incessantly exhibit to the English people the most flourishing colony, the effect of labour for more than a century, destroyed in a great measure within two years ? Why not repeat to them incessantly, " *consider St. Domingo ; that fine colony*

" *colony formed the glory of America; the barbarians wished it to be destroyed, and a*
" *great part of it is so. May this terrible example for ever prove a warning voice*
" *for yourselves and your families dispersed through the Antilles !*"

Why have you not employed your talents in repeating, in a thousand different shapes, that, if the most considerable island is abandoned to the *anarchy of a revolted population of slaves*, such as that of St. Domingo, *Jamaica will be destroyed soon after?* Why, since you are incapable of giving your fellow citizens all the necessary information, in order to prevent, *by the recital of our misfortunes*, every thing which can make them experience them, why have you not wholly consecrated your labours in writing commentaries which your too imperfect account will not allow them to do? But my readers being put upon their guard against your superficial knowledge, by what I have hitherto written, may appreciate the whole of your work. I beg of them to lend me all their attention, as I am going to enter into the most disagreeable part of my undertaking. My answer to the 10th chapter of your book will finally convince your partisans and most sincere friends of its imperfections.

Emigrations from all parts of St. Domingo had indeed prevailed to a very great extent ever since the revolt of the Negros in the Northern province; many of the planters had removed with their families to the neighbouring islands, some of them had taken refuge in Jamaica, and it was supposed that no less than 10,000 had transported themselves at various times to different parts of the continent of America.—CHAP. X. Page 140.

Before I begin to refute this chapter I must remind you, what you very well know, that it was I who, *if I may so express myself*, directed every thing at St. Domingo at the time the English took possession of it. On that account, Sir, I am better able to expose your errors than any other person. I am obliged to call upon our readers before I continue my painful task, which truth and my attachment to my unfortunate countrymen have compelled me to undertake. I must observe both to them and to you, that, if you have hitherto been guilty of negligence and trifling in what you have written concerning this colony, in what follows you are still more so; for it is no longer upon some few and uncertain memorandums that you might and ought to have written the chapter containing the transactions of the English at St. Domingo, as many of the officers who contributed to your country's success in that colony are in England; the principal commanders are likewise returned—and you might have consulted them.

Your work was published in March, 1797, and General Williamson had returned to London near a twelvemonth ; Colonels Whitelock and Spencer, and Captains Mackaras and Smith, with many Englishmen of all classes who have been at St. Domingo, and who by their labours have added a part of the finest and most useful of the colonies to the possessions of Great-Britain, have since resided in this country. You are totally inexcusable then if any errors are found in this part of your work ; particularly if, after having seen you several times, I never refused to communicate to you the knowledge I possessed, as having, according to your own confession, *been sent express in order to conduct this important operation.* With what sensation then will my readers learn that the tenth chapter of your book is that which contains the most errors. I shall now refute you as an ocular and confidential witness. I here oblige myself, Sir, to furnish proofs of every thing I shall advance, in order to manifest the injustice and barbarity of your calumnies against my unfortunate countrymen ; *who, with that loyalty, that frankness, and that bravery, which is natural to them,* gave themselves up to England without being conquered, *even by the excessive misfortunes that overwhelmed them.* I write in England, Sir, and I call down upon me the vengeance of all impartial men if I do not prove that you have unjustly wished to render the fidelity of the Creoles and colonists suspected ; who, by their sacrifices, have done every thing in their power to deserve the support of that generous government which has preserved them from the destruction *to which their country had condemned them.*

If my answer contains errors, *it is I alone that am responsible for them.* I ask not your indulgence, Sir, but that of your readers. In answering you, I am cruelly afflicted, at finding that various interests have made you write against the colony of St. Domingo and its generous inhabitants.

I beg my readers will recollect, as well as you, Sir, what you have asserted in this paragraph ; it will very soon serve to condemn you.

The principal among the planters having other objects in view had repaired to Great-Britain.—Page 140.

I must declare to you that not a single proprietor of St. Domingo had then come from the colony to England ; all had been in France. Those who have since come did not arrive here till after the disasters of our unfortunate King. I came here express in 1791, and was then one of the first to return ; the rest could not till after the commencement of hostilities. Many had not even the means till (by the taking possession of the colony by the English) they could receive succour from the British merchants ; few of those had resided at St. Domingo, and were but very imperfectly acquainted with the colonies.

It is a circumstance within my own knowledge that so early as the latter end of 1791 *(long before the commencement of hostilities between France and England) many of them had made application to the King's Ministers requesting that an armament might be sent to take possession of the country for the King of Great-Britain and receive the allegiance of the inhabitants.*—Page 140.

Few planters had made propositions to the English Ministers in 1791. I came to England at that time, and found myself here alone. The events and the *misfortunes of the colonies* have but too well proved that it was wise to propose to the King's Ministers the taking possession of St. Domingo, in order to prevent not only its destruction, but that of Jamaica and all the other English colonies. The events that have happened since that period have too well proved how reasonable this proposition was ; *Grenada, St. Vincent's, the war of the Maroons at Jamaica,* answer for those who had announced and foreseen the misfortunes of the English colonies. After this, if it was me who presented these observations to the Ministers, my conduct, my constancy ought to have proved to you that the colonists were worthy of succour, and that he, who did not cease *to announce what has happened,* would not deceive the King's Ministers.

They asserted (I am afraid with much greater confidence than truth) that all classes of the people wished to place themselves under the English dominion, and that, on the first appearance of an English squadron, the colony would surrender without a struggle.—Page 140.

If an inhabitant unacquainted with the colonies, if any other than a colonial planter had written this phrase, it might have been attributed to his ignorance ; but that you, Sir, being a colonist of Jamaica, could believe that there was an inhabitant foolish enough to propose to the Ministers what you assert, can scarcely be credited. How could any one attribute to them what you write, that all classes of inhabitants in the colony were desirous of putting themselves under the dominion of Great-Britain, since they knew that the Mulattoes and Negros had revolted, and that it was against them the colony must defend itself ? There is only one sensation, that of personal interest as a planter of Jamaica, that could have induced you to write in this manner. I shall make no other answer ; but let our reflecting readers judge both you and the pretended propositions made by foreigners, to such well-informed Ministers as those placed at the head of the British government.

In the summer of 1793 a Mr. Charmilly (one of the planters) was furnished with dis-
patches from the Secretary of State to General Williamson, the Lieutenant-Governor
and Commander in Chief of Jamaica, signifying the King's pleasure (with allowance
of great latitude, however, to the Governor's direction) that he should accept terms
of capitulation from the inhabitants of such parts of St. Domingo, as solicited the
protection of the British government.—Page 140.

At last, Sir, you introduce me before the scene of your work : this *Mons. de*
Charmilly is not unknown to you; and you knew both by your friends and by what he
had said to you, that he must be perfectly acquainted with the French colony of St.
Domingo. It is he, then, that requests you to recollect what you have written yourself,
that General Williamson should accept, if he should think it proper and useful, the
terms of capitulation of such parts of St. Domingo as solicited the protection of the
British government.

And for that purpose the Governor was authorised to detach from the troops under his
command in Jamaica, such a force as should be thought sufficient to take and retain possession of all the places that might be surrendered, until reinforcements
should arrive from England.—Page 141.

You here admit, Sir, that the governor of Jamaica was authorised to send only
as many troops as should be sufficient, in order " *to take and retain possession of all*
" *the places that might be surrendered, until reinforcements might arrive from Eng-*
" *land.*" Had you taken time to have reflected upon your own phrases, and the con-
fessions they contain, you would have abstained from calumniating those who were
charged with an expedition that has been more fortunately and more completely
executed than those *who proposed it,* and even *the King's Ministers themselves,* expected—That is what I shall prove hereafter.

Mr. Charmilly having thus delivered the instructions with which he was entrusted, sent
an agent without delay to Jérémie, a small port and town in the district of Grande
Anse, to which he belonged.—Page 141.

As, in the following sentences, you accuse those who have pointed out to the
Ministers the advantages of an operation respecting St. Domingo, *with having been*
led away and conducted by their personal interest, I must here particularly set forth
the error into which you lead your readers, in order no doubt to prove your accusation ; which is, that M. de Charmilly sent first to Jérémie, *to which place he be-*
longed.

longed. This phrase tells your readers, that I conducted the English to la Grande-Anse, in order to prove (what you afterwards advance), namely, that I thought of my own interest, in endeavouring to save the dependency, and that part of the colony where my own property lay, first. I must inform both you and our readers, that I never possessed any plantation in this dependency; that Cavaillon, a parish on the Southern coast, where my sugar plantation lies, is upwards of 50 miles from it by land, over the double mountains, where there are only horse roads; and by sea it is upwards of 100 leagues from it. This insidious error is the more notorious, as, had you wished to have informed yourself among the numerous planters of St. Domingo in London, there is not one but would have informed you that, with respect to my property, I was a stranger at Jérémie.

It will no doubt be expected that some account should be given of the difficulties which were to arise, and the force that was to be encountered, in this attempt to annex so great and valuable a colony to the British dominion.—Page 141.

I have read your work over and over again, and have not been able to discover the particulars you promise concerning the difficulties that presented themselves in opposition to the execution of the determination taken by the British Minister. The state which you give of the forces has only existed in your imagination, and I shall hereafter prove it by my answers; but the event has proved it still better, for the English troops were received in the colony without having been obliged to fire either a cannon or a musket shot.

I am well apprized that I am here treading on tender ground; but if it shall appear, as unhappily it will, that the persons at whose instance and entreaty the project was adopted, EITHER MEANT TO DECEIVE, *or were themselves grossly deceived in the representations which they made to the English government on this occasion—* Page 141.

You felt, Sir, how much you were obliged to act with precaution in this part of your work; but you have not the less continued to write at hazard. How can it be conceived that a colonist, that a man who has the honour to sit *in the first Senate in the universe,* can be capable of accusing people without proof, who, by their attachment, have rendered the greatest services to his country? Yes, Sir, if you prove, as you assert you will, that those who solicited the Ministers to accept their project, *intended to deceive them,* or have been grossly deceived themselves, I readily consent to incur *the punishment of a traitor;* for I, Sir, more than any person whatsoever, since the year 1791, solicited, represented, and furnished the plans to

T

the Ministers, in order to commence this great operation, the management of which I undertook myself. I here declare to you, and to all England, that *I could not have been deceived*, for I too well knew the colony and its inhabitants; so that, if any person is guilty, *it can only be me*; and if I am guilty, I ought to be delivered up to the indignation and hatred of civilized Europe. Produce just proofs to the public; I have a right to expect them, and I ask for them. But, if you do not prove what you advance; if, on the contrary, the continuation of my answers confirm how frank, loyal, and faithful, I have been; if I prove that the success surpassed the hopes I had given—deem it not amiss if I appeal to Great-Britain to judge you, and if I give you up to those sensations I invoke upon myself if I am guilty. I have still more reason to complain of you, as you might have known of the Ministers, by your new situation, the means which ought to have been furnished *as serving as a basis* to the success of the proposed projects.

*It is my province and my duty to place the failure which has ensued to its proper account. The historian who, in such cases, from fear, favor, or affection, suppresses the communication of facts, is hardly less culpable than the factious or venal writer, who sacrifices the interests of truth and the dignity of history to the prejudices of party.—*Page 142.

You have here condemned yourself, Sir; prove the want of success of the plans that were proposed, and I am guilty: but, if you do not, what opinion will just men entertain of your work, after what you require of an historian?

I know not, nor will I enquire, whether you have been induced to write against the unfortunate planters of St. Domingo, through that spirit of party which has caused you to say, *that the inferior order of nobility exacted the more in proportion as they had less claim to real merit*; but I must think and believe, according to your work, that your personal interest, as a planter of Jamaica, has contributed much towards making you express yourself as you have done respecting the colonists and the colony.

The republican commissioners, as the reader has been informed, had brought with them from France 6,000 chosen troops, which added to the national force already in the colony, and the militia of the country constituted a body of 14 or 15,000 effective Whites. All these amounting in the whole to about 25,000 effectives, were brought into some degree of order and discipline, were well armed—Page 142.

Before I begin to answer every thing you advance, it is very important to fix the readers' ideas. In page 109, you say that the civil commissioners sailed from France in July 1792: here you say, they were accompanied by 6,000 choice troops, which, added to the force already in the colony and the militia of the country formed an army of 15,000 Whites; you then add to these, the greatest part *of the Mulattoes, which you say,* in page 20 of your work, amounted in all, at the beginning of the troubles, to only 4,700 men capable of bearing arms. You likewise add certain corps of Negro troops which never existed ; and you thus establish an army of 25,000 men, well armed and disciplined : (although there were no corps of Negros till after the civil commissioners had proclaimed their liberty).

But seeing clearly that your assertion would make your readers ask for proofs of what you advance, and where these 25,000 men were assembled, you disperse them in all parts, without informing us in what proportion they were divided throughout the three provinces of the colony ; which was very essential, in order to establish the difficulties and dangers of the project which the English Ministers had been so-licited to adopt, and which was confined, according to your own account, page 141, to the taking *possession of all such places that might be surrendered.* Making use of your own words, in order to destroy the difficulties you create at plea-sure, I shall observe, that in page 140, you set forth that many of the plan-ters had emigrated from the colony, with all their families, after the revolt of the Negros in the Northern part; that they were in the neighbouring islands ; that some retired to Jamaica ; and that it was supposed that 10,000 planters had taken refuge, at different times, in various parts of the continent of America. You forget that you made the population of the Whites amount only to 30,800.

After the emigration which you admit of, how could it furnish the numerous mi-litia you give to the colony, and the powerful forces which you have thought proper to create ? You moreover forget to establish an essential point ; which is, the period when you make this army of 25,000 men exist. We will fix it at the arrival of the commissioners at the Cape, the 13th of September 1792, the time most favorable to your assertion.

But the war did not then exist between France and England, it did not take place between the two nations till February 1793 ; it was not till the June follow-ing, that the Ministers sent me to execute the projects that had been proposed to them, and the plans they had adopted ; *the possibility of their execution being always subject to the opinion of the governor of Jamaica :* who, being upon the spot, could judge of the facility of their execution, and *the complete success of which* depended upon the succours which might arrive from Europe.

We must then fix ourselves at this period, in order to judge what those difficul-ties were that were found in the colony. Now I observe, in page 114 of your work, that the commissioners having subjected Port-au-Prince and Jacmel (you are not ignorant that this operation had likewise produced a very considerable emigration)

3.

arrived at the Cape, on the 10th of June 1793. In page 115, you say, that ten days passed in negociations and hostile preparations ; the governor and his brother landed on the 20th of June, with a corps of 1,200 sailors ; *that, assisted by the mili-tia*, &c. &c. they presented themselves in order to attack the civil commissioners, who had taken refuge in the government, where they were defended by the Men of Colour, and a body of regular troops with *one piece of cannon.*

You have been at the Cape, Sir ; you have seen the court yard, or the garden belonging to the government, and you must know what a small number of troops it can contain ; 1,500 soldiers would be too much embarrassed to be able to exercise : the forces shut up there, had only *one piece of cannon.* If you put to-gether the troops that Galbaud brought, those that declared for him, and those that the civil commissioners had, you will yourself see how inconsiderable at that time was the number of all these troops, and that after the battle which, according to you, was *fierce and bloody*, there could not remain many. If to this you add the massacre you relate in page 116, as having taken place from the 21st to the 23d at night, adding thereto the 12 or 1,500 men which you say (in the note to page 121) retired on board the ships with General Galbaud, you will agree, Sir, that the army of 25,000 men which you created, was very far from being in existence. In short, recollect, and you will perceive, that, according to your own confession, the whole or nearly the whole of the population of Whites, in the Northern part was destroyed at the period of the 23d of June, 1793 ; and that no part of that army created by you, or of that which had really been formed, existed, when on my arrival at Jamaica on the 24th of July, I delivered to General Williamson, the packets with which I was entrusted, in order that he might judge of the utility of the projects and plans accepted by the Ministers in England.

Without making imaginary calculations, you should really have informed your-self of the quantity of troops in St. Domingo, when, towards the end of August, Ge-neral Williamson ordered preparations to be made for the expedition to take pos-session of the colony. You would have learned that there were not 2,000 Euro-pean troops in the whole of the French part ; that there was no militia of Whites nor any corps of Negros or Men of Colour ; that the small number of those who bore arms acted as national guards attached to the party of the civil commissio-ners ; but there was no corps regularly formed and still less disciplined. You might have known that the two thousand regular troops were dispersed in the different parts of the colony in very small and incomplete bodies.

You

You ought, moreover, to have mentioned the famous affair of the 19th of June, which will ever be celebrated in the annals of the colony, for the bravery, courage, and patience, displayed by the inhabitants of la Grande-Anse, and which saved the whole colony. This event will prove, more than any thing I have hitherto said, what few difficulties there were to surmount, in order to execute the proposed plans'; it will likewise prove how much you have exaggerated the force of the Men of Colour, the population of which, on the 19th of June, experienced such a diminution as they have never since been able to recover, and what little danger was to be expected from them, at the commencement of the execution of the projects relative to the colony.

Our readers and you, Sir, should know, that the 19th of June, 1793, 1,200 Men of Colour, accompanied by some Negros, attacked the post called the *Camp des Rivaux*, situated upon the coffee plantation of that name, in the mountains leading from Port-au-Prince, to the town of Jérémie. It was at that time only defended by 3 or 400 of the brave White inhabitants of la Grande-Anse, accompanied by a few of their slaves. The great house belonging to the planter, built upon the top of a hill, served as a guard house: thrice did the Mulattoes come within pistol shot of this house, defended by a two-pounder, and thrice were they shamefully repulsed. At length, the commander of the Whites, who had been *wounded* from the beginning of the attack, having ordered a general sally to be made from the houses in which they were shut up, the Mulattoes were completely routed, leaving upwards of 500 dead upon the spot, and having upwards of 200 wounded, who died in their flight, without reckoning a considerable number of others who saved themselves with difficulty. After this victory the Men of Colour never assembled alone; the lesson was severe, and they never will forget it. The generous defenders of la Grande-Anse saved the colony by this battle ; and I can venture to say, *they that day saved Jamaica and all the colonies of the Antilles.*

These were the first inhabitants of the colony who received the English; it is them in particular who have incessantly fought for them. It was more than a month after this honorable event, when I arrived at Jamaica. The commissioners trembled at such great success, and they continually kept themselves upon the defensive, having every thing to fear from the small number of their partisans. Add to this likewise, that there was only one ship of war of any consequence in the colony, viz. *l'Inconstante* frigate, which was taken a short time after the arrival of the English at Jérémie. You see, Sir, and the reader will observe as well as you, how much you have been deceived relative to the state of the colony, at the time Gene-

ral Williamson thought it useful to his country, to execute the plans of the Ministers concerning it. This worthy general, blessed by the planters, is here, as well as
many English officers who first went to the colony—Let them be consulted—they
can tell *which of us it is that deceives his readers.*

In the additional notes to your work, page 240, you say, that it is *only* in the
Southern part of the colony that the decree (which gave liberty to the slaves) was
put in execution. It is very amazing that, publishing your work in 1797, you
should be ignorant that this law had been put in execution in the Northern part, in
part of the Western district, and in fine at Guadaloupe, St. Lucia, and in French
Guyana. Your readers must be the more surprised at this error, by its being placed
in a note written at the end of the work : it must prove to them how misinformed
you are, concerning the subject upon which you write.

*Yet vast numbers of all parts of the colony (apprehensive probably that this offer of li-
 berty was too great a favor to be permanent) availed themselves of it to secure a
 retreat to the mountains, and possess themselves of the natural fastnesses, which the
 interior country affords.*—Page 143.

Where did you discover that *great quantities of Negros* retired into the mountains, and established themselves in places naturally fortified in the interior of the
country ? The French part of St. Domingo does not contain any such place ; every
part of the colony is perfectly known : it contains no place of difficult access,
where a population of 100 *Negros could establish themselves*; the mountains not
being large enough in the two narrow points of the island, which form the greatest
part of the French colony. In the centre, towards the Cul-de-Sac, is the renowned
plain, perfectly well known, beaten and intersected by many roads. Bring forward
the persons who have so misinformed you : why did you not consult those who have
inhabited the colony since the arrival of the English ? General Williamson, or many
others, could have easily undeceived you.

Successive bodies have since joined them, and it is believed that upwards of
 100,000 *have established themselves in those recesses, into a sort of savage republic.*—Page 143.

Who could have told you *the absurd tale*, that a population of 100,000 individuals had assembled in the savage and inaccessible parts of the colony, and had
there formed a species of *republic still more savage ?*
 You are a colonist, a proprietor of plantations, you have seen and might have
observed the Negros and the climate of the colonies, and you can speak. You ap-

pear to believe in the assembling of 100,000 Negros! No, you do not believe it ; *some motive arising from personal interest made you write this sentence* ; for, where could you first fix upon an inaccessible part that could contain such a population ? Have you calculated the great extent of land necessary for nourishing so many people in the retired parts of the mountains, at a distance from all succour furnished by sea and commerce ? Being a planter in the Antilles, you must know how much vegetable food is required to support a number of Negros who could no longer get meat and salt fish by commerce to add to their support. How could you admit of a sudden assemblage of 100,000 Negros under the same government, without magazines or cleared land, you who ought to have studied the light and fickle character of this species of men who are such enemies to labour ? A republic of Negros ! there is no man who has been in the colonies *but what must laugh at the idea.* What, Sir, have you not examined what has passed since the beginning of the misfortunes of St. Domingo and in the other colonies where the Negros revolted ? How happens it that you have not observed that the Negros, faithful to the character which Nature has given them, are acquainted with only one kind of government, namely, that which is founded upon implicit submission ? What, Sir, are even the present facts and calamities lost upon you ? Observe, read the immense list of their chiefs, or we should rather say, of their most absolute Sovereigns ; they may be counted by dozens, and yet you speak of a Republic for the Blacks! What follows will perhaps discover to us your reasons.

Like that of the black Charaibes of St. Vincent where they subsist on the spontaneous fruits of the earth, and the wild cattle which they procure by hunting.— Page 143.

It is no longer the inhabitants of the colonies, it is no longer the persons who have travelled through the Antilles, whom I call on to judge of the error you present to your readers. The inhabitant of Europe, who has reflected upon human society ; the man who has considered the interests of his country, its resources, and the wretchedness attached to so many unfortunate beings (unremittingly employed in labour to support themselves and their families) will judge full as well as the planter in the colonies of the falshood and impossibility of what you here advance. What ! can you venture to compare a population of 100,000 men to the small number of Caribbee families that live at St. Vincent's, *not by the spontaneous productions* of the fruits of the earth, which would not suffice to support a single family, as is proved by the Maroon Negros in our Colonies, but who with much difficulty live upon those they cultivate with corn and vegetables, and the roots and plantains which they plant ?, State to us, Sir, the spontaneous fruits that can feed 100,000 individuals; add to them all the wild cattle you please, and you will perceive that the *recesses and natural fastnesses* of the whole of St. Domingo and Jamaica cannot support six thousand men. Consider a little what an extent of land is necessary to feed numerous flocks, and what speedy havock a population, equal to what you make so easily live upon the spontaneous fruits of the earth, must occasion ; and likewise, that there are no more wild cattle in any part of the French colony of St. Domingo, nor indeed in the Spanish part, where all the numerous herds have their masters ; and, although wandering, are easily collected when necessary, which indeed is generally done twice or three times a year. These herds are much diminished to what they formerly were, and could not long suffice for a population of 100,000 men, who must subsist principally upon them, as they would be obliged to do if reduced to live upon the spontaneous fruits of the earth.

You ought to have expected that the European reader would ask you how this remote population, without communication with the sea ports, could extend their hunting, and furnish the necessary means for bartering for arms, lead, powder, &c., which they would want, and the necessary articles for cloathing their wives and children ? The informed cultivator will ask you whether at the approach of such a *republic* the Spaniards would remain quiet spectators of its establishment, and particularly if they had given up their cattle to them ?

The Negros, Sir, were so far from acting so foolishly with respect to themselves, that I must inform you they never quitted those parts that were most inhabited, and that their despotic chiefs were solely occupied (and had much trouble to do it) in making their new subjects cultivate a few pieces of ground in order to raise provision, and that even none but the old Negros, children and women could be compelled to this work. I must inform you that in spite of the great number of plantations abandoned to them, and the numerous plantain walks they found there, the Negros have experienced, and do daily experience, the greatest misery from scarcity, although they have been assisted with provisions furnished them by the Americans belonging to the United States. You are but little acquainted with the Negros, Sir ; I will answer for it that it will never be those who have inhabited the rich plantations that will retire into the inaccessible parts of the island in order to lead a savage life. The guilty Negro fearing a severe chastisement, found much difficulty in determining to fly into the woods ; he never ceased to solicit his pardon, when he had hopes of obtaining it ; for Negros hate solitude.

Pra-

Prudently declining offensive war, and trusting their safety to the rocky fortresses which nature has raised around them, and from which, in my opinion, it will be no easy undertaking to dislodge them—Page 143.

A society of 100,000 Negros would be too well known, and the place you allow them for a retreat would be too considerable, not to contain a whole province. In what part of St. Domingo then do you place the rocks and fortresses which nature has raised for them? They exist only in your imagination and in your history : for the very position in which you place them, carries with it the impossibility of raising provisions in the country sufficient for a population of 100,000 men, since the very elevated mountains beyond a certain height produce very few provisions natural to the Antilles.

Of the revolted Negros on the Northern province many had perished of disease and famine; but a desperate band, amounting, as it was supposed, to upwards of 40,000, inured to war, and practised in devastation and murder, still continued in arms. These were ready to pour down, as occasion might offer, on all nations alike.—Page 143.

I observe here, Sir, the same error that guided you in the enumeration of the forces of the colony. You very justly observe, at first, that many Negros died in the Northern part among the rebels. Nevertheless, with a *dash* of the pen, you create an army of 40,000 Blacks, inured to war, and ready to fall upon any nation that might wish to settle in the island.

How ! Sir, after having stated a circumstance so strictly true, that many of the Negros died of sickness, hunger, and in war, and by the cruelty of their chiefs, you add to the 100,000 Negros formed *into a republican society*, 40,000 warriors ! and, in admitting that hunger destroyed many Negros, you are not afraid to say, that 100,000 individuals can live and exist upon the spontaneous fruits of the earth—and all this, in order to make them fall upon those who might seize upon the island ! The best proof I can give of your ill-grounded fears is, that *the Negros* no where attacked the English *alone*, that they only attacked them when led on by the Whites, and accompanied by white soldiers and Mulattoes. The most powerful chiefs among the Negros, never had 100,000 men under their orders. Jean François is the one that assembled the greatest number. Biassou, Toussaint, Macaya, Maréchal, and a hundred others, never commanded 3,000 at once ; and all these chiefs and their subjects were always very jealous and independent of each other. I refer you again to consult those who have resided some time at St. Domingo since the arrival of the English there.

x

Concerning the White proprietors, on whom alone our dependence was placed, a large proportion as we have seen, perhaps more than one half of the whole, had quitted the country.—Page 144.

Pray agree with yourself : two pages from this, you make the Whites in arms amount to 15,000 ; here you declare, that half the population had quitted the country. You ought to have known, and said, that seven-eights had quitted it ; for it is a positive fact.

Of those that remained, some there were, undoubtedly, who sincerely wished for the restoration of order, and the blessing of regular government ; but the greatest part were persons of a different character : they were men who had nothing to lose, and every thing to gain by confusion and anarchy.—Page 144.

Certainly all the planters who were in the colony, wished for the re-establishment of order and tranquillity, and it can only have been in their name that the treaty was made. The others were not proprietary inhabitants of the colony ; they were its enemies : they kept to the commissioners' party ; but I can affirm, that all the White colonists, whatever might be their opinion, wished to belong to England. The fact itself has furnished the best proof, and the sequel of my answers will demonstrate it.

Not a few of them had obtained possession of the effects and estates of absent proprietors.—Page 144.

When one advances a fact, the proof should be adduced. The Mulattoes and the commissioners had alone taken possession of the property of the Whites. The plan which I shall soon discover to my readers will prove it ; but I here declare, that no White (previous to my arrival at St. Domingo with the English) had been put in possession of the habitations of the absent or massacred planters.

From people of this stamp, the most determined opposition was necessarily to be expected, and unfortunately among those of better principle, I am afraid but a very small number were cordially attached to the English. The majority seem to have had nothing in view, but to obtain by any means the restoration of their estates and possessions.—Page 144.

Certainly, the commissioners and their partisans were not those who ought to have delivered up the colony to the English, and it might be expected they would oppose it; as to the others, they have proved by their conduct what might have been expected from them.

. If after what we have hitherto read, we can be surprised at some of your propositions, we must be particularly so at your ignorance of the human heart. Who informed you that the proprietary inhabitants of St. Domingo *were attached to the English before they knew them? Why should they be so? What had Great-Britain done for them?* In what men, in what society have you found that gratitude preceded kindness? What other claim, than that of personal interest, had England to the attachment of the colonists of St. Domingo? Certainly, Sir, self-preservation, so strongly imprinted *by nature* upon the human heart, first engaged the colonists to solicit the British government to take them under its protection, and to receive them among the number of its subjects. The interest of Great-Britain made her accept this offer. The French planters were desirous of having recourse to a mother country that had colonies; and, consequently, the same interest as they had in preserving them, in putting themselves under the protection of the most powerful one, in submitting themselves to the most positive and *prohibitory* laws of its government.

England saw her interest in the acceptation of her prohibitory laws, and she was right in making the necessary efforts in order to secure herself the immense advantages offered to her. Read the capitulation I signed with General Williamson again; it is the basis of the contract which was then made under reciprocal conditions with Great-Britain; if they have been executed, the contract is fulfilled. The sequel will shew *if either has failed*, and *who has failed*; but it was made for the direct and personal interest of each contracting party, and I am not afraid to acknowledge it.

Ought you to be surprised, Sir, that few of the colonists were attached *to the English government*, before they knew the advantages of this government, and to what degree it would contribute to the happiness of those who submitted to it? Can we love that which we are unacquainted with? What was known of the power of Great-Britain, was sufficient to make them desirous of being protected by it; attachment should follow the first service; and it is the paternal care of governments, that attracts the fidelity and gratitude of the governed. Who has felt this sentiment more than the sensible and grateful hearts of the colonists of St. Domingo? The whole of their conduct and devotion to Britain prove it. I have observed in reading over your book, that you endeavour to make the contrary be believed; I have in vain sought for a proof of the inference you wish to be drawn. The shame of the failure in the attempt does not render you less guilty of it towards my generous countrymen, and the continuation of my answer will make it better known. In vain would you wish to throw some suspicion upon their integrity; it is by facts, it is by their actions they will support the reputation which has long since distinguished them; their frankness, their generosity, their bravery, will always be the same. I am warranted in what I say, by every thing that has happened in the colony; and I defy you, Sir, as well as all those who, like you, may be their enemies, to produce a people who, not having been conquered, but who of their own accord, have submitted themselves to a foreign power, can have merited its protection more! As a colonist of St. Domingo, and in the name of all, I call upon you to answer this challenge. But in the mean time, I appeal to the heart of the good, the generous General Williamson who governed, after having saved them, to say whether he doubts their attachment and adherence! Yes, the colonists of St. Domingo, will, for ages, pronounce the name of General Williamson with benediction. He, Sir, has experienced whether they are susceptible of gratitude and fidelity. And why? Because after having, in the name of England, *fulfilled the political part of the contract, agreed upon with him, he merited this attachment* by his kindness, by his paternal care for them, and by the consolations he poured into their hearts; in short, it was by his universal benevolence. His name will never perish but with the colony, it is indelibly engraved in the minds of all the families of the planters of the French part of the island.

*Many of them under their ancient government, had belonged to the lower order of nobles, and being tenacious of titles and honours, in proportion as their pretensions to real distinction were disputable, they dreaded the introduction of a system of laws and government, which would reduce them to the general level of the community.—*Page 144.

Had you written your book in another hemisphere, one might pardon the error you here commit, for one may be ignorant of *that which has no relation to one's self*; but, being so near France, in the midst of your countrymen, informed of what existed there, and being surrounded by thousands of Frenchmen of the order of nobility, that you should write an error so easily to be rectified; that you should say, that many of the planters of St. Domingo belonged to *the lower order of the nobles,* is truly astonishing. There is no person but what could have informed you, that there was no inferior order of nobility in France; that there were poor and rich, ancient and modern, but that their rights were equal. You should also have learnt, that many of the proprietary inhabitants

of

of St. Domingo, had the honour of belonging to the order of nobility; that many of the younger branches of families were managers of the effects, either of their parents or other planters; entrusting their property with greater pleasure to the management of men, who, to their talents, joined those principles of honour, which have ever distinguished the French nobility.

Thus, as their motives were selfish, and their attachment feeble, their exertions in the common cause were not likely to be very strenuous or efficacious.—Page 145.

I have already agreed with you, Sir, *that the contract* agreed upon between the French planters and the Ministers of Great-Britain, was respectively made through personal views; and I am not afraid to repeat it here. But it is in my own name, and in the name of all the planters of St. Domingo, that I shall call upon you to prove that their efforts were not vigorous and efficacious.

Have you, Sir, consulted the Ministers, in order to know what were the conditions with which I set off, as you say, in the summer of 1793, charged with the necessary orders and instructions *for delivering up St. Domingo to Great-Britain?* Have you been informed of the means which I found at Jamaica for fulfilling my instructions? Have you well considered whether some irresistible events have, or have not, counteracted the plans proposed to the Ministers? In short, do you confine yourself to what you have written, in order to state what must have happened at St. Domingo. If I have hitherto proved that no one was so ill-informed as yourself, in every thing you have written upon this subject, I will answer for it that you are still less so concerning what has really happened there; as I shall prove by what is hereafter related.

I first state, Sir, that the proprietary inhabitants of the colony have entirely, and more than fulfilled every thing they promised. A coast of 50 leagues in extent has been delivered up to 560 English troops; with the Mole town, *the Gibraltar of the colonies*, and not a single gun was fired. The troops, both officers and soldiers were quartered by the inhabitants of Jérémie at their own expence : at the Mole, they were lodged in the forts and barracks.

Not a single English soldier was sent out of the town of Jérémie to guard la Grande-Anse; the inhabitants continued (as they did *before they freely gave themselves up* to Great-Britain) *to defend their frontiers* at all the posts, at the Camp-des-Rivaux, at the central camp, and at the Camp-des-Irois. What could they do more?

No attack took place in any part, *but what there were more French* than English ; they always set the example. Envy and jealousy will never succeed, in endeavouring to make their courage and loyalty suspected.

They furnished every thing for the service of government, that was required of them. If their motives were *selfish*, what matters it ? What could they do more ?

I now call upon you, Sir, in my own and their name, to say, *what more the English have done.* They did not go out of the town of Jérémie and the Mole. The war was continued and supported by the planters alone ; and it was at the expence of their blood, that they daily protected the tranquillity the English troops enjoyed in their garrisons. I speak as a witness. Produce others who can contradict this truth, known to all the English and the whole colony.

The commerce between Jamaica and la Grande-Anse, was soon established, and the commodities of this dependency have since found their way to England. In the mean time, the colony was still supported by terror, and the astonishment occasioned by the arrival of 560 English troops, which had been multiplied to as many thousands, and by the stores and provisions furnished to the inhabitants, who themselves defended their property. I ask you again what could they do more ?

I add, Sir, that they incessantly did what was required of them, and I am the more certain of it, as *I was the organ of every request* ; for the two officers who commanded the St. Domingo expedition, could not speak French. Besides, I never quitted Colonel Whitelock ; and, as being member of the privy council at la Grande-Anse, I was the point of communication, through which every thing passed. It is then, with truth I assert, that *nothing was done at which I did not assist*, nor no attack took place at which I was not present.

I do not find that the number of French in arms, who joined us at any one period (I mean of White inhabitants) ever exceeded 2,000.—Page 145.

When the English were put in possession of St. Domingo, on the 19th of September, 1793, there were not 2,000 Whites capable of carrying arms in the whole of the French colony ; and they only took possession of a small part where there were not 700 Whites fit to serve in a military capacity.

But this number very quickly encreased, and I can demonstrate, that at the taking of Port-au-Prince, there were upwards of 5,000 French colonists, bearing arms at the service of Great Britain, in the part then possessed by the English. I am ready to enumerate them, if necessary.

I must add, Sir, that Colonel Brisbane never had, before the month of August 1794, more than 50 or 60 English to defend St. Marc's: with what troops, then, did he do it for a great length of time? At Léogane there were only 50 men with Captain Smith; at l'Arcahaye, at the Vases, at the Boucassin, there were only troops placed there occasionally for a long time; when there were any they were never numerous, and always remained in their garrisons. Seek, Sir, for proofs to contradict me—As to myself, I appeal to the English army and to the whole of the colony.

It were unjust, however, not to observe, that among them were some distinguished individuals, whose fidelity was above suspicion, and whose services were highly important. Such were the Baron de Montalembert, the Viscount de Fontanges, Mr. de Sources, and perhaps a few others.—Page 145.

I can assure you, Sir, that there have been many *individuals* who have shewn the greatest attachment to the interests of Great-Britain. They are superior to your praises, and they despise your censure: but, if you will praise, you ought at least to do it with exactness. The bravery and the honest character of the Baron de Montalembert are generally known; but his services are not more considerable than those of the officers he had the honor to command; and you must be informed, that M. de Montalembert knew but very little of St. Domingo at the time the English took possession of the colony, of which he only became an inhabitant since the Revolution; by having resided there a year upon the plantation his uncle purchased at the beginning of the troubles in France.

When the expedition against St. Domingo was planned at Jamaica in favour of the English, he was gone *upon an expedition* which some of the French planters wished to attempt *in favour of the Spaniards.* You ought to have known, that it was only chance that brought him to Jérémie at the time it was taken possession of. He came in the *Pénélope* frigate, which returned from escorting the ship that carried *the inhabitants devoted to the Spanish party, of which he was one;* that having met us at sea on our way to St. Domingo, the brave and esteemed Captain Rowley was ordered by the commodore to accompany us with his frigate. It was by this means that the Baron de Montalembert found himself at Jérémie without having wished it, and it was only through the solicitation of his friends that he remained there; being a total stranger to, and unacquainted with the place. The fact then is, that he wished to serve Spain, and that it was *only by chance* that he served England; but he served her as a man of honour. All who had the honour of commanding the French did the same. M. le Comte ó ***, M. le Comte de ***, the Viscount de B***, the Chev. de Sevré, *who was afterwards killed whilst commanding; M. de Boisneuf, who* *was likewise killed.* Indeed, all the officers who commanded, and a *thousand colonists* of St. Domingo, did honor to the British arms, as well as the Baron de Montalembert *who more than them* ought to have shewn himself grateful for the confidence placed in him; a confidence still greater, as he was unacquainted with the colony, its inhabitants, their manners, and their political and commercial interests.

The Baron de Montalembert, however, rendered some service; and, if he merited your applause *as did the officers under his orders, and all the colonists,* it was unnecessary to say, that *the fidelity of the Viscount de Fontanges was above all suspicion.* You have never taken the trouble to inform yourself concerning him, for the first colonist or officer to whom you might have spoken of him, would have informed you, that, before the arrival of the English at St. Domingo, he had taken the oath of fidelity to the King of Spain; that myself having made a journey to the Gonaïves, in order to see him and press him to use his influence on his part in favor of the English, I found at his house the Spanish officer *Villanova*; that he freely acknowledged to me, he approved of *my attachment to the British government*; that as to himself, he had taken the oath of fidelity to the King of Spain, that he should keep it, and would consequently serve him to the utmost of his power; that he could see no inconvenience that would arise from the English having one part of the colony and the Spaniards the other; that he would join with me in every thing that could be done that might be useful, and in concert, for the respective interest of those we served; but that he should keep his oath, as a man of honor ought to do. I shall not enter, Sir, into the details of the operations which followed this conversation; I shall confine myself with relating, that the Viscount de Fontanges has strictly kept his word; that he afterwards went to Jamaica, from thence came to England, from whence he repaired to Spain; that soon after his arrival here, he was made lieutenant-general in the service of the King of Spain, with appointments; his son was received among His Majesty's guards; and a part of his appointments granted in reversion to his wife and his son after his death, in the form of a pension. I am ignorant *whether it was at the solicitation* of Great-Britain, and for the services he had rendered her; what I can assert is, *that, if he did not succeed in serving the King of Spain,* it was not his fault; but he has never been in the situation to be faithful to the King of England, whom he never promised to serve.

You could not have too much praised the brave des Sources; this valorous Creole was not at St. Domingo when we arrived there, but came there soon after the taking of Port-au-Prince; and, since that time, he has not ceased to serve with that fidelity *generally found among the planters* of St. Domingo, *whose confidence was merited.*

merited. My countrymen will despise the *perhaps* which relates to all those whom you have not named ; for, *I repeat it,* they are superior to your praises.

All these men were well educated, and nourished deep resentment against the French planters, on account of the indignities which the class of coloured people had received from them.—Note C. Page 145.

Men sufficiently rich to participate in the good education received in France were not unhappy, and could not be more so than the Negros, who were slaves, as you have said. *To the same allegations I shall always make the same answers ;* adduce facts and prove the indignities with which the Mulattoes could reproach the Whites. I shall confine myself to repeating to you, that, if the Whites had been *less kind to the Mulattoes,* the colony would have been preserved ; because they would have been less numerous, less rich, and less informed.

On what follows this note, concerning the Men of Colour whom Colonel Brisbane had taken into his friendship as much as you, (to the great mortification of all the White planters), I remark, that he was very soon rewarded for it. One of these Mulattoes, who was his aide-de-camp, made use of the word of command which he had, in order to enter St. Marc's, and make his comrades revolt against this very Colonel Brisbane, their benefactor. He greatly repented before his death having placed any confidence in them.

At Cape Tiburon, 3 or 400 Blacks were embodied very early under a Black general, named Jean Kina, who had served well and faithfully.—Note C. Page 145.

Here is a man whom you cannot praise too much ; *the good, the brave John Kina.* Observe, above all, that *this is a Negro ;* that he incessantly interested himself concerning his master ; that every thing he gained he sent to his master and mistress at Jérémie. He rested not a moment without giving proofs of his fidelity to the Whites and his attachment to his masters, the whole of whose Negros he has saved, and now employs himself. This Negro is the honour of the men of his colour. Shew me among the Mulattoes a man that can be compared with him, and who is so generous, so honest, so brave ; and who, above all, is so well acquainted with the Men of Colour, *whom he despises as much as they hate him.*

General Williamson has done much for this worthy Negro; he has sown in good ground ; he and his soldiers will be always faithful to the Whites ; they have constantly served in the Camp-des-Irois, and at Cape Tiburon, before the English lost it, and since always at the advanced posts on the frontiers of la Grande-Anse.

From this recapitulation, it is evident that the invasion of St. Domingo was an enterprise of greater magnitude and difficulty than the British government seem to have imagined.—Page 145.

Hitherto, Sir, I see none of the difficulties you speak of, except those that may be created by your own imagination. I find you no better informed of the plans proposed and accepted by the English Ministers, for after having read your work over and over again, I do not perceive upon what authorities your recapitulation is founded. But I perceive, by the facts I have adduced in answering you, that the invasion was performed without trouble, without difficulty, without expence, and without a single gun being fired. I saw Great-Britain the same week in possession of a track of land on the coast containing 50 leagues; I moreover saw her in possession of Mole St. Nicholas, the most advantageous port of all the Antilles—and I only see these facts counterbalanced by your allegations, divested of proof.

Considering the extent and natural strength of the country, it may well be doubted whether all the force which Great-Britain could have spared would have been sufficient to reduce it to subjection.—Page 146.

In what consists the natural strength of a country, full of ports, roads, and bays, and open on all sides ? where the English have been received without battle, but with open hearts; and, above all, where, when they have been obliged to fight, they have not met with an hour's resistance ? I shall hereafter answer the latter part of the article I have here cited *by facts, and in a manner* that shall carry conviction with it.

And restore it at the same time to such a degree of order and subordination as to make it a colony worth holding.—Page 146.

You publish your work in 1797; you ought to have known, that, in the wretched state of the colony, *the exports*, from that part possessed by Great-Britain, amounted last year to 2,000,000 l. sterling.

The truth seems to have been, that General Williamson, to whom, as hath been observed, the direction and distribution of the armament was entrusted, and whose active zeal in the service of his country was eminently conspicuous, was deceived equally with the King's Ministers, by the favorable accounts and exaggerated representations of sanguine and interested individuals, concerning the disposition of their countrymen, the White planters remaining in St. Domingo.—Page 146.

I am now come to the second personal attack made against me. I shall answer for myself, and shall leave your readers and the public to judge. General William-son, you say, " *was deceived equally, with the King's Ministers, by the favorable* " *accounts and exaggerated representations of sanguine and interested individuals,*" &c.—What you here say concerns me personally. I am the only one who can have deceived both the Ministers and General Williamson, being the only person that was sent by them into the colony ; and I am almost the only one who represented to the General the utility and advantages which would accrue to England from taking possession of St. Domingo. I am, therefore, that *sanguine and interested* individual. In answering for myself, I shall confirm all the proofs I have given of your injustice in censuring an operation of which you were totally ignorant.

First, Sir, at a time when governments require the entire confidence of the people, what must your readers have thought at your daring to accuse the Ministers of Great-Britain with fickleness, inconsistency, and want of foresight ? Ought a Member of the British Parliament to accuse the Ministers of his country, with the folly of causing it to be supposed, that they have suffered themselves to be de-ceived by a few foreigners, who consulted only their own interest ? That they have been able to impose upon them concerning the advantages which the colony might be of to England ? and that they have suffered themselves to be deceived by an exaggeration which was always open to detection ? In short, how could you have supposed that Ministers, whom all Europe, as well as Great-Britain, acknow-ledge to have superior talents, could at once have forgotten the political interests of England and its advantages, so far as to adopt the projects of some inhabitants of a foreign colony, without due consideration ?—I repeat it, Sir, both to the people of England and to you, that I am one of those, who, with the greatest perse-verance, since the year 1791, have never ceased to propose, to remind, and to solicit the King's Ministers to fulfil the *happy destiny of England,* by seizing the colony of St. Domingo. If I have been guilty, I am doubly so, in proposing these plans, and charging myself with their execution. For I have said : " *This* " *is what must be done, and I will undertake to execute it.*" It is I then that am doubly responsible, both for the project and the want of success.—I call down upon me the whole indignation of Great-Britain, if I do not prove that I have fulfilled, and ten times fulfilled, my promises to the Ministers, and that without being influenced by any direct view of gain, except the reward which a man of honor has a right to expect for an important service rendered to a powerful nation. This, I acknowledge, I have expected, and do still expect ; as I shall prove that, ay devoting myself entirely to the success of my plans, I have succeeded in executing more than I have promised.

I shall enter into the particulars of my conduct in the briefest manner possible ; and there will only be left you the shame and regret of having sought to render a man of honor suspected, who has constantly shewn the greatest zeal in serving your country. Honest men will judge me. I defy you, Sir, to answer by contrary proofs what I am now going to state.

I had, as I have already told you, ever since the year 1791, endeavoured to demonstrate to the Ministers, that England, more than any other nation, was interested in saving the colony of St. Domingo, in order to *preserve her own colonies*. In 1792, I renewed, with others, my solicitations, with the approbation of a great number of planters at London. After war was declared against France, in 1793, what had previously appeared so difficult, was then found to have become easy ; and after much care, pains, and many memorials, terms were prepared here for the colony, and I set off for Jamaica.

As I am not writing the history of the colony, but am merely answering what personally concerns me, I shall only give an account of that which I can relate with honor ; without endangering those secrets which the confidence reposed in me requires me to preserve, and without speaking of the *positive promises* I had solicited in order to save the colony before I set out on my voyage, and still less without accusing any person of the political events which have happened in Europe ; events which may have prevented the execution of every thing that might have been granted to me. I shall speak only of what is known to all the inhabitants of Jamaica ; of the troops which accompanied me to St. Domingo in the expedition, which has proved so successful ; in fine, I shall speak of every thing that was publickly done and known by the whole colony and its inhabitants, and which, above all, you should have been perfectly acquainted with, as you intended publishing an account of the colony.

I left England in a packet boat, accompanied by two proprietors of St. Domingo, one as my secretary ; the other was my kinsman, with my Negro servant.—I was not ignorant what would have been my fate had I been taken by the French. Being arrived at Barbadoes, I learnt that the attack upon Martinico had failed. I arrived at Jamaica towards the end of July ; where I heard of the destruction and burning of Cape Français, and the flight of the White inhabitants. I there likewise heard of the departure of General Galbaud, and the wretched state of St. Domingo.

The

The projects respecting this colony *continued the same*, but the plans became different. I was received by General Williamson with that kindness, that openness of heart, and that confidence, which make him beloved by all who have occasion to treat with him upon business. After having communicated to him the orders, of which I was the bearer, and my instructions, of which he had a duplicate, and after having had three hours conversation with him, I perceived how much the state of affairs had lately changed, and how many new difficulties the state of the colony at that time presented. Nevertheless the account of the affair at the *Camp-des-Rivaux* once more pointed out to me the means of safety; with courage, resolution and patience, all might yet be well. General Williamson begged I would reflect upon every thing I had just heard, and communicate to him speedily the result of my hopes and fears, and to consider also of the best measures to be taken, which would give us a little time, and which for several reasons we stood in need of.

I must here stop again, in order to relate a fact which will ever deserve the gratitude of the proprietors of St. Domingo towards the inhabitants of Jamaica. During five or six months, and particularly after the fire at the Cape, many of the principal proprietors of St. Domingo took refuge at Jamaica, mostly from the Northern part. They had scarcely arrived there when the Spaniards, who had their views, published, *by the president or governor* of the Spanish part of the colony, certain proclamations, inviting the French proprietors to repair to him; with such advantageous and exaggerated promises, that they must have evinced the falsity of those who published them. In consequence of which many inhabitants repaired there successively; and the first news I heard on my arrival at Jamaica, was, that an armament was preparing to carry the principal inhabitants of St. Domingo, who were at Jamaica, to the Spanish capital of their colony.

Mr. Henry Shirley, member of the House of Assembly, at Jamaica, with a liberality, that will do eternal honor to his heart, began a subscription, and had engaged the principal inhabitants, proprietors, and merchants of Jamaica, to join in it; in order to procure a sufficient sum to equip a vessel and furnish it with every thing necessary for the voyage of the French colonists, who, might be desirous of repairing to the capital of the Spanish colony. This subscription, through the care of Mr. Henry Shirley, very soon amounted to several thousand pounds sterling, and when I arrived, every thing was ready for sailing. General Williamson, with his wonted humanity, had freighted a ship at the expence of government; the commodore appointed a frigate as convoy; arms, ammunition, provisions, and money, had been furnished to each inhabitant, out of the subscription. In fine, every thing was ready for their departure, two days after my arrival. I learnt all these particulars the same evening ; I saw with concern that the Spaniards had long since been before-hand with the English government ; that their agents had laboured with zeal, and that they had at last persuaded many of the inhabitants of the Northern part, almost *in spite of themselves*, by the insidious offers they had made to them. I saw the Spanish agents ; I saw their proclamations, and from that very moment I perceived the snare. I wished to inform the inhabitants, but, I found some minds so prejudiced, that I was obliged to request General Williamson to suffer the armament to sail, and that for very wise and political reasons given to me, and of which I informed the General, who approved of them. What principally decided me was, the engagement they made to rejoin us, should the Spaniards fail in their promises, and not furnish the means for attacking the civil commissioners, according to the assurances given them by the Spanish agents ; and if they did not furnish the means for making an advantageous diversion in favor of the English enterprize. The expedition sailed and returned to Port-Royal. Nothing could persuade the Baron de Montalembert from going to the Spanish governor. Happily for him, after the entrance of the freighted ship, he was received on board the frigate which served as convoy, by which means he escaped the disagreeableness which the other inhabitants on board the transport experienced. On Captain Rowley's arrival at the port, having landed in order to communicate the object of his voyage to the Spanish *president*, he discovered by his ill humours that the new comers would not be well received. He continued to cruise about St. Domingo, and was on his return when we discovered him near Jamaica, on the 15th of September. Whatever may have been the success of this expedition, it was undertaken solely by the generosity and kindness of the planters of Jamaica. The colonists of St. Domingo will ever retain a perpetual remembrance and gratitude for it.

Whilst this was passing, General Williamson was expecting news from Admiral Gardner at Martinico. As to myself, after having well considered and reflected upon the state of the colony of St. Domingo, and the conduct of the inhabitants of la Grande-Anse, I saw that on them alone depended the hope of saving St. Domingo.

The two persons that accompanied me from England, were gone to meet the ussembly of the parishes of la Grande-Anse, assembled at Jérémie, with letters for my friends and the principal inhabitants of the dependency ; in which I encouraged them to persevere, and directed them to send me their full powers and instructions as soon as possible.

Both before and after the departure of my friends for Jérémie, I saw almost every day some fugitive inhabitants from St. Domingo, brought in by the Jamaica privateers; and, within five and twenty days 490 of them arrived from different parts of the French colony, but chiefly from the Northern part. They escaped from one evil to meet a worse; for they were inhumanly pillaged by the privateers, who cast them almost naked upon the shores of Jamaica. General Williamson came forth to relieve these unfortunate inhabitants with a kindness worthy of the greatest eulogiums, in granting to each the pay of prisoners of war. The committee entrusted with the subscription money raised by the planters of Jamaica came forward also with a noble generosity to the relief of my countrymen. Some money being left after the departure of the colonists for the Spanish part of St. Domingo, they begged I would undertake, as being personally acquainted with the proprietors, to verify the wants and condition of each inhabitant; and, at my request, they granted to each a small weekly sum in addition to that allowed by government. It was *these kindnesses that saved the lives of a great number of families of St. Domingo.*

By the arrival of so many prisoners I soon discovered a double plan, separately executed by the republican civil commissioners and the Spaniards; namely, that of depopulating the French colony of all the Whites. The Spaniards attached the rich inhabitants by their advantageous proclamations; and those who, being young and vigorous, required nothing more than to fight in order to recover their property, they engaged to repair to the Spanish part; where they found nothing that had been promised them, nor were they allowed to return again into the French part.

On the other hand the women, children, and old men were compelled by the Negros to quit the Northern part; they embarked on board every thing that could receive them. " *We do not wish to use you ill,*" said they, " *but we will have no* " *more Whites in the colony. Retire and carry with you as much of your property as* " *you can.*"—They even assisted them to embark the very goods which became a prey to the English privateers of Jamaica or Providence.

I saw in this double manœuvre the plan, which I long knew the commissioners had laid to destroy the colony of St. Domingo, by driving away all the Whites and giving liberty to the Negros; and I discovered in the conduct of the Spaniards their favorite desire of ruining the French colony: rather wishing to see it possessed only by Negros, who would soon become like themselves, than to see it inhabited by *such active and laborious people as the French and English*. I saw the time was precious, and that little remained for the colonists; some favorable circumstances that offered determined me still more to take a decisive resolution.

The friends I sent to Jérémie had been gone but a few days, and could not be expected to return in less than twelve days or a fortnight.—I waited for them with impatience, when one evening a flag of truce from St. Domingo was announced. I was considering what could be the occasion of it, when M. le Gras, a rich planter of the Northern part, and formerly one of the council at the Cape, disembarked at Kingston, where his wife and children had been for a considerable time. He informed me, that he came in the name of the inhabitants of la Grande-Anse, to state their wretched condition to the governor of Jamaica, and to solicit assistance. He declared to me at the same time, that it was impossible they could defend themselves another month without assistance. In fact, he gave me all the necessary information; he confirmed me in my opinion, that there was no time to be lost in executing the orders of the Ministers, by assuring me that my two messengers would be joyfully received, and that every thing I had proposed would be granted. A few days afterwards, he informed me that his intention was not to return to St. Domingo, and that he gave up the mission with which he had been charged, by the inhabitants of Jérémie, having no property in that dependency; thinking, *added he*, that I was the most proper person to treat concerning this business. I soon discovered that the Spanish agents had seduced M. le Gras, and that they flattered him that his fortune and habitation, in the North and at Fort Dauphin, would soon be in the power of that government.

I informed General Williamson of every circumstance. At last, an American ship, taken by a privateer, brought in one day 120 inhabitants of every age and sex, masters and servants, who fled from the Northern part, where they had been compelled to embark. On the 12th of August I determined to ask the general to explain himself definitively, concerning what he could and would do for the salvation of St. Domingo. I in consequence wrote officially a letter, which I carried to General Williamson at Spanish Town, in which I informed him, that there was not a moment longer to be lost; that I saw the plan of driving away and extirpating the entire population of Whites in the French colony of St. Domingo, was the end which the civil commissioners and Spaniards had in view; that, without consulting together, they each laboured to accomplish their purpose; that I begged him to read his orders and my instructions, which were, *to take possession of such part of St. Domingo, as might be willing to submit*. I likewise begged of him to give me twenty-five

soldiers

soldiers belonging to the English troops, an officer, and a flag, with as much provisions and warlike stores as possible; that I would go to St. Domingo with this feeble force, and take possession of the colony in the name of the King of England, and there erect His Majesty's standard, and maintain my ground, until the arrival of *the forces which were promised us*, at a fixed period; that the brave inhabitants of Jérémie would receive me with joy and join me; and that the inhabitants of the colony, knowing me to be established in one part of St. Domingo, instead of flying to all the neighbouring islands, and to New-England, would range themselves under the British flag, *which I promised him to defend to the last moment of my life:* observing, that this measure was the more necessary, as by it the good Negros would not be discouraged, and would continue faithful to their masters, when they should know that they did not abandon St. Domingo, and that they were assembled in another part of the colony; and that, above all, *they would have* the hope of seeing them again. In short, I begged him to give me an answer in writing, if he refused my request, and to permit me to set off again immediately for England. I here repeat the answer which General Williamson made, with the same sensibility I then felt. " Yes," said he, " my dear Charmilly, I will assist you to save St. Do-
" mingo; your attachment to your countrymen, and to the interests of Great-Bri-
" tain, merit every effort I can make, and I will not only give you the twenty-five
" men you ask, but I will give you a hundred, if the commodore will transport them
" to St. Domingo, and cover their retreat, in case it should become necessary."

I knew better how to feel than to express the pleasure this answer gave me. From this moment, I vowed to a man of feeling, who, in the manner in which he granted my request, intermixed a kindness I cannot return; I vowed to him, I say, an eternal gratitude, an attachment and respect, which can end only with my life. General Williamson crowned my wishes, by promising me that from that day, he would prohibit (which he did) all privateers, under pain of losing their commissions, from pillaging the personal property of the inhabitants, who might happen to be on board the ships they should take, declaring that merchandize only should be deemed lawful prizes.

It is with joy I take the opportunity this letter gives me of rendering public the eternal gratitude, which both the colony and myself shall retain, for General Williamson's kindness. I declare with pleasure, that it was by his orders that every thing was conducted at St. Domingo, *until the taking of Port-au-Prince*, and that all the colonists have found in this worthy and respectable chief, the care, the kindness of a father, and the protection of a generous commander. His heart will be satisfied, when he learns, that the grateful colonists never mention his name, but with the sincerest wishes for his happiness. The homage I now pay him is as disinterested as my conduct towards him as always been. He is in London; it may be known of him, whether, among the numerous requests *I made* on behalf of the colony and its unfortunate inhabitants, (which he almost always granted) *I added one for myself*; and he can say, whether he has found any other person who has told him the truth with more force, disinterestedness, devotion, and attachment, towards himself, towards England, and towards the colony, than I have done at all times.

As soon as he had kindly given me his promise to succour St. Domingo, I immediately set out for, and soon arrived at Commodore Ford's, to whom I gave an account of my letter, of the kindness of the general in granting me the 100 men necessary for the salvation of the colony, to go there to wait the arrival of other troops, and the conditions on which he agreed to it. He said to me, *with that frankness* which characterised him, " I am very happy in being able to second your resolu-
" tion ; and to secure to it all possible success, I will not only prepare every thing
" necessary in order to transport and convoy the troops, and to guard the se-
" curity of the detachment which the governor has granted you, but if he will
" even increase the number to 200, I will order all the necessary preparations for
" the expedition. Try to persuade the general *to grant them to you:* the more
" there are the less risk they will run." He added many more things full of kindness, and promised me, what he perfectly executed afterwards, to do every thing in order to second my zealous endeavours to merit the confidence reposed in me.

I feel a pleasure in relating that the rapid successes we met with in St. Domingo, were likewise owing to the great care taken by this worthy Admiral, and it is with a sentiment of sincere grief for him, that I lay this declaration on his tomb, as a mark of my gratitude and that of the whole colony.

Satisfied beyond description, I returned without delay to Gen. Williamson, to whom I gave an account of every thing. " Well! ' said he, " since the commodore will
" undertake the care of 200 men, you shall have them, my dear Charmilly; you may
" depend upon them, and that as soon as possible." We agreed that I should send back the ship that had brought M. le Gras, with the news of this intended succour, and the certainty of its speedy appearance ; but that it was necessary that they should immediately answer my first letters, and send me the full powers I had requested, before the general could suffer any thing to leave Jamaica ; and, in the mean time, we might employ ourselves in making the necessary preparations.

This, Sir, is the truth of every thing that passed. General Williamson is in London, he can contradict me, and he owes it to his own character to do so, if I have advanced any thing contrary to truth: he ought to have my letter. If every thing I have just related as having passed between General Williamson and me be true, can he have been deceived by me? It was the extreme wretchedness of the colony that determined me to beg him to declare himself, *and take a decisive part,* which alone could save, as it has in effect partly saved, the French colony of St. Domingo.

You are unfortunate, Sir, in your reproaches! Certainly, both you and the public will be astonished to find that *this interested individual; that I,* of whom you wish to speak, have proposed the plans, and offered to undertake to put them in execution, without ever having made any stipulation with the Ministers respecting my personal interest. In proof of which, I appeal to the Ministers and General Williamson. You, as well as any other person, may receive such information from them as shall appear to you necessary, in order to verify what I here advance.

Instead of the few hundreds of them which afterwards resorted to the British standard, the governor had reason to expect the support and co-operation of at least as many thousands.—Page 146.

It has been seen by my answer to the preceding article, that it is entirely false that the governor of Jamaica could expect that the English troops might be joined by more planters than remained in the colony; for the steps I took to press him to put in execution his orders to take possession of St. Domingo, were with the view of preventing the rest of the colonists from quitting the island. I call upon all the officers who commanded there to contradict me, when I declare, that the inhabitants of la Grande-Anse joined the English. I prove it in saying, that the English troops never quitted their barracks at Jérémie except on very few occasions; that it was the French inhabitants who continued to defend the camps placed upon the frontiers; that in every expedition the French were at least double the number of the English; and that in about six weeks after our arrival, the number of *French inhabitants* at Jérémie, and at all the posts, was doubled, and that soon after it was quadrupled.

In this fatal confidence, the armament allotted for this important expedition was composed of only the 13th regiment of foot, seven companies of the 49th, and a detachment of artillery, amounting, altogether, to about 870, rank and file, fit for duty. Such was the force that was to annex to the crown of Great-Britain a country nearly equal in extent, and in natural strength infinitely superior to Great-Britain itself.—
Page 146.

If General Williamson had been consulted by you, he is too much the man of honor not to have undeceived you respecting the confidence you attribute to him ; which could still less have happened, as he knew, what you allow yourself, that the population of the Whites was diminished more than three-fourths ; as much by the numerous emigrations which took place before the massacre at the Cape, as by the massacre itself and the flight of those that escaped from it. If you, who write in England, have had imperfect information respecting what was passing in the colony, you ought to suppose that the general was too well informed not to know that the population of Whites there had almost become extinct. But he hoped *(and the sequel has proved that he was not deceived)* that the planters would hasten to return to the colony. The confidence which you attribute to the governor of Jamaica might have been criminal, and General Williamson has no reason to reproach himself with such strange negligence as what you attribute to him.

The forces you mention were more than sufficient to fulfil the plans of government ; it was only in agitation to take possession of and retain that part of St. Domingo which should submit, until reinforcements should arrive from England. These are your words, p. 141 : " *such a force as should be thought sufficient to take* " *and retain possession of all the places that might be surrendered, until reinforcements* " *should arrive from England.*" It was not intended to take possession of the whole colony with this small body of troops ; the Ministers never had such an idea ; which indeed you admit, for you say, that it was only to occupy *such parts as should submit* until the arrival of reinforcements. I must observe here, to the honor of the British arms, that this small body of brave soldiers, assisted by the inhabitants, not only sufficed to take possession of and keep, during eight months, that which had been delivered up to them on their arrival, but likewise to take possession of more than a third part of this immense colony ; and that they were capable of supporting themselves, during that time, upon a tract of land upwards of a hundred and fifty leagues long, and to attack and often beat their enemies.

I trust that our readers will readily admit, according to the truth I have here established, that, if the inhabitants of St. Domingo had not been eager to come and fight under the British flag, the small number of troops, which you have yourself stated to have been sent to St. Domingo, however brave they might be, could not have defended and supported themselves from St. Nicholas Mole to Cape Tiburon during the space of eight months.

The truth is (and I appeal to the testimony of the whole colony and the English army), that it was the inhabitants, arriving from all parts where they had taken refuge,

who

who fought in defence of the frontiers and all the posts. After this, the most prejudiced reader cannot but allow, that it was them who preserved to the English government that part of St. Domingo which had been delivered up to it.

Speedy and effectual reinforcements from England were, however, promised, as well to replace the troops which were removed from Jamaica, as to aid the operations in St. Domingo.—Page 146.

The reader will agree, after what you here say, that it was with a very ill grace you exclaimed above, *such was the force that was to annex to the crown of Great-Britain a country nearly equal in extent to Great-Britain itself*, since you so readily agree that it was the reinforcements expected from Europe which were to second the operations at St. Domingo.—It is possible that this might be only irony.

As the propositions or terms of capitulation had been previously adjusted between the people of Jérémie, by their agent M. de Charmilly and General Williamson, it only remained for the British forces to take possession of the town and harbour. Accordingly the troops disembarked early the next morning. The British colours were hoisted at both the forts, with royal salutes from each, which were answered by the commodore and his squadron, and the oaths of fidelity and allegiance were taken by the resident inhabitants, with an appearance of great zeal and alacrity. —Page 147.

The capitulation had been signed by General Williamson and myself, according to the instructions sent me from Jérémie; which were found to be so satisfactory by General Williamson, that he determined, after the most serious consideration, to increase the 200 men *he had previously promised* to 560, amongst which were 30 artillery men, commanded by Captain Smith.

The Europa, a 50 gun ship, which had escorted the Jamaica convoy as high as New England, having returned about the beginning of September, Commodore Ford readily determined to embark in order to command and conduct the expedition, particularly when he saw, by the arrival of many inhabitants from the Mole, who came to solicit *help upon the same conditions* as the inhabitants of la Grande-Anse, the service he could render his country, by taking possession of the most important military and maritime post of all the Antilles.

On the 19th of September, 1793, three months after my departure from London, one of the most important quarters or districts of the colony of St. Domingo was delivered up to the British forces, without risk, without trouble, and without expence.

c c

—I affirm, and am in no fear of contradiction, that it was with sincere joy the inhabitants pronounced the oath of fidelity, which they have since most rigidly observed.

At the same time information was received that the garrison at the Mole of Cape St. Nicholas were inclined to surrender that important fortress in like manner. As it was a circumstance not to be neglected, the commodore immediately directed his course thither and on the 22d took possession of the fortress and harbour, and received the allegiance of the officers and privates.—Page 147.

Had you taken the trouble to inform yourself of facts, you would have known that the agreement for the surrender of the Mole upon the same conditions as Jérémie was entered into before we quitted Jamaica; and that it was the importance of this acquisition that determined the brave Admiral Ford to undertake the superintendance of the expedition, which has put the most important and finest port of the West-Indies under the dominion of Great-Britain.

With the marines only, that were on board his ship, he took possession of a post which the whole force of Great-Britain would not have been able to have conquered; where he found artillery and warlike stores worth ten times more than the sum expended in the expedition. This is what you would certainly have said, had you wished to inform yourself of such an important fact, and which is known by the whole colony.

The voluntary surrender of these places raised expectations in the people of England that the whole of the French colony in St. Domingo would submit without opposition.—Page 148.

Had you taken the trouble to inform yourself of the projects, the plans, and the hopes, of Ministers, concerning St. Domingo, when they dispatched me to Jamaica, and had you known their astonishment at the successes obtained within the space of three months, without expence, and without trouble, perhaps you would have found that the wisest part of the English people had much to hope from such a favorable commencement.

The town of Jérémie is a place of no importance.—It contains about one hundred very mean houses, and the country in the vicinage is not remarkably fertile; producing nothing of any account but coffee.—Page 148.

The town of Jérémie is like all the other small towns in the colonies. Both the Englih troops and officers were very well quartered there; it is very wholesome and is so situated as to render an attack very difficult. In delivering up la Grande-Anse to the English, the town of Jéremie was nothing more than the point which was to serve, and which did serve, as barracks; and where the British flag was displayed, without any danger to the troops.

But if the town be inconsiderable, the plantations of this dependency form of themselves a more useful possession than many of the English colonies of the Windward Islands. Your readers will be very much surprised to find, that you should consider a district producing *as much coffee as la Grande-Anse* of so little importance. Before the revolution, this dependency produced upwards of *twenty millions weight of coffee annually*, beside sugar, cotton, and indigo, and almost all the cocoa which was collected in the French colony of St. Domingo. The districts of Plymouth and of the Cayemites, newly cleared; which promised a considerable produce at the beginning of the revolution, have since yielded it. I am informed that upwards of twenty-five millions weight of coffee came last year from the single district of Jérémie, with a great quantity of sugar, cocoa, &c., &c. A planter of Jamaica *(where so little coffee is produced)* ought not to look upon such a crop with disdain ; and such advantages for the British commerce may make the *insignificancy of the houses* serving as magazines for such noble products, forgot

Unfortunately from the elevation of the surrounding heights, the place is not tenable against a powerful attack by land.—Page 148.

Had you taken the trouble to have made yourself acquainted with the position of the Mole, you would have known, that it is still more difficult to be attacked by land than by sea ; for nature has so provided, that such an inconsiderable force as 500 men, cannot repair there with the necessary ammunition to attack a place which has nothing more than a simple dry wall for its defence. The land which surrounds the Mole, from the sea to the ravine is a stony mountain, called *Roche-à-Ravets*; that is to say, of very hard stones, pointed and sharp ; in the interstices of which grows a forest of Indian fig-trees and all sorts of thorny plants, which will not admit of a passage. There is no road by which cannon can be conveyed, and one must travel, on all sides, a space of upwards of twenty miles, on a sandy soil and under the torrid zone, without finding water, which, with the want of a road is a more secure defence than the best contrived fortifications.

And a Mr. Duval pledging himself to raise 500 men to co-operate in its reduction. An expedition was undertaken for that purpose and Colonel Whitelock with most of

the British force from Jérémie arrived in Tiburon Bay on the 4th of October.
—Page 145.

There are facts which we must ourselves verify, in order to be able to speak of them ; such is the one you mention. Morin Duval was to be suspected by the English, on account of his pretensions previous to their arrival. I must say, that owing to his conduct I was obliged to be upon my guard against him ; but I am likewise bound in truth to declare, that Morin Duval was punctual, and that he had assembled at the Post of *Irois*, a great part of the men he had promised. The good and honest Negro *John Kina* was amongst them ; and this brave Negro had upwards of 280 men with him, of his own colour, with which he had been supplied by the different inhabitants. I assisted in reviewing these Negros ; I was sensibly struck with the speech which *John Kina* made to his soldiers upon the arrival of the English. *I here declare* that I made the strictest search in order to come at the truth of every thing that passed, because it was my duty to get at the knowledge of the conduct and actions of Morin Duval, who, commanding a post upon the frontier of la Grande-Anse, might do us much mischief. I mistrusted him, and examined all his actions, in order to preserve us from the mischief he might have done. It is from respect to truth then, that I declare that the men he promised were assembled at the Camp-des-Irois.

But on this occasion, as on almost every other, *the English had a melancholy . proof, how little dependence can be placed on French declarations and assurances.* —Page 149.

I do not think it necessary, Sir, to answer this fresh insult which you have given to the colonists of St. Domingo as well as to all *Frenchmen.* The folly of this reproach must have occasioned you to have been completely judged by your readers· What I shall hereafter write will prove still more that the inhabitants of the colony have, by their entire attachment, and constant fidelity, merited the protection of the generous nation that supported them. Your readers, Sir, will be more just than to calumniate a whole colony for the faults of a few individuals. Indeed I cannot refrain from imagining, that even yourself, when better informed of what has passed at St. Domingo, will not hesitate to retract the unmerited reproach and obloquy with which you have stigmatized my countrymen.

Duval never made his appearance, for he was not able to collect 30 men. The enemy's force was found to be far more formidable than had been represented,
and

and the gallantry of our troops proved unavailing against superiority of numbers,
they were compelled to retreat with the loss of about 20 men killed and wounded.—
Page 149.

I have the most positive proofs that Duval repaired to the post agreed upon, but
the wind prevented us from hearing the appointed signal. All the English army
knows, that I did not leave the commander of the expedition for a single moment ;
who, not speaking French, I had promised not to quit. Thus I can declare that
nothing was either ordered, or done, without my knowledge. In answering you,
I have not obliged myself to write the history of the colony, nor of every thing
that has happened there since the arrival of the English ; it may be easily known
whether there be any one who can speak of it with more knowledge than me. The
time will come when every thing will be proved. I shall for the present remark,
that Morin Duval, with John Kina, repaired to the post agreed upon; but a
piece of cannon, which we discovered whilst at sea, directed upon the place
fixed for landing, compelled us to land at three miles distant from the appointed
place ; that place was hid by a mountain ; so that instead of making our landing
good by seven or eight in the morning, it could not be begun till near one in the after-
noon; and it moreover failed, by an event common in war, by the arrival of a reinforcement of cavalry from Aux Cayes which appeared upon the shore at the time the
boats for debarking began to quit the ships. Time will discover the particulars of
the whole of this affair.

I shall only observe, that Morin Duval, neither having seen nor heard of us,
waited in a very dangerous position, without eating or drinking till the evening,
and did not return to his camp, (distant above ten miles from the post he had occupied,) until night, very much fatigued, and after having run the risk of being attacked himself.

The defeat and discouragement sustained in this attack were the more grievously felt,
as sickness began to prevail to a great extent in the army. The season of the year
was unfavorable in the highest degree for military operations in a tropical climate.—
Page 149.

The reader will here judge with what attention you write. You forget, Sir, that
you said that we did not arrive at Jérémie before the 19th of September in the evening ; that it was on the 4th of October that the first affair of Tiburon took place,
which makes only fifteen days. You should have known that of all the troops that
came at the time of the first expedition to Jérémie, not one was sick till the end of

February, when we set off for Léogane, which makes near six months, during which time there were only two soldiers buried, who died of consumptions, and they had been given over from the time of their quitting Jamaica, where they had been very ill. Inform yourself, Sir; consult the returns of the hospitals, and you will find that I am right.

The rains were incessant, and the constant and unusual fatigue, and extraordinary duty to which the soldiers, from the smallness of their number, were necessarily subject, co-operating with the state of the weather, produced the most fatal consequences. —Page 149.

At what period, and of what place do you mean to speak? At Jérémie, the weather was almost generally fine, and the air cool. You forget that September, October, November, December, January and February, are the coolest and most agreeable months at St. Domingo. Ask Lieutenant-Colonel Spencer, and he will tell you that he was never so well in the colonies as at Jérémie, where he arrived ill; that he speedily recovered, and that the English troops performed only garrison duty there, never quitting their barracks which were in the best houses in the town; and *the French inhabitants* alone performed *the service* of the camp and the frontiers.

The sudden appearance of a reinforcement in St. Domingo, though small in itself, produced however a considerable effect among the French planters,- by inducing a belief that the British government was now seriously resolved to follow up the blow. —Page 150.

Had you been informed of what had passed at St. Domingo you would have known that, faithful to my engagements, I was incessantly occupied, day and night, in continuing to execute the plans entrusted to me; that accordingly every thing was prepared in order that the greatest part of the colony might revolt against the civil commissioners, and range themselves under the power of Great-Britain, in the course of November, the time when the reinforcements were to arrive. *But we had hopes that were not realized*; and the forces which were necessary, and which I had announced for a fixed time, not arriving, the situation *of many persons* became critical, for the civil commissioners began to be informed, and the dangers increased. Nobody complained, because, as you say yourself, the inhabitants were convinced that the British government had resolved *(according to its interest)* upon seizing the whole colony.

In the beginning of December, the parishes of Jean Rabel, St. Marc, Arcahaye, and Boucassin, surrendered on the same conditions as had been granted to Jérémie; and their example was soon followed by the inhabitants of Léogane. All the former parishes are situated on the North side of the Bight. Léogane on the South.—Page 150.

At last we could *put it off no longer,* and it was necessary it should burst forth at the beginning of December. The parishes you mention shook off the yoke of the commissioners and gave themselves up to Great-Britain. The consequences you should draw from what you here state, destroy what you have said page 149, " that we have had, upon almost every occasion, a proof of the little reliance that " could be placed upon the declarations and assurances of the French." Your account here proves more in favor of the colonies, than any thing I can add to it.

The defeat which our troops had sustained in the late attack of that important post, served only to animate them to greater exertions, but a considerable time unavoidably elapsed, before the expedition took place.—Page 150.

This interval was four months. You forget, Sir, to say, that the Camp-des-Irois was four leagues from Tiburon. Probably, as no English soldier ever performed any service at the posts upon the frontiers, during the four months that elapsed between the first and second attack upon Tiburon, you do not think it necessary to speak about it: but from what you have written in page 149, you compel me to inform you that you ought to have known, that during these four months, five or six hundred French were alone, without intermission, at the Camp-des-Irois, the most unhealthy of the colony; because, for greater security, it was thought most proper to fix the fort in the centre of the marshes, which situation at the expiration of some months caused many fevers, and occasioned the death of many of the planters; that there were several engagements, in which the brigands were always beaten. During these battles the English troops remained quiet in the town and fort of Jérémie. You should have known that it was only upon the representation made by the privy council of la Grande-Anse, that the second attack against Cape Tiburon was determined upon; because the inhabitants wearied of being sick, and seeing their friends and relatives die in the midst of the marshes where they were placed, requested they might go and seize the post of Tiburon, whose situation was more wholesome; the commodore came there with his ship.

You should likewise have added, that the commodore stood out to sea, and that he left the management of the attack to one of the most active and brave officers of the English navy, Captain Rowley; this attack was well directed, and as well executed by the troops under the command of Lieutenant-Colonel Spencer.

*The interval being employed in securing the places which had surrendered.—*Page 151.

Certainly, the time was well employed; but you might have stated *every thing that ought to have been done, and every thing that was not done*; and you might have known the reason why. Above all, you should have been consistent. Since you wished to cast suspicion upon the conduct of the inhabitants of the colony, page 149, it was not necessary to say, that much time was employed in putting the places delivered up into a state of defence. Who delivered them up? Why were they delivered up? It seems to me that it might have been easy for you to have known it; and, as an historian, you ought to have felt that it was your duty to have stated it.

*The enemy appeared in considerable force, and seemed to wait the arrival of the British with great resolution, but a few broadsides from the ships soon cleared the beach.—*Page 151.

It is difficult to shew more courage, more ardour, and more zeal, than Colonel Spencer constantly displayed, in every attack committed to his charge. In this affair he had only six companies of grenadiers and chasseurs: it was necessary to land and take possession of a house the brigands had retired to. They made the descent, overthrew the enemy, and carried the house in an instant: it will ever be difficult to resist the bravery and impetuosity of this officer, who is generally beloved by all that know him.

*By the possession of this port on the South, and that of the Mole of Cape St. Nicholas on the North-Western part of the island, the British squadron commanded the navigation of the whole of that extensive bay, which forms the Bight of Léogane, and the capture of the forts, shipping, and town of Port-au-Prince (the metropolis of the French colony) seemed more than probable on the arrival of a large armament, now daily expected with much anxiety from England.—*Page 152.

You admit yourself by this, that on the 3rd of February, 1794, the English were masters of the whole of the bay of Léogane, except Port-au-Prince. How then could

could you before say, in page 146, that General Williamson *had been deceived by interested men, and that the inhabitants had not made the efforts they had a right to expect from them ?* Observe upon the map the size of the bay, which, within four months after their arrival, the English were in possession of—consider this extent of coast ; and, recollecting that after having delivered it up, the planters continually defended it, tell me what the brave and generous inhabitants who had given them-selves to Great-Britain, could do more ?—I shall add nothing but leave our readers to their reflexions.

In the mean while (the reduced state and condition of the troops not admitting of great enterprise) the commander in chief conceived an idea of obtaining possession of the town of Port-de-Paix, an important station to the Eastward of St. Nicholas by pri-vate negociation.—Page 152.

Had this affair been well conducted, it certainly would have succeeded ; but the orders of the commander in chief, who had written his letter to Laveaux in English, and which I translated into French, were strictly obeyed ; he would not have sent it, could he have thought that it would have been delivered to General Laveaux in the manner in which it was. This was either *a malicious trick,* that an officer wished to play Colonel Whitelock, or at least business clumsily managed.

The town was commanded by Laveaux, an old general in the French service, to whom Colonel Whitelock addressed himself by letter, which he sent with a flag and offered 5,000 pounds to be paid to him in person, on his delivering up the post.—Page 152.

General Laveaux whom you state to be old, is not so. He is of a very good fami-ly, and was captain in a regiment of dragoons in the French service, before the Re-volution ; he was overwhelmed with debt and covered with humiliation for his bad conduct ; this is what made him its partizan. He despises it, but he made an ex-cellent bargain of it. Colonel Whitelock was not in fault in any part of this affair ; I say again, that it was ill conducted : not by him but by another officer ; he wished to serve his country and spare human blood : he was upwards of 120 miles distant from Port-de-Paix by sea, and could only give the first orders ; the means of exe-cuting them were necessarily at the direction of the officer to whom they were ad-dressed.

Colonel Whitelock seems, however, to have mistaken the character of Laveaux, who was not only a man of distinguished bravery, but of great probity.—Page 152.

E C

It is very diverting to hear you speak of General Laveaux, in the manner you do. You ought to have known, that owing to the malicious trick intended against Colonel Whitelock, the letter was presented to General Laveaux in the middle of the day, in presence of all the White troops of the garrison that he commanded; he had no alternative, but to act as he did; being obliged, according *to what he wrote in his answer*, to read this letter aloud to his soldiers. He would be very much astonished at the austere character you give him; you may judge of him by that lately given of him at Paris in the Council of Five Hundred. It was there said, on the 28th of May last, " *Laveaux, who has established a revolutionary tribu-* " *nal at Port-de-Paix; Laveaux who wrote in Vendémiaire, in the 3rd year, a letter* " *in which he proposed to get rid of all the Whites and strip them of their property;* " *Laveaux, who delivered to Santhonax a project, signed, for getting rid of all the* " *Mulattoes, and which Santhonax published; Laveaux, equally abhorred by the* " *Whites and the Men of Colour.*" After this, I leave our readers to determine concerning your judgment!

Unfortunately from the mismanagement of one of the transports, the troops under the command of Baron de Montalembert could not be landed.—Page 154.

This is very true; the captain of one of the transports was intoxicated the whole day; but the captain of the *King Grey*, behaved himself perfectly well; and although we could not land, we kept at bay 200 men, who continued the whole day in ambush, expecting us every moment to make our descent. Hence it resulted, that although we had the mortification not to effect our landing, we kept a corps of upwards of 200 Negros and Mulattoes in check, which prevented them from retiring into the fort.

For the officer who commanded, finding he could no longer defend it, placed a quantity of powder and other combustibles in one of the buildings, which was fired by an unfortunate brigand, who perished in the explosion.—Page 154.

This was a piece of infamous perfidy of the commander, contrary to the rights of war: his order was executed by a Negro from the coast of Africa, who, according to all appearance, knew not the effect of gunpowder; for the unhappy man set fire, not to the powder that was in a room, but to an artillery waggon, which was placed under the gallery of the house, that served as the guard-house in the fort. He was killed as well as thirteen English or Frenchmen who arrived first, besides the officers you have named.

A place called Bompard, about fifteen miles from St. Nicholas.—Page 155.

You no doubt meant to say *Bombarde*. Since you were desirous of writing concerning the History of St. Domingo, it might not perhaps have been useless to have informed your readers of the cause of the establishment of so important a post as the Mole, and how, and by whom it was established. Permit me in very few words to supply the deficiency.

During the war which was terminated by the peace of 1763, the English had nearly established themselves in the port of the Mole St. Nicholas, which was not inhabited, the soil which surrounds it being arid and without water. They made a place of shelter of it, particularly for their privateers. The English ships entered there, and sailed again quietly, as the English and French still do in time of war, in some parts of the island of Cuba. At the peace, the Count d'Estaing, having been appointed governor of the French colony of St. Domingo, was informed of what happened during the war; he caused the port of the Mole to be inspected, and he even examined it himself. He readily comprehended the importance of its situation and strength, both for the colony and for France, and in consequence obtained an order from the minister for erecting the fortifications and the necessary establishments. In order to people it he settled the Acadians there, whose loyalty had determined them to quit their country, when it was given up to a foreign power. He afterwards caused a certain number of German families to settle there; and in order to draw some commerce, and secure a resource to the inhabitants, he made it the only free port in the colony, which very quickly succeeded in making it a considerable staple town. The neighbouring lands are very arid, but at a few miles distance they become a little better; they were divided amongst the Acadians and Germans, who succeeded in cultivating many excellent vegetables and some European fruits, such as grapes and figs. The peace of 1783 ruined the inhabitants of the Mole; for the Americans of the United States, having obtained permission to go to Port-au-Prince, to the Cape, and Aux Cayes, St. Nicholas Mole ceased to be an important staple town.

A detachment of 200 men from the different corps, were ordered on this service in two divisions, one of which was commanded by Major Spencer, the brave and active officer already mentioned, the other by Lieutenant-Colonel Markham.—Page 155.

There are many Englishmen here who have been at St. Domingo, who could have informed you, that the detachment ordered upon this expedition (which was only intended as a *coup-de-main* in order to punish the treachery of the inhabitants of Bombarde) was composed of no more than 300 men, the greatest part of *them marines*, from the different ships performing the garrison duty of the Mole with the regular troops. This detachment was in fact, under the orders of Colonels Spencer and Markham. There were only two Frenchmen concerned in this affair, M. Deneux, the major of artillery, who had contributed to put the English in possession of the Mole, and myself. I was at the Mole with Colonel Whitelock, agreeably to his request, and at a distance from my corps. I requested and readily obtained leave to serve as a volunteer in this expedition, or rather as aide-de-camp to Colonel Spencer, whose determined and enterprising character no one admired more than myself. He was satisfied at having me with him. The detachment set off at nine o'clock in the evening ; we had fifteen miles to march in the woods and mountains. We performed it without difficulty, and arrived at the opening of the wood into the plain, where the redoubt was situated that we were going to attack, at about three o'clock in the morning, at the moment they were relieving guard : we were then very near to it, insomuch, that in a moment after we saw the alarm gun fired, which was repeated every minute. Whether we were discovered by some patrole or advanced post, or by the noise of a corps of 300 men marching quickly, or by the noise of the soldiers arms (for we marched with fixed bayonets); in short, whatever might be the cause, a great part of our project failed from the moment we were discovered ; for it should be known, that we had to attack by night 150 old German soldiers, intrenched, and having three pieces of cannon, and we had none. The brave Colonel Markham took half the detachment, to attack the redoubt in flank, whilst we went to attack it directly by the gate. The enemy suffered us to arrive within half gun shot : their sentinel having thrice called *qui vive ?* Colonel Spencer, at the third time, cried *England !* We then received a fire perfectly well directed, which continued with so much order and briskness, that we were obliged to give up the enterprise. Several of the officers, however, were advanced as far as the ditch, supported by some grenadiers, but too few in number. We were obliged to retire, and disorder ensued. I was at the side of the ditch, ten feet from the entrenchment, which served as a rampart, and was wounded by several musket shot. At this instant I experienced the greatest piece of good fortune, a ball coming flat upon the plate of my belt, and another falling against the barrel of a brass pistol, that was in my pocket, which caused only a considerable contusion. Thus, in the same action, was my life twice miraculously saved, after having received four wounds besides. I with some difficulty rejoined a party of our men, who were still firing from behind a hedge, but whose

position

position was a very bad one ; I apprized them of it. We retired, and in a few moments met Colonels Spencer and Markham, who were extremely mortified at seeing
my situation : it was resolved to abandon our project. Day light appeared, and we
employed ourselves in retreating and collecting our people, who had wandered about
in the dark, and during the attack. Major Deneux, one of the number, was
slightly wounded in the thigh; he did not rejoin us till we were on the high road.
Had the Germans perceived our disorder, they might have attacked us with advantage. The retreat was hastened : grievously, though not dangerously wounded, I
caused myself to be put on horseback, and remained for a long time in the rear
guard ; but when we were no longer in danger of pursuit, I went on before
with my servant, and arrived at the town, being the first who acquainted the
commander with our ill success, after which I went home to get my wounds
dressed. I then received a part of the reward I was most ambitious of, by the attention every one wished to shew me, for I was visited by the whole town, as well
as by all the army and navy.

There were only sixteen men killed and twenty-six taken prisoners. Many
causes contributed to this loss; the principal was, that our attack was made in the
night, by troops that were fatigued, and astonished at the manner in which they
were received. *If there are any others,* time and history will no doubt transmit
them to the public with impartiality.

I cannot, Sir, refrain from reproaching you, for not having made yourself acquainted with all the particulars of this affair ; for you would have communicated
to your countrymen, one of the most courageous military traits of the present war,
which will confer an everlasting honor on the brave and young *English officer*,
who, to the greatest courage, united the most determined character and presence of
mind. I shall endeavour, however, to supply your negligence.

We were obliged to make our retreat rather precipitately, in order that the
enemy might not perceive the disorder, which this attack, made during the night,
had thrown us into. We had no drum, nor any means of indicating a general retreat : the consequence was, that many of our people strayed from us.

A young and brave officer, a lieutenant in the first regiment of the Royal English
Infantry, *M. Garstin,* who belonged to the detachment of his corps that came with
us, found, at day break, that he had strayed with eight men belonging to his company. He, for a long time endeavoured to find the road, in order to return with
them to the town, and followed several paths which led him still farther distant
from it ; when, towards the middle of the day, he fell in with a German patrole,

F f

consisting of six men, who desired him to surrender : he refused, and threatened to fire upon the patrole if they attacked him. Seeing his determination, they contented themselves with following him, but he strayed still more from the road ; the republicans informed him of it, continually advising him to surrender, which he as constantly refused. The Germans, fatigued with having followed him so long in the sandy and dry plain, (which the young officer with his eight men had travelled over) on the approach of night retired. Being thus left alone, these brave men continued to wander ; distressed with hunger and thirst, and overwhelmed with fatigue, it was not till after two days and a night, that they arrived by the greatest chance at the landing-place of the platform, two of their companions having died with fatigue, hunger, and thirst ; for they found nothing but the fruit of Indian fig trees and aloes, wherewith to supply their pressing wants. At this place, which was one of the republican posts, the establishments of which had been destroyed three weeks before, by Captain Rowley, they found an old fishing boat that had been deserted ; these brave soldiers, guided by their young lieutenant, embarked, and exposed themselves to all the dangers of the sea, after having experienced all that can be suffered by land, being without provisions, without fresh water, without a sail, and with bad oars. They arrived on the morning of the third day, at the entrance of the gulph or bay of the Mole, from whence the fishermen brought them to the town. You may easily form a judgment of their situation. I cannot conceive how this instance of courage, perseverance, and the most determined and best supported conduct, can be unknown to you and to England. I am even ignorant whether, at the time, General Williamson was informed of this action, worthy to be compared with any that the history of the present war may transmit to posterity.

I have the greater reason to think that he was suffered to remain ignorant of it, as it was only by accident that he learnt that I had been wounded. The commander had given him an account of what had happened in this affair, and had detailed the number of English that were killed and wounded ; but, we being Frenchmen (Major Deneux and me), he no doubt did not conceive himself obliged to inform him of every thing that had happened to us ; although, like him, I was a lieutenant-colonel in the English army, and was with him at the time, for the public service.

I have reason to complain of you, Sir, and to solicit the just readers to direct their attention towards you, by requesting them to observe your partiality *(unworthy of an historian)* in favor of the King's ancient subjects, to the prejudice of the new ones, who became such by choice.

For you ought to have known, Sir, that whilst a part of the English troops met with a feeble check at Bombarde, a part of the French troops at the fort of l'Accul de Léogane, covered themselves with glory; but it is possible that these troops, being composed only of the inhabitants of the colony, and Frenchmen who had entered into the English service, (in the British Legion formed in order to serve in St. Domingo), and because they were commanded by a French officer; it may have so happened I say, that you thought the recital of this action ought not to be inserted in your Historical Survey, concerning St. Domingo; or you perhaps may have discovered, that it would too completely contradict what you have advanced, relative to the negligence and backwardness of the inhabitants, in joining the English troops. Whatever may have been your reasons, I think I have a right to reproach you with partiality, and to supply your forgetfulness. I must inform you then, Sir, that the republicans, under the command of the lieutenants of Rigault, endeavoured to seize upon the important post of *l'Accul de Léogane*; that he collected 12 or 1,500 men of different colours, and prepared to attack the fort, which had cost the lives of so many brave men; when, on the day preceding the intended attempt, they were themselves attacked by Baron de Montalembert, with only 400 men, of which 150 belonged to the British Legion, and the rest consisted of the inhabitants forming the militia of Léogane.

The brigands being charged with fixed bayonets, were completely beaten; they lost a piece of cannon, and left upwards of 300 dead upon the field of battle. This victory caused them to make a retreat, which for a long time cleared the dependency from them as neighbours, and from their incursions. This action, so important from its consequences, might have been placed in the scale against the failure at Bombarde, and would have proved, *that at all points, although no troops had been received from Europe,* we did not continue upon the defensive; but, on the contrary, that no opportunity was lost for attacking the enemy.

I am ignorant, Sir, whether this affair was ever known to General Williamson, for the commanding officer was not at Léogane when it happened; and as there was not a single Englishman among the 400 men, who crowned themselves with glory upon this occasion, he might have thought it *a matter of indifference to England,* and unnecessary to inform her of it.

This affecting loss was but ill compensated, by the very distinguished honor, which was soon afterwards acquired by the few British troops that had been left in possession of Cape Tiburon, who were attacked on the 16th of April, by an army of brigands, amounting to upwards of 2,000.—Page 155.

I am moreover obliged to accuse you here, of the most unjust partiality; and to remind you that, as a writer, you owed the same justice to all the subjects belonging to Great-Britain; whether it be, that they had submitted to her laws but for a few months, or for a long time past. You owe it particularly to the brave, loyal, and ever active inhabitants of la Grande-Anse, who were the first that implored and accepted the British government, and received the English as brethren at St. Domingo.

The affair you have just mentioned, will confer immortal honor upon the brave Creoles, and the valiant inhabitants of the colony, as well as *upon the small number of English officers and soldiers*, who partook of their labors in this memorable action.

You ought, Sir, as a faithful historian, to have informed your readers that there were only sixty Englishmen at the post of Tiburon, and not by your dolefulness, and the consequence you thence draw respecting the state of the English army *(which in this passage, as in the rest of your work, signifies only the men born in England)* to have suffered it to be thought, that the killed and wounded were all English.

Although not an historian, yet I owe it to the memory of one of the bravest, most active, and most devoted French officers, that served the English cause in St. Domingo, to render him that justice which is due to him, from your grateful countrymen, for the zeal with which he served the King, whom he had chosen for his Sovereign, *and in whose service he was lately killed*, whilst fighting the enemy he had so often conquered; *it is the Chevalier de Sevré of whom I wish to speak*; all who knew him, know that he had the well-merited reputation of possessing the most determined courage.

In publishing his letter, in which he gives an account of this affair *to Colonel Whitelock*, the just and impartial reader will bestow on each the share of glory he merits, recollecting that the number of English in garrison at Tiburon, amounted only to sixty men.

> Copy of a letter from M. le Chevalier *de Sevré*, commander of the colonial troops at Tiburon, to Colonel Whitelock, commander in chief of His Britannic Majesty's troops in St. Domingo.

" Sin,

" Captain Roberts, who arrived this morning in our port (and who has deter-
" mined upon sailing to night) furnishes me with a secure and speedy opportunity

" nity of informing you of the particulars of the attack made yesterday by the bri-
" gands upon our posts, two hours before day light.

" At half after three my advanced post, placed at the Vegie, was surprised by an
" army of at least 2,000 brigands, having with them two field pieces of four pound-
" ers; they surrounded both the fort and the town at the same instant. It was
" with difficulty that I could retire into the fort with my garrison, where I sup-
" ported the enemy's fire for a long time, before I was in a situation to return it.
" The brigands had every thing in their favor; they saw the fort, they commanded
" it on all sides, and as it was not day light, we could not distinguish them. The
" engagement lasted two hours, when two casks of powder caught fire upon the
" great battery, and entirely dismounted it, blowing the guns out of the fort.
" This unfortunate circumstance killed or wounded twenty of my men, and for a
" while discouraged the garrison; they soon recovered themselves, and fired vio-
" lently upon the enemy. I ordered some of John Kina's Negros to sally upon
" the road near the river; they defeated the brigands, and forced them to retire
" upon the heights.

" I then made a sally with about 200 men, Negros and Whites, and marched on
" the side towards the town, dividing my forces into two columns. I gave the
" command of one to Mr. Philibert, and continued at the head of the other my-
" self. I mounted in order to inclose their rear, and to endeavour to seize upon
" their pieces; but the first column, not being able to mount in time, the brigands
" succeeded in carrying off their cannon.

" I was not able to pursue the flying enemy, farther than the plantation *Gen-
" sac*; so much were my men fatigued with incessant fighting during five
" hours.

" About 100 of my men fell victims in this engagement, of whom thirty were
" killed upon the spot; 100 were wounded, many of them mortally. I think they
" must have at least 500 men incapable of bearing arms or dismayed; 150 were
" found dead upon the field of battle; and the roads by which they retreated
" are so covered with blood, that they must have had a very considerable number
" wounded.

" *The English troops conducted themselves with that courage which characterizes
" them every where.* Captain Hardiman is deserving of the highest praise. I am
" vexed you have recalled him; it is difficult to replace him, on account of his ta-
" lents and virtues.

" Immediately after the engagement, I wrote to all the commanders in the dif-
" ferent parts of the dependency, to send me some reinforcements ; I expect some
" every moment ; but I am much strengthened by the presence of the *Alligator*
" frigate, which arrived this morning.

" I am, with respect, &c.

(Signed)　　" Le Chevalier DE SEVRÉ."

Tiburon, April 7th, 1794.

This letter was printed from the original at St. Nicholas Mole, by order of Colonel Whitelock ; it was at that time distributed throughout the colony, and I am in
possession of a printed copy of it, with many other pieces, which will serve for the
History of St. Domingo, when the proper time for writing it shall arrive.

This letter, above all, will serve to convince your readers of your unjust partiality ; for you ought to recollect how few in number, according to your own account,
were the troops which you call by the name of the English army. You should have
said, that in all parts the French colonists, bearing arms, were three or four times
more numerous than the English.

*The whole of the British force at this time, in all parts of St. Domingo, did not, I be-
lieve, amount to 900 effective men, a number by no means sufficient to garrison the
places in our possession, and the rapid diminution which prevailed among them, could
not fail to attract observation among all classes of the French inhabitants, to dispirit
our allies and encourage our enemies. Such of the planters as had hitherto stood a-
loof, now began to declare themselves hostile, and desertions were frequent from most
of the parishes that had surrendered.—Page 156.*

What must the French have thought, who, after the English were in possession
of a considerable part of the colony for seven months, saw no reinforcements arrive ?
What a difficult part had *be* to act, who had conducted them there, and who had
continually exhorted them to place the greatest confidence in the reinforcements
that were to arrive from England ? Had you received any information upon what
passed at St. Domingo, you would have learnt every thing that was done, in order
to preserve the confidence that had been raised ; and, so far from calumniating
those who, by their most perfect attachment, had gained and preserved such a capital possession to Great-Britain, you would have said, that nothing was spared, neither
voyages, pains, promises, solicitations, nor assurances, to counteract the intrigues of the republicans, and those of the Spanish party, who continually de-

clared that England only wished *to ruin the colony*, and had no intention of keeping it: they adduced as a proof, the desolate condition in which it was left. It will appear but little astonishing, if several persons affrighted and discouraged, should have suffered themselves to be persuaded to desert from some parishes; two or three individuals might have been so, but they were not planters.

Eight months had now elapsed since the surrender of Jérémie, and in all that interval, not a soldier had arrived from Great-Britain; and the want of camp equipage, provisions, and necessaries was grievously felt.—Page 157.

It always happens, Sir, that after your accusations against the planters of St. Domingo, comes a proof that you ought not to have suffered yourself to have inculpated them. You give the true cause of their discouragement yourself; *during eight months no succours arrived, and every thing was wanted.* I know not if other colonists would have had so much patience as the generous inhabitants of St. Domingo had. Save a few trifling exceptions, there was neither insubordination, nor even complaints in the part that had submitted to the English. Ought you to reward their zeal and fidelity by your injustice?

And although the regiments newly arrived did not exceed 1600 *men in the whole (of whom* 250 *were sick and convalescent) the deficiency of number was no longer the subject of complaint.*—Page 157.

You acknowledge yourself, that only 1,600 men arrived, of which upwards of 250 were not fit for service, and the courage of the inhabitants was such, that they no longer complained of not being sufficiently numerous to defend themselves. How do you hope to persuade your readers into what you say, page 146? And, if the fidelity, the attachment, and the courage of the colonists had not been true and sincere, what could such a small number of troops have availed them, arriving eight months after the taking possession of St. Domingo?

You should have said, that, during this interval, upwards of 4,500 planters of every age and sex, had returned into the parishes possessed by the English; that this was the cause of their strength, and not the small number of their troops remaining in the garrisons.

The whole under the immediate command of Commodore Ford.—Page 158.

This brave and valiant officer, was at that time very ill; he, however, did not cease employing himself in the preparations for the attack upon Port-au-Prince. He had for a long time blockaded the port, which contributed greatly to discourage the commissioners, and facilitated our enterprise against the capital of the colony.

And the land forces under the orders of General White consisted of 1465 rank and file fit for duty.—Page 158.

It is proper to remind you that there were only 1,465 English soldiers under the command of General White. You ought at least to have informed your readers of the number of French inhabitants : you would have been surprised to find that it exceeded two thousand.

You should likewise have recapitulated how many there were in arms *at the Mole, St. Mark's, Léogane, Jérémie* (where there were no longer any English troops), the *Camp-des-Rivaux, the Camp-du-Centre,* and above all, at *Cape Tiburon*; for it was known that Rigault was to endeavour to make an attack there, whilst the English should besiege Port-au-Prince. You would be surprised still to find near two thousand of them under arms. I can assure you, Sir, it was so ; and, if necessary, can furnish you with the account, for I have been unremittingly employed upon this subject ; and had, strictly speaking, continually been surveying the English possessions in the colony, particularly during the latter months, when confidence appeared to be declining, owing to the delay in the arrival of the reinforcements. You perceive that your calculation, page 103, differs from this. With respect to its accuracy I refer to the English who were at St. Domingo at the time I speak of.

Major Spencer with 300 British and about 500 of the colonial troops was put on shore on the evening within a mile of the fort with orders to commence an attack on the side of the land. A most tremendous thunder storm arose accompanied with a deluge of rain which as it overpowered the sound of their approach—Page 159.

I was fortunate enough to recover from my wounds before the arrival of General White, and to be able to join Colonel Spencer's detachment with my corps. On the 31st of May the fort was cannonaded the whole day by two men of war and two frigates, which entirely dismantled it on the side next the sea ; but on the land side it remained perfect, and an assault at least was requisite to turn it. Night approached, and a storm was coming on ; a council of war was held between the brave Colonel Spencer, the Baron de Montalembert, myself, and an officer of genius (*a man of such perfect talents and cool bravery as cannot be surpassed by any one ; I mean Captain Mackarus, whose activity was always such, that he knew how to be present*
sent

sent every where, when a gun was fired. With such officers one can never fail of success). The advice given *by one of us, who was perfectly acquainted with the cli-mate of the country,* was, to attack with fixed bayonets, at the time when the great quantity of rain, which generally falls, would prevent the men in the fort from using fire-arms and cannon. The action of Captain Daniel cannot be sufficiently praised, it was executed with a courage and alertness which will always do him ho-nor. History will no doubt one day give *further particulars ;* what I have here said is sufficient for the present.

The possession of Fort Bizoton determined the fate of the capital which was evacuated by the enemy on the 4th of June.—Page 139.

We continued in Fort Bizoton till the 4th of June ; waiting till the great body of the army, which was coming from l'Arcahaye, one part by land and the other by sea, made its approach on that side lying towards the plain of the Cul-de-Sac. It was four days in marching six leagues, and was but three from the town, when, on the 4th of June, at ten in the morning, we began our march from Fort Bizoton, with Colonel Spencer, for Port-au-Prince, from which we were only three miles, in order to occupy a post upon the heights behind the town. Having marched half way a Mulatto woman informed us that the Republicans had abandoned it ; Colonel Spencer, (with whom, as he could not speak French, I found a pleasure in serving as aide-de-camp) begged of me to take 50 of the cavalry of the inhabitants of Léogane, which had joined us at Bizoton the day after the fort was taken, and go and ascertain the fact. I executed this order. Two inhabitants who marched before us as guides arrived without difficulty at the ditch of the town situated under the fort, called the gate of Léogane. One of them jumped into the ditch and having entered the fort let down the bridge, the other joined us at the same instant with the happy news that what the woman had told us was true. I sent to give an account to Co-lonel Spencer, and took possession of the fort, having previously taken care to or-der one of the cavalry to examine whether we had not reason to fear some villainy similar to that at Fort de l'Accul. Nothing was then discovered ; but half an hour after Colonel Spencer and all our detachment had entered the fort, a cry was heard as coming from a cellar that was very much concealed ; the door was broke open, and a Negro was found in the midst of several barrels of gunpowder. I have al-ways thought that this unhappy man had been placed there ever since the pre-ceding night, in order to set them on fire at a certain hour, but that his match was extinguished ; for there was not found even the appearance of fire.

Being acquainted with the town I was directed to go and take possession of the Fort of the Hospital which was likewise abandoned; there I discovered that the plan of the republicans, was to blow up all who might have presented themselves at this post. I found a train of powder reaching farther than a gun could carry, beginning at the powder magazine, where there were eleven barrels of powder, several of which had the bottoms knocked out, and a quantity of powder strewed about the floor; this train reached to the thickets behind the fort. It appears the commissioners thought we should attack them sooner, and that this train of powder had been laid for a long time past. The rain had defeated their fatal project, for I found it wet through to the ground, the surface of it only being dried by the sun. I got off my horse and ordered six men to dismount; we swept the door with our hands and handkerchiefs, and watered the front of it, which I shut, and immediately gave an account of this trifling operation to Colonel Spencer.

As there appeared upon Fort Robin an assemblage of 2 or 300 men, who, upon our entering Fort de Léogane, lowered the republican flag, but who had neglected sending some of their people to us, Colonel Spencer directed me again to go and reconnoitre them, whilst he put himself in a state of defence at the door of Fort de Léogane. I took a detachment of 80 cavalry with me, and repaired to the foot of the fort, having caused the governor-general's (or the King's) house to be examined as we went along; it was completely pillaged and abandoned.

Arrived in the street facing Fort Robin I sent two of the cavalry to tell those who composed the assembly to lay down their arms and to send some of their officers. Two of them came, and informed me that they refused to fly with the commissioners, and that they surrendered with joy to the English troops. I then went up with them into the fort, and took possession of the guns. As those that remained with us were far more numerous than ourselves, I told them to go into the guard house leaving their arms at the door, which they all did immediately, and with the appearance of great content. I then sent to inform Colonel Spencer, who dispatched the Baron de Montalembert to take possession of Fort St. Joseph, which commands the gate of the town leading into the plain of the Cul-de-Sac. A detachment of troops from Léogane was sent to Fort de Ste. Claire. Thus in the forenoon of the 4th of June, 1794, the English were in possession of Port-au-Prince, without having fired a single gun.

The commodore who had brought the ships towards the road at the time we set off from Fort Bizoton, took possession of the Fort de l'Islet, and sent an English flag on shore, which I hoisted at Fort Robin in the place where the republican one was displayed *an hour before*. An express was sent by land *to the grand army*, and we remained at our posts till six o'clock, when General White arrived.

I cannot here forbear mentioning to you, Sir, the pleasure I felt at being *the first officer, in the King of England's service*, who entered the capital of the colony, and who first caused *the English flag to be hoisted at Port-au-Prince*. I consider this happy event, as a reward *procured for me by fate*, for all my labors and anxieties to save St. Domingo from its entire destruction.

The commissioners themselves, with many of their adherents, made their escape to the mountains.—Page 160.

There are secrets which cannot be expected to be discovered; I cannot assert then, whether the commissioners, in the numerous flags of truce they sent, during the time we remained at Fort Bizoton without attacking it, had not agreed with the commodore to suffer them *to retire from Port-au-Prince with their enormous riches, without following them*, on condition that they should neither burn the town nor the shipping. If it be so, one cannot but approve of the commodore's wisdom ; but to me, as well as to all the colonists acquainted with the colony, and the road *from Port-au-Prince to Jacmel*, it will ever appear surprising, that they succeeded in saving themselves with the immense convoy of 200 loaded mules, with 1,500 or 2,000 persons of every age, sex, and colour, in their train. Government no doubt is acquainted with the truth ; this is what prevents me from deducing all the consequences which it would be right to state to the public, since I am obliged to defend the planters of St. Domingo from your accusation of not having *actively and in good faith assisted the English troops* ; and being likewise obliged to defend myself, and those who, like me, proposed and advised the projects and plans by which the English might be put in possession of the colony—*but a day will come when we shall know more about it*. At present, I request you to observe, that there were, after the capture of Port-au-Prince, more than 3,000 men assembled in that town, well armed, and ready to undertake any thing to complete the conquest of the colony.

The situation of the town of Port-au-Prince has already been noticed unhealthy in itself, it is surrounded by fortified heights which command both the lines and harbour.—CHAP. XI. Page 161.

Never was Port-au-Prince considered as unhealthy before the English arrived there. The new houses on the sea shore were damp, but they were burnt with a great part of the town, and the air having a freer circulation, the town cannot be unhealthy. Only one of the heights is fortified, which is the hill of Fort Robin, the other forts are in the plain. The disorders that have occasioned such great ravages must not be ascribed to the situation of the town. I shall hereafter state the cause to which they ought to be attributed.

Here (in the heights) the enemy on their retreat from the town, made their stand in the well founded confidence of receiving regular supplies of men, ammunition, and necessaries, from Aux Cayes, a sea port on the Southern coast, distant only from the town of Port-au-Prince by a very easy road about forty miles.—Page 162.

I can assure you, Sir, that the brigands were nothing but Negro troops, badly armed and dressed, without discipline, and without cannon, and if they had any were not able to bring it against the town. You here commit a surprising error in mistaking the town Des Cayes for Jacmel, which is in fact only 40 miles from Port-au-Prince, by a road in the mountains one above another. In your note you entirely confound the town Des Cayes, where the Mulatto Rigaud commanded, with Les Cayes de Jacmel, where Monbrun, Bornéo, and other Mulattoes commanded. The town Des Cayes where Rigaud commanded is the capital of the Southern part of the colony ; but Les Cayes de Jacmel is in the Western dependency. If you look in your chart you will easily perceive the advantages it might have been of to the English and to the colony, after taking the capital, to have profited by this success, and to have sent a part of the 3,000 men, who were assembled at Port-au-Prince, to finish what had been so happily begun. In the events of war there are opportunities which we should know how to take advantage of ; when lost they are seldom, if ever recovered.

And from both those sources reinforcements were constantly poured into the enemy's camp.—Page 162.

The *camps* of the enemy deserved only the name of *assemblies* of Negros. With one hundred men of the Legion and as many inhabitants, we took the strongest of these camps, called *Néret*, in less than a quarter of an hour, where we found nine field pieces which we carried off ; they had been brought to this spot by the commissioners at the time of their flight, and the carriage road not extending farther they left them. The brigands never supported themselves five minutes in these camps ; we passed over three in two days with four hundred men, without once being able to fire a single gun.

The

The brigands received no reinforcements. I again repeat, that, before the month of August 1794, they never had a single camp in the dependency of Port-au-Prince, in which they supported themselves for a quarter of an hour.

On this account, the British commanders found it indispensably necessary to strengthen the lines, and raise additional entrenchments and works on that side of the town which fronts the mountains.—Page 162.

I shall say nothing of the danger there was of *Port-au-Prince being attacked by the brigands*; the colonists never had any uneasiness about it. I shall content myself with observing, that, when we took possession of the town, there were within the compass of its lines 131 pieces of cannon mounted in batteries. After hearing you, Sir, one would believe that the brigands had disciplined troops, provided and well armed with trains of artillery, whilst they were nothing but highwaymen that rifled travellers.

It was fortunate for the British army, that the French troops suffered by sickness almost as much as our own. Port-au-Prince would otherwise have been but a short time in our possession.—Note B. Page 163.

Permit me, Sir, to ask you of what corps and of what kind of men these French troops were composed, and *where you place them?* There were no White troops formed into regiments but at Port-au-Paix, and the remainder of some companies at Aux Cayes; the revolted Negros, of which I have given an account, were not numerous, and could not attack Port-au-Prince with cannon, not having any, and not being able to convey any by the double mountains; in general, their arms were in a very bad state. In fact, they could not be called an army; how then could there be sickness *in an army that did not exist?*

What you say, Sir, in the text, (to which you thought proper to add the note I am answering), is the continuation of that inactivity in which the 3,500 troops were kept during ten days, who were in good health, and satisfied, after the taking of Port-au-Prince; if Jacmel had been taken, as was then proposed, the war had been at an end; if, if, if, if, &c. &c.; one might add a great many. . . . . . . Consider, Sir, with all my readers, what you have said of me, and that I have a perfect knowledge of St. Domingo, and am acquainted with every thing that happened there, &c. &c.

The frigate (the Experiment) in which they were conveyed became a house of pestilence.—Page 163.

This is the true cause of the sickness at St. Domingo. The arrival of this frigate was the source of the greatest misfortunes to the colony, by bringing the pestilential distemper that carried off so many brave men.

So rapid was the mortality in the British army after their arrival, that no less than 40 officers and upwards of 600 rank and file met an untimely death, without a contest with any other enemy than sickness, in the short space of two months after the surrender of the town.—Page 164.

The sickness called the *yellow fever* was never known at St. Domingo; it was brought by the English frigate the Experiment; and it was *the English themselves* who introduced the disease into our unfortunate colony. It is a scourge to which the inhabitants are victims as well as the English, but in a much less proportion, indeed, than amongst them; because the manner of living is different, as the French physicians treat the tropical diseases better, and by processes less violent, than the English. *La Fievre Jaune*, or Yellow Fever, is a real pestilence, brought from Bulam to Grenada in the Hankey. This ship staid so long at Bulam as to contract a disorder, *sui generis*, similar to what is called in England *the gaol distemper*, from the crowded situation the people were in on board her: where they remained many months before they could be accommodated on shore, when, with a very few exceptions, they died; the master and mate, or the mate and another man, were all who remained alive when the ship arrived at Grenada. THE CLOTHES AND BEDDING OF THOSE THAT DIED OF THIS PESTILENCE WERE SOLD BY PUBLIC AUCTION; and, by that means, the contagion was spread over the whole of the islands and great part of the continent.

I am again obliged to repeat, that, if part of the 3,500 troops which were at Port-au-Prince after the town was taken, had been ordered to march, a less quantity of soldiers would have been collected there, &c. &c. Fewer men would have perished, &c. &c. I leave our readers to reflect and to judge of the consequences.

Whatever troops were promised or expected from Great-Britain, none arrived until the expiration of seven months after General Horneck had taken the command.— Page 164.

It is very essential to observe, that General Horneck did not arrive at St. Domingo till the 15th of September 1794; that the troops belonging to the second reinforcement did not arrive there till seven months after; that, after the taking possession of the colony on the 19th of September 1794, nineteen months elapsed before the complement of men promised for the colony arrived. You should have drawn the result, which is, that, arriving by divisions, their number was not sufficient to finish the conquest; every thing should have convinced you, that the French planters did all in their power to accelerate the capture of the whole of the colony, and to diminish the difficulties, fatigue, and dangers, of the English in this expedition; that they braved themselves with a fidelity that deserved that justice from your impartiality which, I fear not to assure you, will be rendered to them by all sensible readers, who know how to appreciate their loyalty.

While Colonel Brisbane was following up his successes in a distant part of Artibonite, the Men of Colour in the town of St. Marc, seduced by the promises of the French commissioners, and finding the town itself without troops, had violated their promises of neutrality, and, on the 6th of September, taken up arms on the part of the Republic.—Page 165.

How happens it, Sir, that you are not informed that there were no commissioners remaining at St. Domingo in September 1794? they set off in June, after the taking of Port-au-Prince. How happens it also that you are ignorant that Colonel Brisbane was deceived by the Mulattoes, *whom he had spoiled by too much confidence?* They were very sensible he could not long remain in error concerning them; we must attribute their revolt at St. Marc's to nothing but their character, which is a mixture of perfidy and atrocity.

This young officer had been often advised to be upon his guard against them; but he thought that courage would make up for every thing. He had still greater reason to think so by the advantages he so easily obtained over the traitors whom he had loaded with favors and kindness.

The garrison, consisting of above 40 British convalescents, threw themselves into a small fort on the sea-shore, which they gallantly defended for two days, when a frigate came to their relief from the Mole of Cape St. Nicholas. The triumph of the Mulattoes, however, was transient. Colonel Brisbane attacked them on the side of the land, and recovered the town.—Page 166.

You forget to say here, whether it was with *the sick soldiers* only, that Brisbane defeated the Mulatto traitors, and obtained a complete triumph over them; you forget to tell us *where the population of Whites belonging to the town, which is one of the most considerable in the colony,* and the militia, *retired to,* and who were *the runaways.* It would be well to know the names of all *who fled.* You forget to say, where the French Legion was at that time, of which Captain Brisbane, of the 49th infantry, was Lieutenant-Colonel. Just and reasonable men cannot fail to blame that partiality, which continually renders you unjust. Know, with our readers, that here, as well as at Cape Tiburon, it was the French, commanded by Colonel Brisbane and some French officers, who defeated the brigands; *and not forty convalascent soldiers.*

Allow, Sir, that it is absurd to write (however cowardly may be the race of the Men of Colour), *that forty men, sick or convalascent, could resist them, and even ob-'tain any triumph whatever over them.*

Allow still more, Sir, that, owing to your unjust pre-possession, you have suffered yourself to be strangely deceived; since you assert, in page 162, that the enemy received regular supplies of men, ammunition, &c. which made it necessary to fortify the town of Port-au-Prince; (" *of receiving of regular supplies of men, am-* " *munition, &c. On this account, the British commander found it indispensably* " *necessary to strengthen the lines, &c*)." If they were so powerful, how do you manage to make a garrison of forty English *convalascent* soldiers enter into a fort, defend themselves there, and then make them quit it afterwards, in order to fight these same Mulattoes upon the arrival of a frigate; without adding whether the frigate had brought any considerable reinforcements, in order to attack these said men; who, a few pages back, you made so dangerous, that it was necessary to fortify at an *excessive expence*, the lines of the capital?

Being joined by the fugitive Mulattoes they soon repassed the river, and having in the beginning of October obtained possession of two out-posts (St. Michael and St. Raphael) they had procured plenty of arms and ammunition, and now threatened so formidable an attack on the town of St. Marc, as to excite the most serious apprehensions for its safety.—Page 166.

What do you understand by *out-posts?* Do you mean to speak of two posts standing without the town of St. Marc? Explain yourself; for the two posts of St. Michael and St. Raphaël, lie within the Spanish colony, and one of them is upwards of sixty miles from St. Marc's, and the other upwards of seventy-five, and it is necessary to traverse the double mountains by the worst roads imaginable. You must likewise observe, that these two small boroughs belong to the Spaniards; whoever at St. Domingo, says a *small Spanish borough*, means the poorest place you can possibly imagine in the world; I have seen them such in the colony's flourishing days, judge yourself what they must be since the troubles in the French part, whose inhabitants no longer purchase their cattle. I assure you, that what ammunition they could bring from the pillage of those two *out-posts*, could not

have

have sufficed them for an attack upon St. Marc's, *and above all, a formidable one.*
What you say about serious alarms that were entertained, *will make the colonists
of St. Marc* and St. Domingo laugh heartily.

*And unhappily, in all other parts of the colony, the weakness of the British was so
apparent, as not only to invite attacks from the enemy, but also to encourage revolt
and conspiracy in the posts in our possession.*—Page 166.

*Colonel Brisbane had scarcely drawn the Mulattoes from St. Marc, and restored order
and tranquillity in the town, before a dark conspiracy was agitated among some of the
French inhabitants under British protection, to cut him off.* Note C.

Was it after having been masters of the colony for more than twelve months,
that the English were still afraid of their possessions there ? It could not be the fault
of the colonists; observe them every where established in camps, *fighting upon
every part of the frontiers,* the posts of which are composed of none but *the proprietary inhabitants,* and consider the English soldiers shut up in the garrisons, and
perishing without having seen the enemy. Admit at least, that if the planters had
begun to lose their courage, it was much less their fault, than that of their unfortunate situation. You have not, however, laid before your readers, the particulars of any conspiracy formed by the inhabitants of the colony.

Among the great number of Whites that returned to St. Domingo, there, doubtless, must have been many bad men, who, not being planters, consider the colonies as their prey, and who are themselves *a scourge to all the colonies.* There might
exist some villains among them, who, enriched by their first pillage during the
troubles of the colony, might wish for a return of those times, which had been so
profitable to them.

But ought a writer to confound this vile horde with the brave and generous
colonists and inhabitants, who have so long fought for the safety of their property,
and *for the support of the power of Great-Britain in the colony?* You should
have informed your readers what kind of men they were who were encouraged to
conspire.

An historian, who pretends to be so well informed as you have assured us in your
preface you are, ought to have been able to have named those French inhabitants
who conspired against Colonel Brisbane. It is not enough, in order to be believed,
vaguely to accuse all the planters of a district; one should be particularly careful,
not to call an individual, who comes into a town only for a short time, *an inhabitant,* or who may even come there upon some plan for a conspiracy; sent perhaps

K k

by the republicans, *in order to get rid of enemies whom they dread,* and whom they have reason to fear, knowing their valour and activity; that was the case with the brave Colonel Brisbane.

That valiant, but young colonel, had greatly alienated the confidence of the inhabitants of St. Marc, *by his connections and ridiculous preference in favor of the Men of Colour*; for he lived upon more intimate terms with the Mulattoes, than ever any White (particularly a French officer) had done, or would have ventured to have done. The inhabitants of St. Marc complained of Brisbane and his inexperience: many quitted the town on that account; but I shall never think that any planter *entered into a conspiracy against him*; they all rendered justice to his qualities; and I will answer for it, that if any one of them had had cause to complain of him, he would have openly demanded satisfaction of them, as becomes a man of honor: but no one was capable of cowardly wishing to conspire against him.

If he had succeeded the loss of the whole of the British army at Port-au-Prince, would have been inevitable.—Page 167.

Had you been acquainted with the situation of Fort *Bizoton,* you would have known, that it in no respect defends Port-au-Prince, from which it is a league distant. On examining this post, it will be found, that its utility is only in defending the great carriage road leading from Léogane to Port-au-Prince.

Had this town been attacked, it would have been defended as Fort Bizoton was, which Captain Grant so well supported against 2,000 brigands. If such a bad post as Fort Bizoton was defended with the feeble garrison it would contain, what might not have been done at Port-au-Prince, whose strong garrison was augmented by the great quantity of people who assembled there, after the town was in the possession of the English?

You forget, Sir, that in page 161, you say the enemy had retreated into the mountains behind Port-au-Prince, and that they received regular supplies of men, ammunition, provisions, &c. from Aux Cayes; you mean to say from Jacmel (*" receiving regular supplies of men, ammunition, and necessaries"*). Nothing prevented Rigaud following that road, or passing even behind Fort *Bizoton,* in order to go to Port-au-Prince; he had neither interest nor advantage in attacking Fort *Bizoton,* if he had wished to seize upon the town; he was master, as he still is, of all the country round it. He could attack it then, when and how he pleased, without possessing Fort Bizoton.

2

But you determine, I am ignorant why, that if Rigaud had succeeded in carry-ing Fort Bizoton with two thousand brigands, *the entire loss of the English army was inevitable*; you forget that the English garrison in that town was always the most numerous of any in the whole colony, and that there were a great number of English soldiers in good health, who would at least have been able to have done what you say, *forty sick or convalescent men* had done at St. Marc's.

Make yourself easy, Sir, there was a very good English garrison in Port-au-Prince, and there were likewise many *French planters*, who, as I have proved by facts, knew how to defend themselves. It will never be 2,000 brigands, nor ten times that number, that will take Port-au-Prince, provided they have no cannon nor White troops with them.

His intentions were known, and his project might have been defeated, if any one English ship of war could have been spared to watch his motions off the harbour of Aux Cayes, from whence he conveyed his artillery, ammunition, and provisions. He proceeded, however, without interruption, in his preparations for the attack, and his armament sailed from Aux Cayes on the 23d of December.—Page 167.

You should have asserted, Sir, and often repeated to your readers, that since *the arrival of the English at St. Domingo*, the French have been *absolutely passive in the administration and government* of the colony; that having given themselves up to Great-Britain, the commander in chief from that moment directed all the interior and exterior operations *according to his pleasure*. The French confined themselves to execute the orders given them.

Certainly, if a small frigate had been sent to protect *Tiburon*, Rigaud never could have taken this post. Do you put this fault to the account of the inhabitants, who never had the power of defending the colony but by land? When a colony gives itself up to a powerful country, it is particularly to have its protection by sea. Where then were the English ships? How happened Rigaud to have a small squadron? You should have put these questions, and have answered them to your readers. There are many other questions that might be put: for example, why, at the time Port-au-Prince was attacked, was not a frigate or a corvette cruis-ing off the port of Jacmel, or towards Altavala, in order to carry off *the commis-sioners with their treasure*, at the time they were making their escape?

History will, doubtless, one day, establish the truth of things, so that the faults may be attributed to those who have committed them; in this case, I previously assure you, that they will not fall *upon my companions.*

The garrison, consisting of only 480 men, made a vigorous defence for four days, when having lost upwards of 300 of their number, and finding the post no longer tenable, the survivors headed by their gallant commander, lieutenant Bradford of the 23d regiment, with unexampled bravery fought their way for five miles and got save to Irois.—Page 168.

You have already seen by the copy *of the Chevalier de Sevré's letter*, that it was he who commanded at the post of *Tiburon*; a lieutenant of infantry only commands a feeble detachment of his corps, *and the Chevalier de Sevré* was the commander in chief in this district, and at this post ; for you will not accuse the English commander in chief of leaving the chief command of such an important frontier post to a young man, who, although very brave and courageous, was ignorant of the resources of a country unknown to him, and being with a people whose language he was perhaps unacquainted with. Add to this, Sir, according to what you say yourself, that it was Lieutenant *Bradford* who commanded, you prove that the number of English soldiers was very small; for a lieutenant cannot, by martial law, command more than 50 men ; now you admit that there were 480 men : you ought then to have said, that there were but few English in garrison at Tiburon, commanded by Lieutenant *Bradford*, but that the greatest part of the garrison was composed of the brave and loyal inhabitants of la Grande-Anse, under the command of the *Chevalier de Sevré*, who, for a long time had commanded at this post ; and with which he was the better acquainted, having been born in the neighbourhood, and where also his property lay.

Alas ! How many of their youthful associates in this unhappy war.—Page 170.

The day will doubtless arrive, when the history of what has passed at St. Domingo, will discover the causes of the misfortunes that happened there, after the island was placed under the protection of England, and will point out those which afterwards interrupted her successes. I shall then make such observations as would at present be too long for an answer to this sentence.

The diseases in which so many gallant men have perished, is commonly known by the name of the yellow fever.—Note F. Page 170.

It is very essential, that I should repeat to our readers, that the Yellow Fever was known only by name at St. Domingo, before the arrival of the English ; that it was not really known there till eight months after they had taken possession of Jérémie.

It

It was brought by an English ship of war, the *Experiment*, after the taking of Martinico; it was the English themselves who introduced this scourge into the colony, and which is generally more fatal to them than the French colonists. The regimen and habits of the two nations contribute much to it, but more than all the difference in the remedies employed by the physicians.

I shall adduce a proof generally known. The brave and amiable Colonel *Markham*, one of the best informed officers in the British army, being in garrison at l'Arcahaye fell ill ; he was soon in the greatest danger, and given over by the English physician that attended him, and the delirium had already begun. I arrived at l'Arcahaye two days after the commencement of his illness ; on my going to see him after my landing, I endeavoured to persuade him to place himself under the care of the French physicians. He would not, and two days after he was given over by his physician. I then pressed his friends who surrounded him to call in *M. de la Croix*, a physician who had lived twenty-five years in St. Domingo, where he had obtained a merited reputation on account of his great experience, particularly in fevers incidental to the colonies. I went to fetch this worthy man, who came immediately. After having considered the patient for some time, he convinced me it was almost too late ; but, that he, however would try, on condition that the patient should be entirely given up to him. The first thing he did, was to order the drugs, that covered the tables to be taken out of the patient's room : he next ordered his own bed to be brought in the room, and had it placed near the colonel's, to whom he himself administered such relief as he judged necessary. The first three or four days, he did not leave him for a moment, on the fifth he declared him out of danger ; and on the fifteenth the Colonel was restored to his friends, in such a debilitated state as is difficult to describe, not being able either to get up or to dress himself. During this time many soldiers were interred every day, and many officers died at l'Arcahaye.

These reflexions and observations are not written in the spirit of accusation against men in authority ; nor (if I know myself) is there any bias of party zeal on my judgment. Page 170.

You only indirectly accuse the men in power ; but why, before you publish such incorrect notes, did you not endeavour to inform yourself whether they were guilty of that trifling and negligence you tax them with, in pretending that they were deceived by persons, who, according to you, in page 141, *either meant to deceive, or, &c.* and instead of injuriously writing against the Ministers and those who advised

L !

the plans, why not, I say, have taken the necessary time to inform yourself whether the Ministers were deceived ? Why not have endeavoured to gain intelligence of what was done ? You might have learnt the substance of my answer to what you have advanced in your work, and you would not have deceived the public. The historian, who so inconsiderably advances matters of such importance, has reason to reproach himself perpetually ; for many readers, having neither the time nor the inclination to investigate what has amused or surprised them, suffer themselves to be led away *by their first judgment,* which always leaves an impression difficult to be removed, because it forces him who had admitted every thing upon the word of an author, to accuse *himself* of imprudence ; and it is with difficulty that three-fourths of mankind recover from their first prejudices.

I am far from asserting that the situation and resources of Great-Britain were such as to afford a greater body of troops for service in St. Domingo, at the proper moment, than the number that was actually sent thither.—Page 170.

Why not have reflected upon the situation in which Great-Britain then was, and has since been in ? Why not, I say, have collected information concerning the resources, and *the means she was able to employ ?* Above all, why did you not inform yourself concerning those who were requested to execute the proposed projects ? In short, Sir, why not have done the Ministers the justice to think that they had taken *a long time* to consider the projects and determine upon the plans they thought to be advantageous to Great-Britain ? And why not have been informed of them ? *And whether events of greater moment* did not prevent the means of executing their plans, at the time intended, *as being the important moment in order to make them succeed ?*

In short, why do you accuse, as you do, in pages 141, 145, 146, the generous inhabitants of St. Domingo, who have unremittingly and faithfully served both the interests of Great-Britain and the colony ? Why do you accuse the colonists who advised the operations relative to St. Domingo ?

I presume not to intrude into the national councils, and am well apprized that existing alliances and pre-engagements of the state were objects of important consideration to His Majesty's Ministers.

Neither can I affirm that the delays and obstructions which prevented the arrival at the scene of action of some of the detachments, until the return of the sickly season, were avoidable.—Page 170.

In every page you furnish those you have accused with the strongest arguments against yourself, and you prove that a little reflexion would have sufficed to have prevented you from publishing your work. I leave our readers to reflect upon what you say in what I have just copied.

A thousand accidents and casualties continually subvert and overthrow the best laid schemes of human contrivance.—Page 170.

I shall refer to your own confession ; and, since you allow that a thousand unexpected events overturn the wisest plans, why not have rendered justice to the Ministers, and to those who proposed the plans they adopted ; particularly when those who proposed these plans undertook (at the risk of every possible danger) to execute them ? What will you say, if it is proved to the public, that, without having been able to possess (and that for reasons of greater moment than you admit of) the means that had been promised them, they have done a hundred times more than they had given reason to hope for ; without ever having *complained, publicly or privately*, that the means were not furnished which were to enable them to undertake an expedition of such magnitude ?

We have seen considerable fleets detained by adverse winds in the ports of Great-Britain, for many successive months, and powerful armaments have been driven back by storms and tempests after many unavailing attempts to reach the place of their destination. Thus much I owe to candour.—Page 171.

You admit yourself a great truth ; you acknowledge that fleets were detained in port, others destroyed in part, and obliged to return ; in short, you admit of every thing that counteracted the projects and overturned the plans, notwithstanding which, you have published your book !

I have sought from the beginning of your work, in what part of the operation against St. Domingo is to be found *the ill success* which accompanied it. If it be not accomplished, I certainly cannot discover the cause in your book ; I observe, on the contrary, that *every thing that was wished to be done there succeeded*, during the period of time comprised in your work. Because troops were afterwards sent, which perished without fighting, it is not a reason for saying that the operation against the colony was in no degree successful ; every thing I have said, proves that its success at first was beyond what could have been expected. If afterwards it did not succeed more completely, it was not the fault of those who had advised it, nor was it moreover that of the inhabitants, who, unremittingly supported all the fatigues of war.

if from the ill success which has attended the attack of St. Domingo, a justifica-
tion of the original measure shall be thought necessary, it ought not to be over-
looked that General Williamson, among other motives, had also strong reasons to
believe that attempts were meditated by the republican commissioners on the island
of Jamaica. He, therefore, probably thought that the most certain way of prevent-
ing the success of such designs, was to give the commissioners sufficient employment
at home.—Note *, Page 171.

General Williamson could not do more for St. Domingo than he did. Every
plan he adopted succeeded. He had orders (as you have yourself observed in page
141, chap. X. line 2) to send troops to take possession *of such parts of the colony* as
might be willing to put itself under the power of Great-Britain, until the arrival *of*
reinforcements which should arrive from England. He did so; I challenge you, Sir,
to say, whether there has been an expedition in this war *that has succeeded more*
completely, that has been more perfectly executed, that has cost less, and yet has
been of more importance to Great-Britain in its present and future consequences.

You have already twice nearly avowed the most important of the reasons which
determined the Ministers to endeavour to seize upon St. Domingo; and the justice
you here render to General Williamson, he has completely deserved, but the Ministers deserve it likewise. For do you think, Sir, that they did not make the reflexions which in your preface you admit Lord Effingham had made from the commencement of the ravages of St. Domingo? Do you think that those who proposed, advised, and solicited the expedition against the colony, whose situation and
resources they were perfectly acquainted with, and who above all knew the influence
that the destruction of the first sugar colony must have upon the others; do you
think, Sir, that they did not furnish the Ministers of Great-Britain with every
reason that might support their political reflexions concerning the danger of
the Antilles? Do you think that the Ministers did not feel the consequence
and the truth of them? Do you not think that it was this which determined
them to carry the theatre of war into St. Domingo, which would have been in-
evitably carried to Jamaica?

How is it possible that you, personally, *being a colonial planter at Jamaica*, can
have been so far ungrateful as to accuse those, who advised an operation that saved
your individual property, of having deceived your government, when it is by the
effects of their advice that the whole of your fortune has been preserved?

I appeal,

I appeal, Sir, to all who have read your work, and who are acquainted with what has happened at St Domingo and the Windward Islands ; I appeal to the planters of all the English colonies that have been ravaged ; and I say, that *Santhonax* and *Polverel* are acknowledged as having been two men *of the greatest talents,* and the latter in particular, as possessing an *astonishing and incomparable firmness of mind :* these are the men with Hugues, whom the Jacobins had entrusted with the destruction of the colonies. You are acquainted with every thing that Hugues has done ; he had no other means but what were furnished him from Guadaloupe, nevertheless the planters of Grenada and St. Vincents will remember him everlastingly, as will also those of Martinico, St. Lucia, St. Christopher, Antigua, &c. They are not yet delivered from the terrors caused by the proximity of this villain. *Well then, Polverel and Santhonax* having means far more powerful than what *Hugues* had, would have displayed them against Jamaica, which is only thirty leagues to leeward of St. Domingo, and where one may repair without difficulty in twenty-four hours, in open canoes. The two commissioners had the remains of a population of 500,000 Negros or Men of Colour, and all the riches and resources of that immense colony, at their command. I ask you, Sir, as well as all judicious men, whether you think *they might not have obtained the same success at Jamaica as the jacobin Hugues did in the Windward Islands ?* Do you think that Jamaica would have continued to be a sugar colony, useful to Europe, and that it would be in a preferable situation to St. Domingo ? The revolt and the war of the Maroons in Jamaica will answer for you ; and all reflecting readers will say to themselves, that the Ministers, in causing St. Domingo to be attacked, and thereby carrying the seat of war there, *have saved Jamaica.* I appeal to the colonists of the latter island, to all the numerous English merchants and manufacturers interested in its commerce ; in short, to every Englishmen, to render justice to those who advised an undertaking which, whatever may have been its consequences since the period you wrote, has had none equal to what the destruction of Jamaica would have produced to Great-Britain.

In order to prove it, I shall ask, 1st. If it was desired to save Jamaica, could it have been done ? Since circumstances prevented the sending of troops there, as well as to St. Domingo, before the 19th May, 1794 ; it is probable that before that time Jamaica would have already been destroyed by Santhonax and Polverel ; particularly, if we take notice, that at the end of July 1793, there was only one. frigate at the island ; that Admiral Gardner had returned to Europe from the Windward Islands ; that the commissioners could have had the command of the French squadron which was at New Englend ; and that in order to land the brigands at Jamaica, it is not necessary to proceed to Kingston, which is in the center of the coast : the French might land any where on the North and North East. In May 1794, war had been declared between England and France fifteen months.

2dly. Supposing the colony of Jamaica was not then attacked, would the forces which have since been sent from Europe have been sufficient for its protection ? And the unfortunate ship which brought the Yellow Fever to St. Domingo, would it not have carried it to Jamaica ? and would not the mortality, which was the consequence of its arrival, have been greater in that island, it being much more unhealthy than St. Domingo ?

3dly. Who would have supported the war at Jamaica ? The militia, as they did in the Maroon war. Upon whom would the loss of men at that time have fallen ? upon the inhabitants. Great-Britain then would have lost, with the men she lost at St. Domingo, the population of Jamaica. The war being carried to St. Domingo, occasioned only a part of the misfortunes which England must have experienced at Jamaica, *whose population and property she has preserved.*

As to the expences, the *French colonists never had the administration of a guinea at St. Domingo* ; they were all ordered and payed by the English. I am ignorant of what the expence of defending Jamaica would have been to England ; *but I can affirm, that the expences incurred in seizing upon all that the English possess in St. Domingo, and what they have lost since I quitted the colony,* do not amount to the sum of 40,000 *l. sterling,* which has been more than paid for by all the warlike stores, &c. &c. which were found at the Mole, at Jérémie, and at Léogane. I do not speak of upwards *of a million sterling* taken at Port-au-Prince, and other ports, and carried either to Jamaica or to England.

The expences which have been made *since my departure from St. Domingo,* by the English Government, have in no respect *contributed to the taking of the colony,* they are entirely distinct from it, and have nothing to do with the advice of those who undertook to put a part of it under the dominion of England. I shall be told that they were necessary for its preservation ; that may be ; *I speak not my opinion,* but I have a right to think and to assert, that a part of these same expences would have been necessary for the preservation of Jamaica, and to carry on the war there against the brigands, as the English have done against those of St. Domingo.

I shall go still farther, Sir ; I declare, and even affirm, *that, admitting the greatest exaggeration* of the expences incurred on account of the colony, the Ministers of Great-Britain have rendered her, as well as the inhabitants of Jamaica, the greatest service, by carrying the war to St. Domingo ; since the safety of Jamaica is the consequence. The expences incurred in order to insure its success, are considerable; without examining to what degree they were useful, they are at least in a great measure counterbalanced by the productions saved from the most considerable of all the English colonies in the Antilles. Let us reckon the productions for nearly four years, which have arrived in England from Jamaica, since the landing of the English at St. Domingo on the 9th of September 1793; add to them those of the latter colony during the same space of time, whose exportations for the part they possess, amounted last year to 2,000,000 l. sterling. Let it be considered, if the expences incurred by Great-Britain have not been almost entirely repaid; perhaps we shall see that the expences have been much diminished by the duties upon the imports from Jamaica and St. Domingo since the period above stated: to which may be added what has been paid upon the produce arising from the prizes made since the same period; perhaps we shall find that the expences of the government are very inconsiderable, and have all turned to the advantage of England, and been shared among the people in it.

After having calculated the expences incurred in taking possession of the colony, and *for supporting the war there, which has saved Jamaica,* let us compare them with *the immense capitals* which have thereby been preserved to Great-Britain, and her inhabitants, as well as those of the colony of Jamaica, whose productions are continually renewed; let us attentively observe the evils which would have arisen to the manufactures of Great-Britain, if, simultaneously by the destruction of Jamaica, they had been without business, with so many thousand hands unemployed, and so many families ruined.

After having reflected upon all the evils which might have befallen England from the loss of Jamaica, there is no prudent man who loves his country, who will not tremble at the idea, and who, far from blaming *one of the greatest and most useful operations of the war,* will not thank the King's Ministers for having undertaken it, according to the projects and plans of those who advised it, and who charged themselves with the execution of them.

Let the planters of the English and French islands that have been ravaged, *be consulted;* they will declare with what pleasure they would have lost all the annual productions of their plantations, in order to recover, *at the peace,* their capitals in the value of their plantations that have been preserved. You are, no doubt, acquainted with some of them, Sir; you ought then to put yourself in their situation, as a specimen of that in which you would have been placed, by the destruction of Jamaica; and far from casting a ridicule of inconsistency and levity *upon the conduct of Ministers,* by accusing them of suffering themselves to be deceived,

2

you ought to vow an eternal gratitude, both to them and those who advised the undertaking ; since it is to them that you, and all the planters of Jamaica, owe the preservation of your own and your families' fortunes.

That they placed (the Ministers) great dependance on the co-operation of the French inhabitants, and were grossly deceived by agents from thence, I believe and admit.—Page 172.

By what you here advance, I find myself more directly and more personally attacked, for you announced (page 140), that *I had been sent by the Ministers to act with General Williamson*; and that (page 147) you set forth that I was *the agent of the inhabitants of la Grande-Anse*. I acknowledge it ; I am then the agent, who, according to you, *deceived, grossly deceived the Ministers*. I ought then, in a direct manner, to answer this accusation ; the injustice of which you may believe, has caused me the most painful sensations. Although I hope, in the preceding part, to have convinced our readers, that it was without foundation, I shall enter into more particular details in order completely to refute your reproach : my answer will serve for all the articles in which you have not so directly accused me.

I do not know, Sir, what right your rank among the legislators of your country may give you to be authentically informed, whether the King's Ministers really think *they have been deceived*. Before you had stated that they had been so, you should have informed yourself whether they believe it, and have acquainted your readers with your proofs in order to assert it : you then could have said whether they agreed with you concerning *the folly, the incapacity* and *the ignorance*, with which you indirectly accuse them. Until you shall lay before the public the proofs you have of the opinion of Ministers, that they have *been grossly deceived* ; give me leave, Sir, to qualify with inconsistency the accusation you direct, without proof, against a man (wholly devoted to the interests of your country), and against the brave, generous and loyal inhabitants, who, led on by interest and gratitude, have incessantly fought, *almost alone*, for the protectors who were to save them.

You ought and might have known from the Ministers the particulars of the projects, plans, and conditions which had been proposed to them for the expedition against St. Domingo ; then, had you discovered any proofs whatever, that the persons who advised them had deceived them, or wished to deceive them, you might have accused those who had advised them. Instead of that, you might

have

have seen, that far from having deceived the Ministers, they spoke to them with a noble frankness. I will go farther, Sir, and maintain, that never did so important an operation either succeed more completely, cost less, or surpass all that was expected and hoped for from it, than this has done. I shall again speak of myself, since it is necessary that I should repel your unjust and un-merited accusation.

You admit (page 140), that I was sent in 1793, by the Ministers, to Ge-neral Williamson, with the necessary orders and instructions to undertake an expedition against St. Domingo. I doubtless did not leave England without the plans for this operation being arranged—it was no doubt subject to certain conditions, which were to facilitate its execution ; and you rightly think, that I should not have set off for the colony, without the positive assurance *of these means :* since the plans that were adopted, and which I was to execute, depended *upon them.*

Let us see then, Sir, whether I have fulfilled what I might have promised. I left England on the 12th of June 1793, in a defenceless packet boat, *and exposed to all the vengeance of Robespierre,* had I been taken. After having been several times pursued, I arrived at Jamaica towards the end of July. *I see, by your work,* that in less than two months, *from the day of my arrival at Jamaica,* the British flag was flying upon the bastions of the Gibraltar of the Antilles, and upon an ex-tent of coast very fertile, of upwards of 150 miles long ; I see, *by the Court Gazette,* that the guns *of the Tower of London* proclaimed this great event throughout Great-Britain, and that it is there ackowledged, that *it did not cost the English the firing of a single gun.* I perceive that very large magazines of warlike stores and artillery were delivered into their hands, and I do not observe a single expence that can be adduced to diminish the enjoyment of the possession of such great advantages. We were only to take post *until the arrival of reinforcements from Europe :* and in less than four days, Great-Britain, without risk, without trouble, and without expence, is mistress of the most important post of the colony, and of the Antilles ; the seven or eight transports which brought the troops, are laden with the revenues stored in the colony, and carry the first productions of the finest country in the world to Jamaica.

The promised troops were to arrive at a time, no doubt fixed upon. What was done whilst they were expected ? *The Gonaïves, St. Marc's, le Monroui, les Vases, l'Arcahaye, le Boucassiu, and Léogane,* were disposed to surrender ; these districts waited with impatience the time fixed upon for the arrival of the reinforcements, which should enable them to declare themselves. The time passed on, *events of greater moment, which happened in Europe,* prevented their being sent. What was the consequence ? it was necessary that the plans, arrived at maturity, should be executed for the security of the inhabitants, as the barbarous commissioners were acquainted with them ; thus these districts, forming three-fourths of the great bay of Léogane, courageously delivered themselves up *to a protection that was not furnished them* ; and at the time agreed upon for receiving the troops, *which did not arrive,* upwards of one-third of the colony was under the dominion of Great-Britain. Time continued to slip away ; the terror with which the arrival of the English had inspired the Republican commissioners diminished daily ; the division of the small number of English soldiers, forming the garrisons, and the length of time taken to send reinforcements, made the French commissioners suppose that the English *knew not, or did not set a great* value upon St. Domingo. From that time they spread a report, that the English only wished *to destroy the colony.* Uncertainty diminished confidence, and prevented other districts from surrendering : the brigands reinforced themselves, and established that fatal correspondence with the United States, which has furnished them with the means of supporting this devastating war.

In the mean time, what did the generous and courageous inhabitants of St. Domingo do ? Being grateful, and confiding in their protectors, *and hoping every thing from what their agent incessantly* repeated to them concerning the intentions of the King of England and his Ministers, they waited patiently ; and, leaving the English troops quiet, and enjoying plenty in their garrisons upon the sea-shore, they went *themselves* to defend the frontiers in the mountains, reduced to the most disagreeable and confined allowance ; fighting the brigands every where, and often alone, and always joining the English when they were going to fight, who had only one single engagement (that of Bombarde), in which there were no colonial troops composed of the inhabitants *(in greater numbers than themselves).*

This is, I affirm, what passed until the arrival of the reinforcements, which came on the 19th of May 1794.

I call upon the whole colony and the English army, to declare how the agent was employed, whom *you accuse of having deceived the Ministers,* during the eight months that succeeded the taking possession of St. Domingo, by the English. I shall confine myself, by saying, that scarcely a single action took place with the brigands, in which he was not present ; and that, when a sufficient interval occurred between the actions, his activity unremittingly carried him to all parts where he could be useful to his countrymen, and to the interests of those who had reposed *their con-*

fidence in him—encouraging some, assisting others, and supporting their hopes by promises and personal services.

At length, Sir, the 1,600 men, sent from Martinico by General Grey, arrived ; they were joined by the colonial troops, and the capital was soon in the possession of the English ; the commissioners, in their flight from it, were obliged to quit the colony. This happened within fifteen days after the arrival of the weak and *first* reinforcements ; and then, I solemnly declare, the power of the French in the colony, was upon the point of being totally destroyed.

I ask you, Sir, and every Englishman, as well as all reasonable men, what more could have been expected ? when, in less than nine months, the most considerable places in the colony were in the possession of the English, and the Republican chiefs put to flight ; when the French only continued to possess, in the Northern part the town of Port-de-Paix, with a garrison of 1,000 or 1,200 men, of which only 500 were Europeans ; when the remainder was abandoned to Jean Français and to Biassou : in fine, when, if I may be allowed the expression, it belonged to nobody. In the South was Rigault, with 300 White troops, and a corps of Negros newly raised, without arms, without discipline, and unable to make any resistance against the triumphant troops, and the numerous planters from all parts of the colony, who had joined in order to attack the Southern part upon four points at once. What more could the planters of St. Domingo do, than every where to give an example of activity and eagerness to attack their own and England's enemies ? Where have these brave and valiant colonists betrayed the confidence that had been placed in them ? and *how have their agents grossly deceived the Ministers ?* What could either do more than to be continually ready for fighting, perpetually armed upon the frontiers ? On the whole, what more could Great-Britain expect, than to be mistress. of one-third of the richest colony in the Antilles in less than nine months, without expence, as well as without an extraordinary armament ?

I shall now go farther, Sir, and maintain, and I offer to prove it, that the French planters carried on *actively and almost alone the war in the colony*, that their agent, in fact would *perhaps be right* in complaining that *he was not better seconded.* What answer will you make to your readers, if I prove, even by your own work, that in less than four months, the English, without having more than 900 men at St. Domingo, were masters of almost all they *ever possessed* there, and more *than what they at present enjoy ?*

What answer could you make, Sir, if I tell you, that troops ought to have been sent to St. Domingo towards the month of November or December 1793 ? Had they arrived to the amount of 4,000 or 3,000 men only, at that time, (the most proper for carrying on the war, and the most favorable to the Europeans, who till the month of May, suffer nothing from the excessive tropical heats); what might not these 3,000 men have done, since 900, assisted by the planters, were put in possession of more than a third of the colony? And if 1,350 English, with the inhabitants, took Port-au-Prince, compelled the commissioners to fly, *without firing a gun*, after having possession for eight months, what might not these troops have done in November, (two months after our taking possession of Jérémie) when the brigands and their chiefs were struck with the general terror occasioned by the arrival of the English troops? What might have been the consequences of such an important operation against St. Domingo? Let the eye of the observing politician judge and decide whether the colonists or their agents can be accused, and whether it be possible better to fulfil every thing that was expected from, or promised by them. They have *never complained* of the forsaken situation in which they were left; they knew better than any one that Great-Britain had the greatest interest in following the plans that Ministers had adopted; they foresaw what has happened, which is, that extraordinary events in Europe absolutely disconcerted the wisest plans—and, Sir, *without complaining*, they patiently redoubled their zeal and courage.

Is it possible there can exist a man who has ventured to accuse them so rashly, without adducing a single proof against them?

What answer will you make, when I shall advance and prove, that the arrival of 1,600 men would have completed what had been so happily begun? . . . . But I forget that I am not writing the history of the colony; that I only wish to prove your injustice and partiality, which many, no doubt, will attribute *to your interest, as being a planter of Jamaica.* I shall confine myself then to putting the following questions to you:

Immediately after the arrival of the 1,600 men on the 19th May 1794, why did they not march against Port-de-Paix, which was only fifteen leagues from the Mole, where we had a correspondence, and which, had it been attacked, would have surrendered?

Why did they prefer going sixty leagues to attack Port-au-Prince, since the taking of Port-de-Paix and the departure of Laveaux and his soldiers from the colony, would have left the Northern part without a single White republican soldier? which would have contributed still more to complete the intimidation of the republican commissioners in Port-au-Prince, as they continued without any resource in order to receive news and reinforcements from Europe by the North;

observe,

observe, moreover, that this attack upon Port-de-Paix would not have delayed the taking of Port-au-Prince a fortnight, according to the arrangements that had been made.

Why did they prefer taking the whole of their forces to the attack upon Port-au-Prince, *thereby exposing such an important post as the Mole* to be attacked by Laveaux, which he could easily have done, as he knew that all the troops were taken to besiege the capital, except a feeble garrison, in which were many sick ; the Mole being in a condition to be attacked with advantage by the Negros upon both points at once, of which Laveaux was master, that is to say, on the side of Jean Rabel, and by the inhabitants of Bombarde, who had greatly tormented the garrison for a long time ?

It will not be said that the French were too powerful at Port-de-Paix and Bombarde (for it would be admitted that for that very reason *they ought not to have gone far from the Mole,* without having finished the war on that side) as they went sixty leagues from the enemy, whom they left on one side at Port-de-Paix, at fifteen leagues distance, very strongly posted, and at five leagues on the side of Bombarde.

Why, Sir, when it was so imprudently determined to go and attack Port-au-Prince, was not a frigate sent to cruise off Jacmel, in order to intercept the supplies, the dispatches, &c. &c. ?

Why, Sir, since Port-au-Prince was taken without a single gun being fired, (except at the affair of Fort Bizoton), why, with upwards of 3,500 men in good health, encouraged by the success of their expedition, did they not immediately march against Jacmel, which is only fifteen leagues from Port-au-Prince, where the commissioners retired in disorder with the immense convoy of their property, accompanied by 2,000 women or children ? In fine, how happened it that these commissioners escaped so quietly from the colony nine days after their arrival at Jacmel ?

Why did they wish, against an enemy having no corps of an army, no regular troops, no magazines, no artillery ; why did they wish, I say, to carry on a regular war against a troop of brigands who always fled, at the latest, after the third discharge ?

Why did they not take advantage of the favorable disposition of the inhabitants of the Southern part, who offered to take possession of it by themselves ?

You, Sir, who have ventured to write concerning St. Domingo, why did you not say that upwards of 2,000 known inhabitants, independent of those who came

o o

to the attack of Port-au-Prince, were assembled at various points in the Southern part for this enterprize, which was the more easy, as I had two deputies with me, Men of Colour, and considerable planters, *supported for two months past at the expence of government,* who had engaged to deliver up the principal districts?

Why did you not inform yourself of all the particulars concerning the conduct of the brave inhabitants of the colony? you would have known that there were,

600   proprietary inhabitants or colonists at Cape Tiburon, commanded by the brave Chevalier de Sevré and M. de ———. That

300   inhabitants were at Jérémie, commanded by him, who so completely beat the rebels at the Camp-des-Rivaux. That

300   inhabitants of the Southern part, particularly of Cavaillon, were at the Camp-des-Rivaux, ready to re-enter that parish, under the command of a Creole, known by his valour, M. de ———. That

180   men from the camp of the Center, would have descended under the command of M. ———. In fine, Sir, that upwards of

550   inhabitants of Léogane and Jacmel, almost all on horseback, offered to march against this last town.

———

2130 : This amount is independent of the armed inhabitants who were present at the taking of Port-au-Prince, except the cavalry of Léogane.

All these different bodies of inhabitants, marching at the same time upon different points against *les Cayes,* need only have taken a gentle walk, and the Southern part, attacked on four sides at once, would have left Rigault the only choice of doing what *Laveaux himself would have been very glad to have done,* after the example shewn him by Rochambeau at Martinico, and Collot at Guadaloupe, who capitulated and retired, carrying with them their immense fortunes, the fruit of their pillage.

I assure you, Sir, that all this could have been done, that history will some day or other relate and prove it, *in answering the questions I have just proposed.*

I shall at present confine myself to request our readers, (whilst waiting your answers) to consider the advantages that might have resulted to Great-Britain and the colony, if that had been done *which ought and might have been.* The brigands were dispersed, the power of the French was destroyed without remedy : diseases could not have affected the troops so much, as they would not have been collected together in Port-au-Prince ; although those which arrived with

Colonel Lenox in the most dangerous month of the year, with the epidemical disease on board of one of the frigates that brought them, must have lost a considerable number; but not being confined in a single town, and admitting of distribution in various parts and at divers posts, they would have been less subject to the influence of this species of plague : the war being finished in the West and South, the provisions, vegetables, and refreshments, would have been very plentiful in the garrisons : no forced service would have taken place, nor would there have been any privateers; in fine, none of the evils that have happened to the English in the colony would have been known. *By this, we may judge how much expence would have been spared*; but because the unfortunate colonists have been the victims of every thing that took place, and which ought not to have happened, it does not follow *that they or their agent ought to be accused of it*; for the directing was independent of them; they knew only how to offer themselves, to fight, continually to obey, and have patience. Reflect, Sir, upon all the questions I have just proposed, and endeavour to answer them; if then, being better informed, you find just proofs in order to accuse the *French planters and those who have been their agents*, do it : but prove that they were able to do something more than to serve and fight every where with patience.

Since, as far as relates to me personally, I have been obliged to answer your accusation *of having grossly deceived the Ministers, in my capacity of agent of the colonists*, I must also answer your accusation, page 146, where you say, that General Williamson was deceived as well as the Ministers, by *eager and interested* individuals.

I think I have proved beyond reply, that it neither depended upon the inhabitants nor their agents, that the colony was not wholly and very speedily, *as well as without expence*, under the power of Great-Britain.

I confess to you, Sir, that I could never have thought that you, or any one whatever, could have been capable of accusing me of being *interested* * : for by *these*

---

* I cannot, according to this accusation, help observing to our readers, how little it becomes you; for, according to my answers, they have a right to think with me, that it is only an interested speculation, which has made you take advantage of the circumstances, that have rendered St. Domingo so very interesting to the European powers, in order (by the reputation you may have gained by your work concerning Jamaica) to risk the writing concerning a colony, with which you are so little acquainted, with so much negligence and inattention, and with such indifference for the respect which every author owes to the public. By forcing me to refute your book, you have initiated me into the secret of the typographical expences of this country. With what astonishment will *individuals, influenced by this vile motive, who have deceived Ministers and General Williamson,* you could mean none *but me,* since it was I alone that treated with him and them.

No doubt, Sir, the enormous expences which it is asserted have been incurred on account of St. Domingo, have made you admit, what was so wickedly spread abroad in America and Europe, that I was partly the cause of them, and that I had received from the British Ministers *a considerable sum* as the fruit of my services in transferring St. Domingo to the British Government. Doubtless you, like many others, judging what ought to be the reward *by the importance of the service,* have thought that mine had been very great. Well, Sir, undeceive yourself; and learn, that I made no stipulation for my attachment, that none was proposed to me, *and that I have received no reward,* nor even any gratification whatever *for this undertaking.*

You should know that the expences of my voyage to Jamaica, and of those who accompanied me, are all that have been paid, and that they did not amount in all to 330 l. sterling. You were likewise able to inform yourself perfectly concerning this, since, as a Member of Parliament, you might have seen the account of the expences incurred by the operation against the colony; had you done it before you wrote, you would have known, that even no appointments had been granted to me, that I asked for none, and that I received none till after taking possession of la Grande-Anse, when I was made Lieutenant-Colonel of the British Legion, in order to raise that corps with the Baron de Montalembert. You might have known that never did General Williamson, nor the Colony, nor the Ministers, grant me the least recompense during my stay in the colony.

You might moreover have been informed, Sir, that the Ministry having placed a considerable sum at my disposal, which was to be delivered to me on my giving receipts, in order to defray *the secret expences* of the important operation I had undertaken, only a small part of it was expended, and the rest was never made use of by me; and that I gave the most exact accounts of the expences I made.

You might have known that, appointed by the colonists, in July 1794, to come and lay at His Majesty's feet their sentiments of gratitude and their wishes, in order

---

not our readers learn, that the work which you have sold so dear, cost you only one third of what it has produced, even including Faden's map (which is not your property). In fine, Sir, when, in order to gain a profit of 300 l., a person sells a work so filled with errors, as yours is concerning St. Domingo, all our readers must think that he has but little right to accuse any one whatever *of being interested!*

to solicit sufficient aid from His Majesty and the Ministers, to finish what was so happily begun: you might have known, I say, that I came to Europe at my own expence, government having only paid for my passage on board the *packet*, which I preferred to the convoy, as being more expeditious, notwithstanding *all the particular dangers to which I was exposed*, had I been taken prisoner and sent to France, or to the French part of the colony. This passage, and that of the servant, who accompained me, cannot have amounted to 120 l. at most. The colonists offered me no entertainment; I asked nothing of them, because I knew, *better than any person living*, how much they were embarrassed and unable to bear expence. You might have known that, being a member of the privy council of the government of St. Domingo, I not only never received any pay from appointments, except that of lieutenant-colonel of infantry, but that I always represented how neccesary it was to observe economy, and to be careful not to swerve from it. In fine, Sir, you ought to have known, since you published your work in 1797, that the taking possession of St. Domingo, and of nearly one third of the colony (when I quitted it in August 1794, and which was then much more extensive than it is at present) with all the expences incurred by government till my departure, required either for the expedition or for the preservation of its possessions, during ten months, *did not amount to* 40,000 *l. sterling*.

The inhabitants of the colony however, at my request, granted very considerable rewards out of their own revenues, such as the sum of 26,000 livres *currency* of St. Domingo, given by the inhabitants of Jérémie to Colonel Whitelock, in the form of a stipend, as commander of la Grande-Anse, and a more considerable reward, amounting to 400,000 livres of St. Domingo, was granted to *La Pointe*, by the inhabitants of l'Arcahaye, les Vases, and le Boucassin, as a pledge of their gratitude for the services he had rendered them.

You ought to have known and stated all this. You ought to have known that I lived in London, in a manner suitable to a man entrusted with the confidence of the inhabitants of the first colony of the world, and honored with that of the Ministers; you ought to have known and said, that I had no stipend more considerable than that of lieutenant-colonel ; that when the Ministers, on my requesting them to determine the lot of the British Legion, and to grant *the King's commission* to the officers, judged that, in the ordinary course of the English service, the matter could not take place but by dividing the Legion into three separate corps, according to their service; being willing to reward the officers of the Legion for their attachment and services, they ordered that the three corps of which it was composed should form three regiments, which should be placed upon the same footing as the English army in the colony, and should always be attached to St. Domingo. Then, Sir, being second officer of the Legion, and having served in it from the commencement of its formation, *and been several times wounded*, I was made colonel of the cavalry ; it was then that I enjoyed the advantages granted in the British service to the commander of a corps. *These same advantages* have been granted to a great number of officers who have been made colonels, and to whom regiments have been given in the colonies, without having served in, even without being at St. Domingo, at the time the English came to take possession of it, nor even when I quitted it ten months afterwards ; what was granted to them might, and ought to have been granted to me, according to the laws of military service ; and was absolutely foreign to my political services relative to the possession of the colony by the English, *as the Minister himself kindly assured me*, when he thought it necessary to reform my regiment and to allow me a gratuity, too small to indemnify me for the expences I was obliged to be at in Europe, and particularly in America, where I had the happiness to oblige many of my countrymen ; insufficient, moreover, to pay the securities for the advances which the desire of attaching the most considerable planters of the colony to the interests of Great-Britain, made me ask of my friends, who thereby deranged their affairs, but who, well informed and rendering justice to the principles which actuated me, wait patiently and without tormenting me for the time when they shall be reimbursed.

You ought to have known *that my attachment to the interests of England* has been the cause of the destruction of my fortune *both in France and at St. Domingo*. In fine, before you accused me *of being interested*, you ought to have known what indemnification I had received for it ; then, weighing the reward against the services, you could have pronounced upon my conduct.

In the mean time, I must confess to you, Sir, that though *I never made any bargain or condition with His Britannic Majesty's Ministers* for the important services I was going to perform, I was assured, at the time I set off to embark (when I took leave), I had a verbal promise, I say, from the Ministry, that, in any case, *the King would remember my zeal* and the fidelity with which I endeavoured to serve him ; but that, if I had the happiness to succeed, *I might expect every recompence that such an important service deserved.*

Believe me, Sir, I was not actuated by this promise ; I had a motive far greater and more noble : that of saving the colony, of being useful to my countrymen, of attaching my name to that of the prosperity and happiness of the colony ; in fine, of rendering an important service to England. These, Sir, are the original sentiments *of interest* that actuated me! This is the first recompence I expected, and this is what rendered every thing easy to me! I have arrived nearly at the height of my wishes; if they have not been completely fulfilled, futurity *and history* will doubtless prove whether I have been in fault, and whether I did every thing in my power to succeed.

Perhaps, Sir, even without being liable to be accused of being actuated *by a vile motive*, I might and ought to have expected that, in rendering an important service *to a great nation, to the generous King of a powerful people, and celebrated for his generosity*, I might have expected that a great reward was the more certain in proportion as I served him *with greater disinterestedness*. Well, Sir, I should not be afraid to acknowledge these expectations, without their giving you a right to accuse me of having substituted my own interest for that of Great-Britain, in the expedition I advised and so happily executed against the colony of St. Domingo. Neither am I more afraid, Sir, that you should interrogate the Ministers concerning my zeal and attachment, than my disinterestedness, in serving Great Britain.

By what I have just said, all honest men may be undeceived and enabled to judge of your accusation, as they can verify what I have advanced, by referring to General Williamson, who is in England, and likewise to the King's Ministers.

Besides, it is easy for you and for many others to see whether in the pretended *immense expences*, incurred on account of the colony of St. Domingo, my name is set down for any sum whatever *on my own account*. It is moreover easy to observe, *from what time these enormous expences commenced*; we shall then see that they were all incurred since the English were in possession of Port-au-Prince, and after having been put in possession of all they *lately* possessed in the colony; moreover, that they were all incurred *since I quitted St. Domingo* in August 1794.

Both your readers and you, Sir, must perceive, that you have been equally incorrect in your accusation respecting what concerns me personally as in every thing else you have advanced in your work. It was, however, very easy for you to have been informed of all you might have wished to have known; you needed only to have asked people of information among the English, or the numerous class of Frenchmen residing here.

I shall continue the painful task I have undertaken *(the refutation of your errors)*, in order to enable my readers to form an irrevocable opinion concerning your work.

But they ought to have surely foreseen (the Ministers) that a very formidable opposition was to be expected from the partisans and troops of the republican government.

And they ought also to have known, that no considerable body of the French planters could be expected to risk their lives and fortunes in the common cause, but in full confidence of protection and support.—Page 172.

I certainly think I have proved that, in every thing that happened at St. Domingo after the arrival of the English, the efforts of the republicans were very weak; and I have demonstrated that there were neither troops nor ships there on our arrival. I must repeat to you, that never was there a more favorable opportunity for a great operation upon St. Domingo than the time of the departure of Galbaud and the French fleet, after the fire at the Cape, the commissioners being left without either land or sea forces to oppose the English; in short, they did not, in any circumstance, make what might be called a resistance, and, when they were attacked, they fled and abandoned the colony.

No reliance could then be placed upon the inhabitants of St. Domingo, being almost all absent at the time of our arrival in the colony. The event, however, has proved, that they alone really carried on the war upon the frontiers, at the advanced posts, and in all parts where any engagement took place, the English seldom quitting their garrisons. Immediately upon the arrival of the English in the colony, all the planters being invited to join them, repaired with eagerness to fight with their protectors, and, as you say, *they did so, and were invited to come to St. Domingo,* upon the assurance and confidence *which was given them,* that powerful succours would arrive in order to protect and replace them in their possessions.

If, according to the variety of information that can be obtained, if, even according to your own work, I have proved that the colonists have unremittingly fought in all parts, why have you accused them, in order afterwards to seek to throw the failure upon others, and particularly for the want of reinforcements, which never depended upon them? Truth often triumphs, in spite of you, over your prejudices and partiality.

In my own judgment, all the force which Great-Britain could have sent thither would not have been sufficient for the complete subjugation of the colony.—Page 172.

The use, Sir, that you have hitherto made of your judgment, gives you no right to offer your opinion to your readers. You are neither a military man nor a statesmen, and you are totally unacquainted with the colony. Why do you risk an appeal to yourself? I maintain, by adducing as a proof every thing that was done in four months, that, if reinforcements had arrived in November, and even in December, the colony would have been entirely conquered. The easy conquest of Port-au-Prince,

eight

eight months after the taking possession of Jérémie by the English, the flight of the republican chiefs upon the arrival of 4,600 men, prove what might have been done, if . . . . I shall stop here, *as I am not obliged to declare every thing*, and what I have just written is sufficient to destroy your accusations against the planters of St. Domingo and their agents, and to refute what you advance through your own judgment.

It is asserted, by competent judges, that no less than 6,000 men were necessary for the secure maintenance of Port-au-Prince alone.—Page 172.

I am unacquainted who the judges are whom you call *competent* to pronounce concerning the troops that were necessary to defend Port-au-Prince *alone*. As you do not state against what enemy it was to be defended, I can only answer to what you insidiously advance. Six thousand men would certainly be necessary for the defence of Port-au-Prince, if attacked by land and sea by an European army supplied with all the artillery, artillerymen, and engineers, and, in short, every thing that constitutes the art of war in Europe.

Six thousand regular troops to defend Port-au-Prince against a few thousand brigands, without cannon, without artillery, badly armed, without stores of provisions, without magazines of ammunition, and who could only attack it by land ! Why, Sir, *they wished to laugh at you*, unless there be *some other reason*, which time will doubtless discover, for your making this assertion. I shall here confine myself to assure you, that it is false, not to say ridiculous; example has proved it, since the brigands have never attacked it, although they were well informed that not a sixth part of the English garrison you require was in the town.

But you perhaps wished to strengthen what you before said, that, if Fort Bizoton had been taken, Port-au-Prince would have been so likewise ?

Yet I do not believe that the number of British, in all parts of St. Domingo, at any one period, previous to the month of April 1795, exceeded 2,200 men; of whom, except at the capture of Port-au-Prince, not one half were fit for active service, and, during the hot and sickly months of August, September, and October, not one third.—Page 172.

Since you assert, that the English never had but such a small number of troops, why were you so thoughtless as not to consider how forcibly your unjust partiality would strike your readers ? Since the English were so few in number, and the brigands so dangerous, that it was necessary they should fortify themselves *at such an enormous rate*, in order that they might not be able to seize upon Port-au-Prince, had they carried Fort Bizoton, it follows then, *that there were other forces to oppose them with*, which is very true ; all the French inhabitants were under arms ; they likewise carried on the war with the garrisons. You ought to have done them justice, instead of endeavouring to render them suspected ; and to have said, that these brave and faithful colonists have continually supported *the weight and misfor-tunes of the war*, in order to ease the nation that came to protect them, and to which they had taken the oath of fidelity.

Perhaps, the most fatal oversight in the conduct of the whole expedition, was the strange and unaccountable neglect of not securing the town and harbour of Aux Cayes, and the little port of Jacmel, on the same part of the coast, previous to the attack of Port-au-Prince.—Page 173.

I again repeat, Sir, that the force of truth overcomes you, contrary to your inclinations. Since you are informed of the faults you relate, why did you not attribute to them, and to others of which you are perhaps ignorant, the want of success in the expedition so happily begun ? and if, reflecting for a moment that the *colonists were absolutely strangers* to these faults, and many other events, why not then have rendered justice to those who, I repeat it, have only obeyed and fought ? Read the questions again, Sir, that I have written above ; reflect upon them well, inform yourself, and you will be compelled to allow that you have been very unjust towards my countrymen.

As to Port-au-Prince, it would have been fortunate if the works had been destroyed and the town evacuated immediately after its surrender.—Page 173.

There never was a more singular proposition written with more levity ; the map of St. Domingo will prove it to every attentive reader better than any thing that can be said, and I beg leave merely to say, that, if it is from a transport of humanity for the unfortunate individuals who have perished there, it is not very rational ; for the yellow fever, brought from Martinico by an English ship, might likewise have been brought to the Mole, St. Marc's, Jérémie, and Jamaica, and might have smitten the same victims there, had it not found them at Port-au-Prince. I shall only observe to you once more, and assure our readers, that the colony of St. Domingo is one of the most healthy of the Antilles ; that, previous to the arrival of the English, the pestilential disease, *which you call the yellow fever*, was NEVER KNOWN in the colony, and that it operates much more upon them than upon other

people, and that for many reasons; in fine, during its greatest ravages, it is well
known that it made less havock among the French than the English. The particulars of these causes would lead us too far; I have stated the fact, it may be verified,
and they may be enquired into.

*The retention by the enemy of Aux Cayes and Jacmel not only enabled them to procure
reinforcements and supplies, but also most amply to revenge our attempts on their
coast by reprisals on our trade.*—Page 173.

You always state, contrary to your intentions, something which proves the advantage, the necessary utility, and the importance, of the expedition of the British
Ministers against St. Domingo. Why were not the towns of Aux Cayes and Jacmel
taken? the whole colony as well as myself will ask you this question, which I have
already anticipated among my other questions.

*It is known, that upwards of 30 privateers, some of them of considerable force, have
been fitted out from these ports, whose rapacity and vigilance scarce a vessel bound
from the Windward Islands to Jamaica can escape.*—Page 173.

I shall here observe to you, that, ten months after the arrival of the English
in the colony, there were not three privateers in the French ports armed by the
republicans. I must tell you, that, when I quitted the colony, not one had yet
appeared in the Bay of Léogane.

Why have there since been any? Why, since the English had so many ships
of war, was there a single privateer? Is this likewise the fault of the colonists?
&c. &c.

Why did the American ships continually bring provisions, arms, and ammunition
to the brigands, although the colony (which was in fact attacked on all sides) might
have been declared in a state of siege, and the English, masters of the sea, could
have enforced the observance of this declaration?

If, near a twelvemonth after the colony had been delivered up to Great-Britain,
the French republicans succeeded in doing all the mischief to the English commerce
you mention, at a time when the English navy was mistress of the Mole and the
sea, and the French possessed but few maritime ports, and had no naval force; in
fine, that their population and army was destroyed, that France had almost abandoned the colony; what would have become of the commerce of Jamaica and
Mosquito Bay, supposing a contrary situation? What would have become of your
islands, had not St. Domingo been attacked and the Mole taken; if the French
ships, retiring there, could have protected the immense flotilla of canoes, or em-

barkations, which in one night could have devastated, burnt, and destroyed Jamaica
in several places at once ?

How could prejudice make you write a single line that could cast blame upon the
authors of a project that has been the most useful to the colony of Jamaica, to its
inhabitants, and to the merchants of the mother country ; whilst you and all the
colonists of Jamaica ought for ever to bless the wise foresight of the Ministers, who,
by an expedition against St. Domingo, have preserved your property from total
destruction ? I put the question to you, Sir, whether you think, that, if France
had not been deprived of St. Domingo, Jamaica would now be in existence ? I know
not what your answer in writing will be ; but I am sure your heart says : *no, Jamaica would no longer exist as a colony useful to Great-Britain.* Nevertheless, Sir,
you have blamed this expedition, and the agents, and all those who have contributed to the success of the plans ; who have not only preserved your revenues and
your capitals, but who have doubled your fortune by doubling the value of your
commodities, the price of which, you may rest assured, will be no longer diminished. It is he, who has tried every thing to make the plans succeed, that has
preserved your fortune, *whom you accuse !* The reader will be more just. Satisfied
with having done well, I forgive you what concerns me ; my countrymen will also
forgive you ; henceforth endeavour to merit the good fortune which our labours
have procured you.

*After all, though I have asserted nothing which I do not believe to be true, I will
honestly admit, that many important facts and circumstances, unknown to me, very
probably existed.*—Page 175.

Why did you not take time to be informed of what *you here acknowledge yourself
ignorant of ?*

Was your work then of so much importance that you could not postpone its
publication till you had authenticated all the facts you made use of in it ? Should
you not have consulted those who were necessarily better informed than yourself,
and who would have taken pleasure in communicating to you what they must
have known more particularly than any one else ?

But I am obliged to declare, that the partiality with which every page of your
work is written—your invectives against the brave, generous, patient, and faithful
colonists, and against those who have had the happiness to succeed in serving England : in short, all proves, that the *interested uneasiness of a Jamaica colonist* has
guided your pen. Fearing, but convinced, that the colony of St. Domingo would
speedily

speedily recover its former prosperity in the hands of the English, you thought that your revenues would then diminish ; you wished, spurred on by that unjust fear, to prevent them from re-establishing it ; for you have endeavoured, by your book, to persuade your countrymen that no kind of advantage could ever be derived from it ; and, not being able to deceive people respecting the excellence and fertility of the soil, you have thought proper to accuse the inhabitants !

You ought, however, to have expected that we should appeal from your judgment. I was in London ; and what you knew of me should have persuaded you that I would not suffer the very numerous errors of your work to remain unanswered ; that *both in my friends name and my own* I should appeal to the public, whom you have misled and deceived—to a just public, now better informed. Let us wait their judgment—you, in avowing, as you here do, that you are not informed of many facts and circumstances that have occurred, *but which might alter every thing you have written*—and I, in offering to prove all I have advanced in this letter.

An acquaintance with which is indispensably necessary to enable any man to form a correct judgment on the measures which were pursued on this occasion.—Page 175.

This confession is still stronger ! Why, according to this, Sir, should you be in such haste to publish and offer your judgment ? How, after the confession in this paragraph, could you venture (after leading your reader on from one error to another for two hundred pages) to come and say to him : " but I am ignorant of many facts that were indispensably necessary to enable you to form *a judgment of what has been done*, and concerning what should have been done, *in such circumstances* as those that have occurred."

To a writer sitting with composure in his closet, with a partial display of facts before him, it is no difficult task to point out faults and mistakes in the conduct of public affairs ; and even, where mistakes are discovered, the wisdom of after-knowledge is very cheaply acquired.—Page 175.

When the force of truth thus leads you to admit the facility with which an author in his closet can quietly select the best materials from those he has collected, and how easy it is to avoid faults, how could you determine upon writing from such incomplete materials as those you possessed ? and why not have endeavoured to acquire that wisdom, that prudence, which you assert results from the instruction acquired after events? You have had two years to select information, and likewise to prepare yourself so as not to deceive your readers.

If, led away with the desire of causing our writings to be read, one is weak enough to offer a work to the public which is not only imperfect but filled with errors, why injure any one? why blame those who, by their knowledge, are equally capable of judging of the utility and advantages of what has been undertaken? In fine, Sir, when a person has been reasonable enough to make such reflexions as I here state *you to have done*, why not have been sufficiently so to obtain the necessary information? why not have waited some time, in order to collect every thing which might be useful for the instruction of your readers?

It is the lot of our nature, that the best concerted plans of human policy are subject to errors, which the meanest observer will sometimes detect.—Page 173.

According to what you here admit, before you accused the inhabitants of St. Domingo with not being faithful and sincere in their attachment to the government that protected them; before you accused the Ministers of *having suffered themselves to be grossly deceived by the agents of the colonists*, why did you not make use of your own reflexion? why did you not first discover the error? and, if any, judge of the intention, and then accuse, if it should prove to be a guilty one? but if the best combined plan, for the interest of those whom it concerned, has met with all the success that could be expected, how much more culpable are you for publishing your book, after the confession you make?

For whether we consider the possession by an active and industrious people of so vast a field for enterprise and improvement, on the one hand, or the triumph of successful revolt and savage anarchy, on the other, it appears to me, that the future fate and profitable existence of the British territories in this part of the world are involved in the issue.—Page 176.

This is, Sir, one of those great political truths which it was necessary to unravel: three pages written upon this subject with attention and reflexion, would have been more interesting and advantageous to your readers, than twenty editions of your work will ever be. This is the question, or, rather, the truth of the business, which it was requisite for you to have demonstrated to your countrymen: you should have made use of your talents in order to write and merit the attention and confidence of your country, by completely disclosing the consequences that this incontestable truth must be of to Great-Britain, viz. *that, henceforth, upon the fate of St. Domingo depends the fate of Jamaica, and all the English colonies.* You should have traced the mischiefs which their loss would occasion to the English commerce, navy, and manufactures. This is, Sir, what you should have disclosed in a thousand different shapes, and have repeated continually—then you would have been really useful to your country, and to all the European colonies; fame would have joined your name to the establishment, the existence, and the prosperity of the colonies of the Antilles.

On all these various and collateral subjects, I regret that I do not possess the means of giving much satisfaction to the reader.—Page 176.

Why make your readers pay *so dear* for the confession you here make? For you have not in the least prepossessed them concerning what you acknowledge yourself to be absolutely ignorant of; but they have been obliged to read what you were so imperfectly acquainted with; and their confidence in a man of your years, now placed among the number of British Senators, who has written a work concerning Jamaica, (perhaps not very correct, but agreeably enough written), has occasioned many of your readers to suffer themselves to be prejudiced against St. Domingo, which they would not have done, had you not written. For instance, a man of honor has lately made public quotations from your book: he would not have done so had he been acquainted with all the errors it contains. Both him, and all who have read it, will be obliged, in addition to the loss of time you have occasioned them, to give themselves the trouble to read my answer, which I do not present to them *from any rage I have for writing*, but from a duty I owe the colony, the interests of England, the honor of the generous colonists of St. Domingo, as well as for my personal character, so forcibly attacked in your work.

In which frantic pursuit, they murdered at least a million of the peaceful and inoffensive natives.—CHAP. XII. Page 177.

I cannot here refrain from observing to our readers, with what indifference you write upon history. How is it possible that you, Sir, who have the honor to be a Member of the first learned Society in the world, being a colonist, living at the close of the eighteenth century, and having long resided in the West Indies, can take up your pen to follow the steps of the monastic and superstitious ignorance of the first writers upon the colonies of the Antilles? for it is not possible but that your reflexions must have been founded upon the absurdities written and reported by the first Spanish historians. Why, making use of sound criticism, and guided by pure taste, did you not reject the absurd fables contained in the history of the first European establishments in the Antilles? After having maturely weighed them, you should have been very careful how you asserted, that the Spaniards *caused upwards of a million of men to perish at St. Domingo.* Never did there probably exist a million of Caribbees together in this beautiful island.

But you might and must have easily repeated the error of others, which rendered your own less surprising, when, by a dash of the pen you establish a savage Republic at St. Domingo, consisting of 100,000 Negros, retired into the inaccessible parts; after having written this, you might be credulous enough to believe, that they easily destroyed a million of men. If I refute what you have advanced, it is not for the purpose of attenuating the crime of the Spaniards, *for I shall not be accused of being their partisan;* I have given many proofs to the contrary. The crimes with which they have sullied themselves at St. Domingo, and to which I have been witness, make me think them capable of all those which the history of America accuses them of. At St. Domingo they were guilty of having entirely exterminated the inhabitants; *a greater or less quantity of men destroyed, makes no difference as to the enormity of the crime;* for they would in like manner have assassinated the whole population, had it been a hundred times more numerous; but truth, and the fruit of reflexion made upon many observations during twenty years, enable me to assure you, that there never was, nor could have been, a population of 300,000 Caribbees in the island; indeed, I am well convinced, that at the time the Spaniards arrived there, the population never amounted to more than the number above stated.

The following are part of my reasons. You are a colonist, Sir, you might have observed the population of the small colonies of the Maroon Negros of the Blue Mountains in Jamaica; you must have known, at least you have spoken, of the mixt population of Negros, cast upon St. Vincent's (about a century ago), intermixed with the Caribbees; you are acquainted with their number; you could calculate the difference between the strength of the Negro and the native of the Antilles: you could reflect upon the advantages which these people must have derived from being visited by the Europeans for these 300 years past. You could reflect upon these societies, and after all this how could you believe, repeat, and write, that St. Domingo contained upwards of a million of inhabitants at the time it was discovered. I have reason to think that you have never considered what so numerous a society is, particularly in a savage state. If, since you have become a Member of Parliament, you have considered for a moment what the consumption of provisions is for a population of a million of men, you would have shuddered in reflecting

flecting upon it, *and would have shed many tears* for the lot of the unfortunate inhabitants, who live in a state of nature.

You-no doubt know, Sir, that before the arrival of the Spaniards, the inhabitants of St. Domingo were reduced to live upon Indian wheat, plantains, small millet, potatoes, and particularly upon *cassavi* and Caribbee cabbages, which were almost their only provisions, as they are to this day among the Negros. The three former and the Caribbee cabbages, are subject to the hurricanes, and are less certain than the others. To these provisions the inhabitants added the abundant fishery in the bays and creeks of the colony, where, it is necessary to observe, there were only five quadrupeds. We are acquainted with the names of three; the Agouti rat: the lizard of a foot and a half long: a small short tailed dog, which did not bark, and whose race is destroyed; the names of the other two are not known, and cannot have been very numerous. You see by this, Sir, how precarious the resources were for the support of a people *consisting of a million of individuals* :—be so kind as to reflect upon the consequences.

You know as well as I do, that, although the Indian wheat yields plentifully, it requires to be planted in a great extent of cleared land, and at more than a foot distance from each other, as the potatoes do, and particularly yams; the plantains, in order to yield plentifully, ought to be planted at least twenty-five feet distant from each other, and the small millet at a foot and a half; judge, Sir, of the quantity of land that must be cleared to support a million of men. Unfortunately no appearance of these cleared lands exists in the colony: and as, according to the Spaniards, St. Domingo was divided into seven governments, whose chiefs or princes called themselves Caciques, one may according to Christopher Columbus's first voyage, (concerning what he says of the distance of the places inhabited by these princes) suppose, that this related to the seven greatest plains of the colony upon the sea coast, and that they were peopled by the subjects, more or less numerous, of these princes, but divided along the coast into small villages, as the savages are in America, Africa, the Society Islands, the Friendly Islands, and New Holland. After mature reflexion, we shall see that these people can only have inhabited the bays and creeks, as they found those resources in the sea, which their provisions on land could not procure them, part of which was subject to the annual hurricanes of the country, and the whole to the frequently excessive droughts in these climates. By the number I allow to the island at the time of its conquest, we shall see that each prince had a population of 43,000 individuals, which, being in a savage state, is very considerable. Let travellers who have visited the

islands of the New World : let the readers of voyages judge whether the population of St. Domingo could have been more numerous : when they recollect, that it
was subject to that *cruel disease*, which makes such dreadful attacks upon generation : which must, however it may be lessened in the blood of the Caribbees, considerably diminish their increase, by keeping them in that state of debility, which
not only prevented them from increasing to a numerous society, but which, (added
to the imperfection of their tools and their laziness, caused no doubt by their
natural disease and the climate) must have impeded the progress of their population. Even the history written by the first conquerors of St. Domingo, in-
forms us, that they were of a cold and weak constitution, and had but few children;
it likewise states the causes of the successes of the first Europeans to be owing to
the ardour with which the female Caribbees preferred them to the natives of
the islands.

All these advantages, and likewise the quickness with which this unfortunate
race of men was destroyed, proves, that they were not very numerous, for the
mines were not opened all at once ; many men cannot work together in a mine till
it has been opened to a certain depth, and from the first moment the mines were
so, complaints were made of the diminution of the men : add to that, that in one
single chain of mountains, called Cibao, the mines which were opened at St. Domingo are situated, and are only four in number; which (admitting them all to have
been opened together) can only have required, for a long space of time, a number of workmen, less by far than a million, which you pretend have been destroyed.

In fine, Sir, I found my estimate of the number of Caribbees upon the total population of St. Domingo at the time of the terrible revolution of 1789. 600,000 individuals of all colours inhabited the French colony ; 60,000 the Spanish part. For
more than a century past, two parts of the world contributed to people this beautiful
island ; every thing that human industry could invent, for the happiness of society,
was carried to St. Domingo : cultivation had rendered the cleared lands of the French
more numerous in the mountains than the plains, where the natives of the country
had never been even able to penetrate ; 8,000 and some small societies or villages,
larger than those of the savages, had left but little habitable land in the French colony uncleared ; and in order to feed this population, Europe and North America
brought upwards of 200,000 barrels of flour and 50,000 quintals of salt provisions ;
add thereto the cattle and every thing that the European resources have been able
to procure in order to support life, and the poultry and vegetables of the country
and other parts of the world. Hence your readers may judge of the consumption

occasioned by a numerous population; for, in spite of all this, the most cruel scarcity has often been experienced, although the cultivation of food and the provisions natural to the climate and the colony have always been attended to. The strongest and most active Whites; the most healthy Negros, assisted by a climate rendered more wholesome from the ground being cleared; all the new inhabitants of St. Domingo, having many children; in fine, every thing united has not been able to make the population of the whole island amount to 700,000 individuals; and yet you can write that the population of St. Domingo formerly amounted to a million of men! It is owing to your not having observed Jamaica, to being totally unacquainted with St. Domingo, and to not having reflected upon the happy and united causes that are requisite to make the savage population of an island amount to a million inhabitants. On observing the places most inhabited by the natives; their tools; the caverns where the greatest number of their collected bones have been discovered; the sight of the country; and particularly the smallness of the shells heaped up in places where they most abounded, and where they have been found whole—every thing convinced me, that these people never lived collectively, except in small families, which can never have been numerous. The history of St. Domingo will collect these proofs, which, added to others, will confirm what judicious, informed men, who have long observed, think as well as myself, viz. that St. Domingo never contained a population of more than 300,000 Caribbees, if even it ever contained that number. The Spaniards themselves have pronounced concerning Oviédo and his historical amplifications.

*The country itself being evidently more mountainous in the Central and Eastern, than in the Western parts, it is probable that the Spanish territory, is, in the whole, naturally less fertile than that of the French.—*Page 178.

You would doubtless have avoided writing your pretended Historical Views, had you considered how imperfect and faulty were your documents relative to St. Domingo. I am ignorant who can have informed you of what you here advance: for the Spanish part, in proportion to its extent, is much less mountainous than the French part, whose plains are very small, and always interspersed with hills and small *mornes*, and which, as one may say, are only the feet of mountains more or less extended. There is no real plain, that can be compared to those in the Spanish part, except the beautiful plain of Artibonite; the others are only appendages, more or less extensive, of mountains; the plain of the Cul-de-Sac is rather long, but very narrow.

2

You might and ought to have known to a certainty, that the Spanish part is the most even, the most productive, and the best watered. This would have proved to you, that the French colony owes its prosperity to nothing *but the industry of the French colonists*; the same industry, employed upon the Spanish territory, would have doubled or tripled the productions of the commodities of the island. It is impossible, unless it were seen, to form an idea of the fertility, the extent, and the beauty, of the plains of the Spanish part, which have no very large mountains, except towards the sea-shore, on the North-East and towards the South-West. St. Domingo, the capital, is situated in a very beautiful and very extensive plain, and at a great distance from the mountains.

And vast numbers (as I believe I have elsewhere observed) are annually slaughtered solely for the skins.—Page 184.

You no doubt speak of the original state of the island, at the time the Freebooters established themselves there as Buccaneers. For many years past, they have discontinued killing the beasts at St. Domingo for their tongues, fat, and skin. The Spaniards, for a long time past, have never been able to supply all the animals necessary for the butchers at the Cape and Port-au-Prince : although the butchers had a considerable number of men employed in fetching them from the most distant parts of the Spanish colony. If you would have recollected, as an inhabitant of Jamaica, that, if the French part could not consume all the beasts belonging to the Spanish part, Jamaica was to leeward of St. Domingo, and that a secure opportunity was always open to the merchants, you would not have written this phrase. You might have learned that, for a long time past, the Spanish herds of horned cattle have diminished in the colony belonging to that nation, first by the great consumption in the French butcheries, next by the use made of them for carrying the sugars and the works of the plantations ; but still more because, for a considerable time past, the Spanish *hatiers* have found great advantage in having horses, and particularly mules, which sell at a high price, without giving more trouble to rear than cattle do ; the herds of horses and mules living, like the herds of horned cattle, free, in the same savannas, which support the one as easily as the other. *This error will make your readers think and believe*, that you have not been more correct in your other works than in this.

Perhaps it were no exaggeration to say, that this and the former districts are alone capable of producing more sugar, and other valuable commodities, than all the British West Indies put together.—Page 185.

You may very positively assert, Sir, that the Spanish part of St. Domingo would not only yield more sugar than all the English colonies put together, but even more than double.

I have already proved, by the report made by Mr. Henry Shirley to the assembly of Jamaica, and by your own estimate or *average* of the productions of the French colony of St. Domingo, that it made annually more sugar than all the English colonies in the Antilles united; and likewise that, at the time of the Revolution, it furnished double the productions of all the colonies put together; and the Spanish part, which is three times as considerable in extent as the French, is so in plains and lands proper for cultivation in a quadruple proportion to the French colony. If the other colonial commodities were not double those of all the European colonies and the French part, they would at least be equal. Two pages written to propagate this truth, and to draw the natural consequences from it, would have been very useful to your country.

Thus scanty and uninteresting is the account I have to give of the territory itself; nor is my information much more perfect concerning the number and condition of the people by whom it is at present inhabited.—Page 186.

It would have been better not to have written, and, above all, not to have announced a work respecting St. Domingo, since you acknowledge you know nothing concerning the Spanish part of it. The reader, according to this letter, will judge how little you are informed respecting the French part.

In 1717, the whole number of inhabitants under the Spanish dominion, of all ages and conditions, enslaved and free, were no more than 18,410; and, since that time, I conceive they have rather diminished than increased.—Page 187.

You acknowledge, Sir, that, in 1717, the population of the Spanish part did not amount to 18,410 individuals, and yet it is you who, a few pages before, allowed a million of inhabitants to the island before its conquest! What! the population of the Spanish colony, increased by that of Africa and Europe, supported by innumerable flocks and herds, having the arts and resources of Europe, enjoying the same climate as the natives of St. Domingo without their diseases, has not, in 220 years, carried its population beyond 18,410, and yet you state the natives to amount to a million! This would astonish those readers who might not have read the preceding part.

T t

However degraded the Spanish nation may be in America, it has considerable advantages over all others in peopling this country. The Spaniard is sooner inured to the climate, is sober, strong, and nervous: he intermixes without distinction with every species and every colour; and neither scarcity nor sickness destroys his population. How happens it, however, that they compose so small a population, when the natives, weak, sickly, subject to such frequent dearth (the consequence of the imperfection of their social system), are reported by you to have formed a million? Let the reader reflect and judge! Why, and upon what principle do you establish your opinion, that the population has rather diminished than augmented in the Spanish colony? Ought your readers blindly to believe in your conceptions, and without your furnishing them with any foundation; when three pages back (in the note, page 184), you acknowledge that, since 1757, the Barcelona company received the exclusive privilege to trade and conduct the other affairs relative to St. Domingo? You ought to have concluded from thence that some change had occurred favorable to the Spaniards, which is the truth: they now cultivate more sugar, more indigo, and more cotton; they are, moreover, more employed in the care of their animals; they have caused a great acquisition of Negros, both in the French part of the island and Jamaica. Since the American war, there has been a more numerous garrison of European troops, and the whole population may be stated to amount to 60,000 individuals. This is what I have seen in part, and what I was assured of in 1786, in one of the tours I made in that part of the island. Since the Revolution, Spain has augmented the number of her troops there; without reckoning them, the population of Whites does not amount to 2,000, the Negros to 30,000; the rest is of a free race of mixed blood, from the mongrel to the *Marabou*, which compose 12 or 14 different mixtures.

It is probable, however, that the knowledge of that circumstance, created greater reliance on the co-operation of the Spaniards with the British army than was justified by subsequent events.

It was evident, at the same time, that they were almost equally jealous of the English, betraying manifest symptoms of discontent and envy, at beholding them in possession of St. Marc and the fertile plains in its vicinage.—Page 169.

Your consequences are truly extraordinary; you admit that the Spanish planters hate the French ones; and you thence conclude, that this must have produced confidence in the co-operation of the Spaniards with the English, in order to restore the property of those French planters whom they hate, whom they had contributed to ruin and assassinate!

You think, that the assistance of the Spaniards might have been expected! Those who could assert it, wished to deceive; for, if they be colonists, they must have known the inveterate hatred that exists between the inhabitants of the two colonies, one of which has cowardly and traiterously bathed itself in the blood of the other.

The government of this country could not have been deceived: for I have constantly informed it of every thing, and I brought and delivered to the Ministers myself the authentic particulars of the assassination and massacre of the French at Fort Dauphin.

As you very justly observe, Sir, the continuation of events has proved who best knew and judged of the Spaniards, and what might be expected from them. History will soon lay before the public every thing that intrigue was capable of promoting respecting this subject.

But in all cases, be well convinced that it has long been proved, that the Spaniards were still more jealous of the English than the French, and would be much more afraid in having them for their neighbours. The informed planters of St. Domingo have long since known, that the Spaniards no longer wish to have either the one or the other for neighbours; their hope was, that the French part would be destroyed, and that it would remain abandoned; that then their *hatiers* and the reliets of the French population, would divide the devastated land among them. They first thought that the French planters would be involved in the destruction of France, and that they would be incapable of preventing the Spaniards from seizing upon this spoil. Fearful of being deceived, when they saw the planters implore the protection of Great-Britain, they revenged themselves for it by causing a part of them to be massacred at the Gonaïves and at Fort Dauphin; but feeling their danger greater, should the English be masters of St. Domingo, they wished, when they acknowledged the new power in France, *to attract her entirely towards St. Domingo*, being persuaded that, so long as this beautiful colony should belong solely to the French, their possessions upon the continent would be safe, and it was as an allurement that they ceded a territory to the French, which, far from being useful, had long been a burden to them. The Spaniards preferred the destruction of St. Domingo to every thing, on account of their hatred to the French; but they like better to see the whole island in the hands of the French, than a part of it in the hands of the English. The Mole, whilst in the hands of the former, gave them no uneasiness; in the hands of the English, it is the key to the Gulf of Mexico. Their colonies upon the continent will still exist for a long time to come, if St. Domingo remains in the possession of the French; the Spanish colonies in the Gulf of

Mexico will no longer continue *under the power of the Spaniards* than it shall please Great-Britain, when she shall be mistress of the island.

They proceeded, however, and took the town and harbour of Gonaïve; but their subsequent conduct manifested the basest treachery, or the rankest cowardice.— Page 188.

You have been deceived in the recital of these matters.

You wish to make your readers believe that the Spaniards seized upon the Gonaïves at the request of Colonel Brisbane; whilst, on the contrary, they took it by fraud, at the time he was going to take possession of it. At the time the English arrived at St. Marc, the greatest part of the inhabitants of the Gonaïves had resolved to put themselves under the power of Great-Britain, as well as the inhabitants of St. Marc, in spite of the intrigues of the Spaniards. When the English went to take possession of the Gonaïves, Toussaint, the Negro, arrived, directed by the Mulattoes, and took, as a Spanish general officer, possession of the town; whilst the Spanish party wished also to hoist the flag of that nation at St. Marc's; but here, they were not the strongest, as at the Gonaïves; Toussaint, having seized the fort belonging to this town, pretended that it ought to continue in the possession of the Spaniards, since every part of the French colony which each of the two nations might seize upon, ought to belong to it. This Negro had not a single Spanish soldier with him, either White or Mulatto; it was not till some time after that a Spanish garrison arrived there, commanded by Villa Nova and another officer, whom I saw at M. le Vicomte de Fontanges', when I made a journey to him at the Gonaïves; it was soon after the brigands came to attack the town, that the Spanish garrison made its retreat by capitulation, and that the French were massacred. A part of these troops retired to the Vérettes; and it was not till after I quitted the colony that the Spaniards came to St. Marc's, no doubt with the view of repeating there what they had already done at Fort Dauphin and the Gonaïves, but which the zeal and activity of Brisbane prevented them from executing.

There is not an Englishman who was in the first expedition against St. Domingo, who will not give you the particulars of this affair.

*On the whole, there is reason to suppose, that a great proportion of the present Spanish proprietors in St. Domingo are a debased and degenerated race, a motly mixture from European, Indian, and African ancestry.—*Page 189.

You might have asserted as certain what you here state with doubt; you need only have conversed with those who have travelled in the Spanish part

of

of the island, and you would have obtained the particulars necessary to confirm
your assertion. You must likewise know that the Spaniards are the only Europeans
who are not prejudiced against *the mixed blood in their colonies*, on which account
they have never flourished; the priests are more masters of the Negros than the proprietors; there are but few sugar plantations and few works of consequence; that
in which they are most employed at St. Domingo is to collect the animals of the
hates together.; they live, like their masters, in the greatest indolence, and the child
born from the connexion of a Negro woman and a free man is a Spaniard, and enjoys all the rights of a Creole, which, it must be acknowledged, are reduced almost
to nothing for people of all colours. The European White being the only one that
enjoys the rights which the Creole Whites enjoy in the other European colonies,
occasions that immense difference between the Spanish and other governments, viz.
that the prejudice against the White Creole in her colonies is nearly the same as that
of other nations against the Man of Colour. Every thing born in the Spanish colonies is quite struck with the civil and military incapacity that exists against the Men
of Colour in the Antilles, except that they may be priests; but the Whites, as well as
the Men of Colour, are seldom employed either in a civil or military capacity. The
fact is, that there is such a mixture among the Creole families in the Spanish colonies, that none but the original shades can be traced. It may with truth be said,
that in her colonies is the greatest mixture of people in the universe, and the most
contemptible by their vices: this might morally resolve the problem of crossing the
breeds too frequently.

*And it grieves me to say, that the present exertions of Great-Britain on this blood-
stained theatre, can answer no other end than to hasten the catastrophe.*—Page 190.

The catastrophe which you foresee (upon what foundation I am unacquainted) will
not happen at St. Domingo: as you clearly perceive, that, during nearly four years
that the English have been in possession of part of that island, the republican principles have made no progress, and that the Negros, who had not risen at the time it was
taken possession of, continue to be submissive and faithful; that the French have
almost given up the idea of sending any forces there, and that it is no longer they
who carry on the war against Great-Britain, but many of the brigand chiefs, who
obey nobody, and who are employed in enriching themselves, in order that they
may go elsewhere to enjoy the fruits of their plunder. The brigand Negros are
every where tired of the condition in which they are held by their chiefs, and no

great efforts are requisite to terminate the war in the island ; it only requires proper
measures to be taken and well combined.

Whatever might be the danger in forming Negro regiments, since that measure
has succeeded, great sacrifices will not henceforth be requisite on the part of England, nor a great number of European troops, in order to terminate the war.

Your foresight arising only from your uneasiness, founded upon erroneous pre-
mises which you have established yourself, I shall here beg leave to assure you
that, as you are in no respect acquainted with the colony of St. Domingo, nor
its interior situation, your complaints are without cause, as they must be without
effect. I shall repeat to you, since you have a right to verify the amount of the
productions exported from the colony last year, that you may readily conclude from
thence, that a possession which, in its unfortunate state, has produced such a considerable mass of merchandise, merits preservation.

*Experience has demonstrated, that a wild and lawless freedom affords no means of
improvement, either mental or moral. The Caraïbes of St. Vincent and the Maroon
Negros of Jamaica, were originally enslaved Africans ; and what they now are, the
freed Negros of St. Domingo will hereafter be, savage in the midst of society, without
peace, security, agriculture, or property ; ignorant of the duty of life, and unacquainted with all the soft and endearing relations which render it desirable ; adverse
to labour, though frequently perishing of want, suspicious of each other, and towards
the rest of mankind revengeful and faithless ; remorseless and bloody-minded, pretending to be free, while groaning beneath the capricious despotism of their chiefs,
and feeling all the miseries of servitude, without the benefits of subordination.—*
Page 191.

This is the paragraph in your work which contains the most truth ; this is what
you ought to have written and repeated continually.

To all the examples you adduce of the Caribbees of St. Vincents, and particularly
the Maroon Negros of Jamaica, you may add what happened at St. Domingo since
the innovators, who have caused its devastation, have been able to make the cruel
experiment of their plans. It is impossible to describe all the evils which have
befallen the Negros, and every thing they have suffered, not only from hunger and
want, but still more from the capricious barbarity of their numerous chiefs. The
history of Africa proves, that the Negros are not susceptible of the same degree of
sociability as the Europeans. When we consider that the Creole Negro, transplanted into our colonies for 150 years past and upwards, has not made one step towards
civilization, that he is still encumbered with all the superstitions of his brethren in

Africa, we must believe that they form a separate species amongst the numerous beings that people the globe.

The Negros are, in every respect, what you here describe them to be; if it is from your own knowledge, you have observed them well. This is what you should have represented without end to those pretended philanthropists who have deceived Europe by their abstractions, made in the midst of the pleasures and corrupted morals of the Europeans. This is what that society, truly worthy of the respect and admiration of the whole universe, will, before long, discover; the generous and truly philanthropic society of *Sierra Leona*, deserves the encomiums of all sensible men, and the blessings of every class of society; soon, and perhaps already, the experiments made by their orders have solved the problem concerning the impossibility of forming Negro colonies, civilized and divided into societies, useful to themselves and others. Their Memoirs will soon prove, that this people, stronger and more active than the people of Paraguay, whom the Jesuits had civilized at the foot of the Cordeliers, are not however, like them, susceptible of any of the institutions of other civilized people; and that it is continually necessary that the foresight of their founders should watch, in order to support their social system : or the labours of many years will be destroyed in a few moments.

But the attempt is good : it is grand, it is noble : it is worthy a great nation and true humanity; it will do eternal honor to the members of that respectable society. I wish well to its success, but I have no faith in it. In fine, if it is owing to the sugar made in Africa that the colonies in the Antilles must lose their prosperity, I shall no longer consider it as a misfortune, and shall even bless the true philanthropists who may have been the cause of it; but who ought never to be compared with that swarm of hot-headed, vain, light, and cruel men, who are incapable of serving their country either by sea or land : and who, eat up with pride in causing themselves to be talked of, have, on entering into the world, looked around them with a view to discover some easy means which they might make use of, in order to attract the attention of the multitude towards them, without risk and danger, as well as without trouble and expence. In fine, these egotists, these proud and superficial beings, who have made themselves the Negros' champions, and who, cold and insensible *to the numerous evils* that surround them, have been seeking for a people (the White Creoles), at two thousand leagues distant, in order to ruin them, without paying attention to the real barbarity of their hypothesis, which (even if their system could have been established) would ruin a considerably greater number of White families, and in a much greater proportion, than it would contribute to the happiness of a few Negro families, remaining slaves in Africa ; in fine, which would be the cause of the destruction of the Creole planters, who, by the blood of their fathers and their friends, have acquired the property they cultivate, by the hands of servants rather than slaves, which they have brought from Africa, and whose condition they have changed by treating them as members of their families, and in making them enjoy a part of the European institutions of which they were susceptible : particularly in putting them under the protection of the laws, which preserve them from the barbarous caprices of their original masters ; in short, by becoming provident protectors, who supply the defects in the character which nature has given the Negros.

Repeat, Sir, comment upon, and amplify, for the happiness of the colonies *and true humanity*, the truths you have here written, and increase your proofs ; the misfortunes of St. Domingo will furnish you with many ; and the death of 500,000 Whites, Men of Colour, or Negros, victims (in the colonies) of the experiments of the pretended philanthropists, will convince them of the falsity of their new systems : but, if not them, they will at least judicious and humane beings, who value the lives of men as something, and who respect the laws of society.

If what I have thus, not hastily, but deliberately, predicted, concerning the fate of this unfortunate country shall be verified by the event—Page 191.

I repeat it, that what you have ventured to predict will not happen. You have made use of incorrect documents in order to produce a work, the errors of which I have demonstrated. You have no knowledge of St. Domingo, particularly of what it is at this moment. I refer you to the produce of its exportations, and to the conduct of the Negros at Jérémie, at l'Arcahaye, at the Vases, and at the Boucassin, and still more to the fidelity of the Negro regiments, in order to prove, that a prediction made in England by your fire-side will not be realized ; the principle of which being erroneous, the consequence must be so.

All other reflections must yield to the pressing consideration, how best to obviate and defeat the influence which so dreadful an example of successful revolt and triumphant anarchy may have in our own islands.—Page 191.

Certainly, you ought to attract and fix the attention of the English government to the consequences it would be of to all the European colonies to abandon St. Domingo to the anarchy and despotism of two or three brigands who now command there. What danger would not the example of a triumphant revolt occasion, and particularly when supported by a numerous population, which would take advantage of it ? Being a Jamaica planter, you ought (more than any other) to know the

danger

danger of it, and to publish at all. times, *that Jamaica, lying to leeward of St. Domingo*, and at a small distance, would find herself speedily destroyed. The English Ministers did not wait for your book to be acquainted with the risks you have set forth ; and, if it was from their knowledge *that they directed their first operations*, you ought to consider how far you were wrong in asserting, that they were grossly deceived by bold and interested foreigners. At this time, when you acknowledge that the British legislature should take into consideration the state of St. Domingo, what would you have said, had the Ministers waited till you had *appeared and announced the danger yourself*, before they had attended to it ?

You, Sir, as well as the inhabitants of Jamaica and all the English merchants and manufacturers, would have had just reason to. reproach the King's Ministers, had they suffered Jamaica to have been destroyed. I hesitate not *in declaring to the whole of Great-Britain*, that this colony would have been, and that for a very considerable time past, in a worse state than St. Domingo, if the theatre of war had been carried there, and the commissioners Santhonax and Polverel had continued to command in the French colony. The wretched example of the Windward Islands, and the Maroon war in Jamaica, will be sufficient for reflecting minds to perceive the consequences, and judge of them ; particularly to judge of those that would have happened, if the Ministers, wanting foresight, had, like you, waited for the effects in order to judge of the causes. What evils would not their tardy reflexions have exposed you to, as well as all the planters of Jamaica ?

I think then, Sir, and I publicly declare it, that all the inhabitants of Jamaica owe an everlasting gratitude *to the English Ministers and General Williamson*, for having, by carrying on the war in St. Domingo, averted this scourge from their island ; in short, for having, by this great operation, secured, augmented, and consolidated their fortunes.

If such shall be her good fortune, it will not require the endowment of prophecy to foretel the result. The middling, and who. are commonly the most industrious class of planters throughout every island in the West Indies, allured by the cheapness of the land and the superiority of the soil, will assuredly seek out settlements in St. Domingo ; and a West Indian Empire will fix itself in this noble island, to which, in a few short years, all the tropical possessions of Europe will be found subordinate and tributary. Placed in the centre of British and Spanish America, and situated to windward of these territories of either nation which are more valuable, while the commerce of both must exist only by its good pleasure, all the riches of Mexico will be wholly at its disposal.—Page 192.

x x

I admit, without thinking it necessary to be a prophet, what you here advance, that a great part of the planters of all the islands in the Antilles will be eager to repair to St. Domingo, *but not if the island returns under the power of France,* whose constitution cannot agree with the existence of the colonies, even if by a new law she should establish the only regimen suitable to the island; as that state will be for a long time a prey to the revolutions and uneasiness that accompany new and democratical governments. As the law which might be now repealed, might be re-established after a popular commotion, it results from thence that the riches of the colonists and the colonies will always be causes for jealousy, which will attract and fix upon them the envy of the party chiefs, who will long reign in France.

The industrious, active, and laborious planters, who now cultivate a soil that is exhausted, impoverished, and dried up in the Windward Islands, and who turn their eyes upon St. Domingo as upon a promised land, since the English have possessed a part of it, would soon turn them back again, if the French were to regain possession of it; for they would rather live as they have done for a long time past, than risk their labours upon a soil which might again experience all the horrors which have devastated it. The situation of Jamaica would again become as dangerous. as it would have been, had not the English established themselves at St. Domingo, and seized upon the Mole. But the possibility of establishing an empire there is a dream. This island may be very flourishing under the protection of a powerful mother country; but a soil that produces nothing but objects of luxury, and no article of the first necessity; which depends upon Europe for its manufactures, as well as for its means of subsistence; which has neither navy, nor wood for building; in short, whose chief productions may be reduced to four or five articles, will never form an empire. If you will take the trouble to consider, Sir, how many advantageous circumstances, and what great means are necessary to form an independent state, you will yourself banish this empire with the savage republic you have created of 100,000 Negros, inhabiting mountains that produce nothing useful in the places where you have fixed them. But if after profound reflexion you address what you here say to your countrymen, not for the purpose of establishing an empire, but to engage them to render St. Domingo one of the most important parts of the British possession, then you would have told a great truth, and very easily to be executed; for what France will never do to St. Domingo, England may easily perform, and enjoy all the advantages which you acknowledge to be attached to the possession of this colony. She has moreover the ready means for doing this, as she has preserved her commerce free and unmolested; she alone has the manufactures, and particularly the capitals that are absolutely necessary for the re-establishment of the colony, and to raise it to what it ought to be under so powerful a mother country.

England is the only power that has a navy capable of defending such a great colony, on which the fate of Jamaica absolutely depends; for *I repeat it to you,. Sir, to all the colonists, and to Great-Britain, the fate of Jamaica will follow that of St. Domingo.* Should the latter be re-established the former will be saved; if it be delivered up to the French, *Jamaica will speedily be destroyed,* and so far from a powerful empire being established in that island, such as you here speak of, I predict that *all the colonies in the Antilles will be entirely and speedily ruined and annihilated.*

And Great-Britain find leisure to reflect how deeply she is herself concerned in the consequences of it.—Page 193.

Your duty as an Englishman, your interest as a colonist and as a planter, should rouse you to be continually declaring to Parliament, and to Great-Britain, that the future prosperity of her colonies absolutely depends upon the part she may take respecting St. Domingo. She has, without trouble, without expence, and with incomparable good fortune, been put in possession of the principal places in this island. If she renounces these immense advantages, to which a considerable loss of men, and *an enormous expence since incurred,* ought to attach her still more; if, I say, she abandons such a capital possession, for which she is alone indebted to the brave and generous inhabitants, who have placed their entire confidence in her; if she thinks, *by such a great sacrifice,* to diminish her risks and dangers, she will only increase them, by leaving an example to the world *of loyalty and fidelity, betrayed by a powerful Government,* to which unfortunate and confiding men had surrendered themselves, in order to escape from the fury and vengeance of the destructive executioners of their country.

But whatever the issue may be in all the varieties of fortune, in all events and circumstances, whether prosperous or adverse, it infinitely concerns both the people of Great-Britain and the inhabitants of the British colonies, I cannot repeat it too often, to derive admonition from the story before us. To Great-Britain I would intimate, that if disregarding the present example, encouragement shall be given to the pertinent doctrines of those hot-brained fanatics and detestable incendiaries, who, under the vile pretence of philanthrophy and zeal for the interests of suffering humanity, preach up rebellion and murder to the contented and orderly Negros in our own ter-

2

ritories : what else can be expected, but that the same dreadful scenes of carnage and desolation, which we have contemplated in St. Domingo, will be renewed among our countrymen and relations in the British West Indies.—Page 193.

As you are a colonist and a Member of the British Senate, be so kind, Sir, as to repeat these phrases there, which I have here extracted from your work, and, above all, mention that in certain circumstances there are questions which are as dangerous as useless to be agitated, since necessity has no law, and that such is the situation of the European colonies, that all the powers of Europe must renounce them together, or neither. No, Sir, not one can renounce them alone. Set forth in particular, that England is not even in so fortunate a situation as the French, who, in case of necessity, can do without the colonies ; but as to Great-Britain, *whose power and prosperity depends solely upon her commerce,* the destruction of any one of her colonies is a great misfortune to her. What would be the consequence then to Great-Britain, if the whole were destroyed, and if that commerce were to cease, which is so necessary to her manufactures, to her navy, to her industry, and to her population ?

The misfortunes which the French revolution has occasioned to Europe and America, form too severe a lesson, for true humanity not to be upon her guard in future against the incendiary ideas of pretended philanthrophists and innovators. Let us hope that the British Government will preserve itself from their cruel experiments : which, however unfortunate they may have been for a country so extensive as France, and which has various resources, would prove mortal to a country like Great-Britain, which can only rank among the great powers by means of her commerce and her colonies.

I call on them with the sincerity and affection of a brother, of themselves, to restrain, limit, and finally abolish the further introduction of enslaved men from Africa.— Page 193.

Why, Sir, do you wish what cannot exist ? You are not ignorant that your appeal to the planters of the Antilles will not be heard ; that it cannot be executed without destroying the sugar colonies ; for you would by that means stop the supplying of the vacancies occasioned by the loss of the Creole Negros, who by their forced inclinations perish in the colonies in a greater proportion than the bills of mortality, considered in Europe as correct, calculate for the ancient hemisphere.

The

The late misfortunes of the colonies, the epidemical diseases, and the clearing of the lands will require many Negros for a long time ; why do you wish to impede the industry of the Europeans, and the augmentation of the White population in the colonies where it is in general so successful ?

I am of an opinion quite contrary to you, Sir ; and, as being the true friend of man, I solicit the continuation of a trade which snatches so many victims from the most absurd despotism, in order to give them kind masters, and procure them enjoyments unknown to the inhabitants of Africa ; in short, to place them in a situation incontestably more happy than that to which they are condemned in those barbarous countries.

You are a colonist, and you know as well as I do, that there is *no distraining law possible*, capable of preventing the planters, who should be in want of Negros, from procuring them by smuggling from foreign nations : *for the preservation of their property depends upon it.* You ought then, as a colonist and legislator, to oppose with all your might the making of any laws which would be attacked by all the planters ; a wise man ought not to contribute to the making of a law, which from its principle would be despised or disowned by those for whom it be established.

Towards the poor Negros, over whom the statutes of Great-Britain, the accidents of fortune, and the laws of inheritance, have invested them with power ; their general conduct for the last twenty years (notwithstanding the foul calumnies with which they have been loaded), may court inquiry, and bid defiance to censure.—Page 194.

Had you, in a hundred different ways, repeated the truth you here advance, you would have rendered great service to the colonists of all the Antilles, and have merited their gratitude. You should moreover have continually repeated, *that personal interest*, that great principle of human actions, watched over the security, the preservation, and the happiness of the Negros.

For calumny, though a great, is a temporary evil, but truth and justice will prove triumphant and eternal.—Page 194.

Although I think and maintain, after twenty years observation and reflexion, that the colonies cannot exist *without the continuation of slavery*, and the regimen

Y y

they have adopted and followed till the year 1790.; yet I do not pretend that the laws may not be watchful in augmenting and ameliorating the condition of the Negros; on the contrary, I solicit the planters of all the colonies, as well as all the European governments, to consider of it. Some new laws are necessary; but impartial, enlightened, and just observers (whom the European governments should send to the different islands, in order to be informed of the truth), will agree, after having staid some time in Africa and the colonies, that the Creoles have been calumniated; and the greatest justice would be rendered to them, as it would be founded in truth: which is, that, in all the French or English colonies, the Negros are not only more happy than in Africa, but even than *three parts of the men forming the class of peasants and day labourers in Europe.*

If I require the continuation of the trade, I likewise require that it should be carried on under laws more rigid than the existing ones, for the benefit of the Negros; in short, that well digested laws be established, which should regulate the tonnage of the trading ships. It would not be necessary for them to be more than 300 tons, nor less than 200; for, if the ship be large, it continues trading too long, and the scurvy and other diseases breed among the Negros first purchased; if it be too small, the Negros are not sufficiently accommodated. It ought to be settled how many Negros should be carried in each ship, according to the size, without its being possible for a captain to carry more than the number prescribed by law. The exportation of Negros from Africa above twenty years of age should be prohibited; a man of that age is still susceptible of attachment to a new country, the climate has but little influence over him, and he leaves fewer objects of his attachment, than the Negro more advanced in years, who often leaves a wife and family.

No Negro should be embarked without having been inoculated in Africa; several surgeons should belong to a ship; they should all make oath, before the sale of Negros begins in any colony, where they may be brought, that they have not by any artificial means *driven in or repelled the disorders of the Negros*; by which means great numbers are killed. These measures, I admit, would be more expensive, and the fitting out a trading ship would at first cost the person equipping it a considerably greater sum, which would finally be borne by the planter; but he would be well indemnified; for, instead of purchasing two or three Negros, he would only purchase one, whom he would more easily preserve, and who would sooner work, &c. &c. In short, it is not the expence it will be of to the planter that must be considered; the Negros are necessary for their works; whatever may be the price of them, they will pay for it. We ought to apply ourselves then in regulating every thing than can be useful to humanity. Wise laws made for well conducting the Negro trade will be more serviceable to them than *all the debates which have taken place concerning them for these fifteen years past,* through a false, idle, cruel, ignorant and absurd philanthropy.

I here finish, Sir, my Answer to your pretended Survey of St. Domingo. Whatever may be the number of errors I have refuted, *still many others remain—* but our readers are now in a situation to judge of your work.

As to myself, I have fulfilled the task I undertook; and think I have answered you so as to prove that *your book is filled with errors.* It was a duty I owed *the colony, England, and myself,* to undeceive the public respecting what you had advanced. I think I have proved, that the inhabitants of St. Domingo, in voluntarily delivering themselves up to England, *have not ceased to fight for her interests.*

I have proved that you were wrong in accusing those who advised *the Ministers to undertake the important expedition to St. Domingo;* that *they have not deceived them;* and that *they never wished to deceive them. I have proved that, if St. Domingo had not become the seat of war,* the colony of Jamaica had necessarily been lost, *which is an absolute truth.* I repeat it, Sir, and *I hesitate not to affirm:* that, if St. Domingo were abandoned, or restored to the French, *Jamaica would speedily be destroyed,* and, soon after, all the colonies in the Antilles.

I have proved, that the Ministers, who had observed this truth, have not been deceived by honest foreigners, who are devoted to the interests of the colony and Great-Britain. I have proved, that those who *advised and undertook the execution* of this great operation have not deceived themselves respecting its advantages and consequences, and that *their attachment* deserved a different reward than the calumnies interspersed in the materials which have been furnished you, and which you have collected with too little circumspection.

In short, I think I have proved, that *it is not a sordid interest* that influenced him who has braved and done all in his power, in order to put this immense and rich possession under the government of Great-Britain.

I have only to regret, that my Answer could not appear sooner, as it might have prevented many worthy people from being led into error. I should, moreover, have prevented a respectable character from depending upon your work for the purpose of speaking publicly of St. Domingo, *with which he is unacquainted ; which you, Sir, and few persons in England are acquainted with.*

I need hardly assure you, that your book has caused me real vexation, by compelling me to refute a *part* of the errors it contains ; it would have been much more pleasant to have praised it. .Whilst I acknowledge that your style is very easy and agreeable, I cannot but regret that you did not employ your talents in writing upon subjects which might have been more useful to your country and the colonies. For example, being a colonist and a legislator, and being desirous of writing, could not you, at this interesting moment, in various ways, *daily renewed,* have acquainted your fellow citizens, *with the dangers of the Peace that is spoken of?* Why not have employed your talents in exposing to your country the fatal consequences this peace would be of to Great-Britain and to all the colonies in both the Indies ?

Why, Sir, did you not call the attention of Great-Britain to the happy situation in which she finds herself, in spite of the war ? Why did you not publish this great truth, viz. that the commerce of all Europe has centered in England ? Why did you not draw the attention of the public to this happy and important fact, that she - *alone has preserved her manufactures,* and increased her commerce ? Why did you not exhibit the English navy as being more flourishing than ever, and that of her enemies almost destroyed ? The Dutch navy annihilated ; Spain flying before the British flag, blocked up in her ports, or reduced to burn her ships with her own hands, to prevent their falling into those of her conquerors, as at la Trinité ? In short, why did you not call the attention of your country to her flourishing situation, the true period of her glory, in being mistress of all the European colonies, her flag flying triumphant in every sea ? What could the friends of England desire more ? What could a commercial nation hope for more than to be mistress of the commerce of the whole world ? Did those who laid the foundation of this amazing power *hope or foresee,* that your Navigation Act would have produced so many and such glorious successes to Great-Britain ? In short, *why do you not repeat to your readers that* PEACE ALONE *may make you lose, in a very little time,* all these mighty advantages ?

Why do you not draw the attention and thoughts of your readers to the gigantic power of the French upon the Continent ? Why did you not exhibit the critical situation of your country fallen from her power, *if peace* gives her enemies the means of recovering *their losses, their manufactures, their commerce, and particularly the re-establishment of their navy, by recovering their colonies ?*

Why

Why did you nôt repeat to your countrymen, that England can only lose, and
gain nothing by peace? Why did you not remind her that she can only make resti-
tution without receiving any thing in exchange? In short, why did you not prove
that no peace with the Republic can be made with safety, from the uncertainty of
her situation and her government? that, being surrounded with many exterior enemies, *and having many interior ones,* a civil war in France is every moment ready
to burst forth?.... Even in this situation, *will England venture to disarm?* And, if she
does not, what advantages will indemnify her for the sacrifices she must make *for a
peace,* which will never be of long duration; but which, doubt it not, would bring
upon her greater dangers than the war?

For, *according to what is going on in Italy and Germany,* you should remind your
readers that the French Revolution is more dangerous for all the European nations
by a peace than by war. If England were to make peace, how could she preserve herself from the poison which would soon be brought to her by a French Ambassador
and that heap of Jacobins that would be attached to his suite? How could she preserve herself from their principles, if, in spite of the war and her careful watchfulness,
this country has several times been upon the point of being overturned? In short, how
could she prevent, in the people of this country, the consequence of this *dreadful
reflexion,* (supported by the example of the success and presence of Republican
Envoys): they were desirous of placing themselves in the situation of those who
possessed every thing, and they fixed themselves there *by assassinating, by pillaging, and by forcing them to wander far from their country;* they wished it, and
they have succeeded. . . . .

In fine, Sir, why do you not rouse the public spirit of your country against her
real enemies? Why do you not remind your countrymen of that profound hatred
which has for so many ages existed between the two countries? Why do you not
animate their courage by reminding them of the wars for these 300 years past, in
which the English have so often triumphed? Why, above all, do you not continually repeat to the English, that *the nature of her government, her position, her
population, and her climate,* destined her only to be *a secondary power;* and say
to her: "in spite of the efforts *of a numerous, brave, and active nation,* we are
become the *first maritime power in the world?* Why should we not support ourselves in this happy situation, since we are enabled so to do by all the united advantages arising from circumstances? Would it be more difficult for us to preserve
the situation in which we have placed ourselves *than to attain it?*" — War

alone, I repeat it to you, Sir, can enable you to preserve that noble and magnificent position—*with peace*, you will soon descend from it.

May Great-Britain and her chiefs reflect upon the fate of Carthage! There is a greater similitude than one is disposed to believe between the situation of the French and English, with that of the Romans and Carthaginians. Let England cast her eyes upon the new Republic that has just established itself at her doors! Let her consider the effects of that force (of a nation consisting of twenty-five millions of souls) which, whilst forming itself into a Republic, has from the beginning of this government, *uneasy from its nature*, given *to the bravest and most turbulent people in the world* those successes which Rome in her most glorious days never surpassed! Let England for a moment reflect upon the power of this people, who, by their Revolution, have made themselves *the friends of the populace in all nations!*

In short, consider, Sir, and repeat in the bosom of the Senate of your Country, to your friends, and to your readers: that France, in spite of the misfortunes attending her Revolution, in spite of the destruction of her finances and commerce, is arrived at such a height as to be able to extend her frontiers, and has acquired a new population, consisting of upwards of eight millions; represent to your readers and the English in general, that the Scheldt, the Maese, and all the coasts and ports, from the Texel to the *Straits of Gibraltar, and the Adriatic*, are now in the power of her natural enemy. I ask what degree of force must that nation attain after ten years *peace, which she alone hereafter will be able to break?* What will become of all the neighbouring States, *if her finances, her commerce, and her colonies*, and through that *her navy*, are restored? Do you think that England can long remain free, ruler of the seas and the commerce of the universe? It is not difficult to foresee her fate, if the French Republic, from her foundation, is more powerful than all Europe. What will she be, when *order in her finances, her agriculture, her commerce, manufactures, and her navy*, are placed in such a situation as the efforts of the peaceable French government are capable of raising them to? What will soon be the fate of England, when we know that the French are, of all other people, the most active, the most uneasy, and the most ready for war? Yes, the ostentation of Rome will soon be eclipsed: if England, *who alone can, and ought, to stop the increase of this inimical power*, does not support herself in the happy situation in which chance, circumstances, her constitution, her manufactures, and her commerce, have placed her.

If England does not say to France, you have rendered yourself *the most considerable* power upon the Continent; *what right had you?* Strength and courage.

Well! then by the same right we are sovereigns of the seas. We will preserve our power; we will respect yours, if you will respect ours, *which our situation renders absolutely necessary.* You will soon be masters of the interior commerce of Europe; well then! we will be masters of the exterior commerce! Our 660 ships of war *will secure to us our maritime power*, in the same manner as your two or three millions of national guards will secure to you the sovereignty of the Continent! Your conquests, your activity, *and our safety*, demand and require, that we suffer neither you nor your allies *to have more than a certain number of ships of war*; and that you possess no colonies; the time is come when England, from necessity, must concentrate all her power and force within her walls and wooden fortresses.

The English nation is arrived to the highest degree of prosperity, and the cruel revolution which has ruined *every other nation*, has enriched the English nation; *her commerce, manufactures, and agriculture*, are in a flourishing state: her credit is unimpaired in spite of her enemies; her troubles are domestic, and are, as to herself, a family concern, and with which, her situation prevents foreign powers from interfering. She has nothing to fear then—*peace, yes, peace alone :* this precious blessing so advantageous for all people, is dangerous for her. This is *the agreeable and smiling enemy* whom she should mistrust, *whom* she ought to dread more than *France and her warriors.* Let her secure herself in her true situation, let all her efforts be directed towards her commerce, her navy, and her possessions in the two Indies, and she will soon see her enemy reduced to the necessity of receiving *such commercial laws* as her interest and her situation will dictate to her to prescribe!

You might explain these simple truths to your readers in a hundred different ways, and which you might support by a comparison between the situation of the two nations. Both the warlike and mercantile navy of England, are carried to a height beyond any example ever mentioned in history. France furnishes an absolute contrast to this situation; without finances, without credit, with few raw materials, without manufactures, with a declining agriculture : she is without commerce as well as without either *a warlike or mercantile navy*; and, whatever may be said of her, without the means of procuring one. Why then should not Great-Britain say to France: " By the extent of your European conquests which you have kept, you are become too powerful for us to make peace by restoring to you any of those we have taken, either from you or your allies in the two Indies : consequently we will make peace only upon condition, that one of the fundamental bases shall be, that you and your allies shall, at no period whatever, have above a certain number of ships of war?" *then the peace may be both honorable and useful to England,* and without danger to her. If she makes any other, she will soon lose her power in the Indies and her Western colonies; for if, forgetting *her true situation, her glory, her interest, and the immense power to which she is raised*; if, in order to obtain a momentary peace, Great-Britain restores the Cape of Good Hope, Trincomale, and Ceylon, to the Dutch, what will be the consequence ? Why, in less than twelve months these possessions will be occupied by French garrisons, which will be voluntarily received by the Dutch, or by the supreme order of the French Republic, that domineers over them.—What must be the consequence that will ensue ? Why, 12 or 15,000 French will be carried to the East Indies, both by these ports as well as by the islands of France and Bourbon ; that the French will by every possible means treat with the Marattas, and endeavour to seduce Tippoo Saib. In short, if the French should at any time hereafter penetrate into India, *I can venture to predict,* that the English would soon after possess no territorial property there.

But let England not deceive herself ! *the natural hatred between the two nations has attained to that degree among the French, which is the cause that republics never forgive.* It is at present then a deadly war *between the two powers,* in which England will come off victoriously, *but by making only a conditional peace,* and preserving the means of causing it to be observed. Moreover, in the treaty which she may some time or other conclude, she cannot and must not forget to have a positive determination concerning the measures she is to take to preserve herself against *the catechism of the French Revolution and the catechisers.* Upon any other conditions, war is much better for England than peace.

Why did you not, Sir, employ your talents in enlightening and informing the English concerning their real situation ? And why did you not point out to them, that though they pay many taxes, they are a proof of their safety and flourishing situation? Germany, Holland, Flanders, Italy, Spain, and particularly France, all powerful as she is, *are ruined :* no taxes can be paid there, because almost all property is annihilated, as well as the manufactures and commerce ; no taxes are paid in these unfortunate countries, as in England, because all the capitals are destroyed. These unhappy people would be glad to be able to pay the same taxes as the English, and like them to have preserved, unimpaired, *their power, their glory, and their property :* to have increased their commerce *from that of their enemies, and from the wrecks of their manufactures,* and to have amassed riches, which cannot be even

des-

destroyed but by peace. Why, Sir, did you not remind the traders who lose some ships, that England, possessing all the trading ships of Europe, must naturally lose some ? Why do you not say to the people paying taxes : *your capitals are entire, your agriculture and manufactures furnish you with certain means to work upon ; you are the best fed, the best lodged, and the best clothed people in Europe :* nay, *even in the universe* ; what could you desire more, after all the misfortunes that have afflicted and ruined all the neighbouring nations ? What better fortune could you have hoped for, after a dreadful Revolution, and five years terrible war, than to have increased *your navy* from that of your enemies, *your power* by the destruction *of their commerce and manufactures,* and by the capture *of all their colonies ?* In short, could you have expected that the horrible Revolution, which has devastated Europe, would only have served to raise *you alone* to the highest pinnacle of power ? You have purchased *this happy situation* at the expence of some taxes : do not complain then any longer.—This is what you should have published with the thousand voices of fame, for the information of your countrymen.

If the East Indies are exposed to the greatest dangers *from a sued for and shameful peace,* the Western colonies will be much sooner and more certainly exposed by it, as it would allow the French to re-enter their colonies. In order to convince both you and our readers, particularly those who know that *the regimen of slavery is absolutely necessary in the colonies of the Antilles,* let them read what judicious and informed men, acquainted with the colonies and the interests of France : men possessing great talents, and having the interest of their country at heart, have lately said, in the councils of the Republic, respecting the importance of the colonies to France.

M. de Vaublanc, in his speech on the twenty-eighth of May, in the Council of Five Hundred, said, after having spoken *of the ruin and the loss of the French colonies :* " Certainly these truths are very forcible, and their consequences are " such *that they alone counterbalance the advantages the French* have acquired in " Europe."

After such an acknowledgment, will England furnish France with the means of recovering her losses, in order that she may increase her immense power ? If, by their conquest, the French are masters, so as to give law to the Continent, what does there remain for England, in order to balance this new power, but to preserve the empire *of the seas,* which henceforth nothing can deprive her of, *without producing her certain destruction ?*

3 A

Independent of the laws *for her own safety*, which point out her immediate preservation, her interest *and a wise policy*, is not to permit either the French or her allies to re-enter her colonies, in order to restore their navy; there is a law still more essential *to the safety of Great-Britain*, and which does not allow her the possibility of restoring them; which is, that the French, by their constitutional laws, have pronounced, by one act, the destruction of all the colonies of the Antilles, *in pronouncing the liberty of the Negros*, founded upon the pretended Rights of Man; nothing is changed in their principles in this respect, and they lay the foundation of the future prosperity of their colonies (if they should recover the possession of them) upon the *chimerical basis of a modified slavery:* their orators pronounced it on the first of June. Bourdon de l'Oise said, after having spoken of the unhappy situation of St. Domingo under the government of Santhonax : " No one " pretends *to bring the Negros back to slavery:* his voice would remain unsup- " ported in the bosom of this assembly."

Tarbé said the same day, upon the same subject : " Already have some evil- " minded persons reported that it is intended *to re-establish slavery, a thought that* " *will never enter our heads*"

What then is the consequence of this confession ? Why, that the French, by a continuation of their experiments, would deprive the other nations of the benefits they might derive from the losses the French should sustain in their own colonies. Let not England suppose that this loss might be replaced by the advantages she possesses in the East Indies.

You might have proclaimed simple truths, *established particularly* by what Mr. George Dallas proved in his speech, at a meeting of the proprietors of the English East India Company. You ought, Sir, as a colonist and a member of the legislature of your country, to have commented upon, and published, the truths clearly demonstrated in this speech, which interests Great-Britain far more than it does the India Company. Mr. George Dallas has clearly proved, that, if the East Indies could do without the sugar colonies, *Great-Britain could not.* You might, and you even ought, to have *deduced an important consequence from it*, which is, that the sugar colonies are *more useful* to England than the East Indies are : the one enormously enriches a few *private individuals*, but the West Indies cause several million *hands to be employed, and gives bread to upwards of a million of individuals* ; because the sugar colonies consume four times as many raw materials and articles of European manufacture as the whole of the East Indies. You should have declared,

Sir, that the French colonies, under this point of view, are of far greater advantage to England than the Cape, Ceylon, and all the other conquests in India; the monopoly of sugar securing still greater advantages to the English commerce, as they would be distributed amongst a greater number of traders, manufacturers, and workmen, than what the East India trade either does or can do.

In fine, Sir, you ought to fix the attention *of your countrymen* upon the dangers of any peace whatever with the French nation, and prove to them *(which I think is easy)*, that no war has ever been *so advantageous to them*, because no one has placed them in the situation in which *they must have been ambitious* to find themselves; in short, because no one ever rendered them alone the absolute sovereigns of every sea.

Why, Sir, in drawing the attention of your fellow citizens towards your country, did you not repeat and prove to them, in a hundred different ways, that Great-Britain *never was more flourishing*; that, if the war has occasioned, and still occasions, some embarrassment in her finances, she is however the only power in Europe whose paper currency *is at par with money?* If England compares her situation with that of every other power, she will be very careful how she makes a peace that will deprive her of all the advantages of an unprovoked war; *which alone has preserved her from complete destruction,* and procured her those advantages which, as a commercial nation, she could, and ought never, to have expected; advantages *(and I think I have proved it)* which are, and will be more *serviceable to her* than all the conquests of the French will ever be to their Republic, and which she has purchased at so dear a rate; whilst England *is sound in all her parts, and is mistress of all the colonies which belonged to her enemies,* and thereby mistress of their commerce, that is to say, *of their real power.*

This is what you might have explained, have commented upon, and easily have proved to your readers; then would your talents, tending to enlighten and inform your fellow citizens, have merited the respect and gratitude both of your country and the colonies.

My unfortunate countrymen at St. Domingo would not have been under the disagreeable necessity of considering you as their enemy, and of blaming the vanity and various sentiments which have occasioned you to write a succession of errors, such as no book ever before contained. I should never have been *compelled by honor and duty to answer you,* which, at the same time that it is a proof of my feeling is a proof of your injustice—for I have written it for the sole purpose of enabling our impartial readers to judge between us. Believe me, Sir, it would have been more agreeable for me to have praised such parts of your work as. deserve it.

I have the honor to be,

S I R,

Your very humble and very obedient Servant,

DE CHARMILLY.

NO. 188, OXFORD-STREET.

THE END.

www.ingramcontent.com/pod-product-compliance
Lightning Source LLC
Chambersburg PA
CBHW030605040726
47497CB00008B/2851

* 9 7 8 3 3 3 7 3 3 1 6 1 0 *